The INDEPENDENCE CLUB

A NOVEL

The INDEPENDENCE CLUB

A NOVEL

RACHEL ANN NUNES

DESERET
BOOK

SALT LAKE CITY, UTAH

Library of Congress Cataloging-in-Publication Data
Nunes, Rachel Ann, 1966–
  The Independence Club / Rachel Ann Nunes.
    p. cm.
  ISBN-10 1-59038-709-0 (pbk.)
  ISBN-13 978-1-59038-709-2 (pbk.)
  1. Women—Fiction. 2. Friendship—Fiction. I. Title.
  PS3564.U468I54 2004
  813'.54—dc22   2006031832

Printed in the United States of America
Publishers Printing, Salt Lake City, UT

10 9 8 7 6 5 4 3 2 1

To all my readers who loved Maxine in By Morning Light
and wanted to know what happened to her and
the rest of the Independence Club!

CHAPTER

1

Maxine

I haven't kept a journal in more than thirty years, and I should have. I know a lot of secrets. Anyway, all of us in the Independence Club have agreed to keep our journals more faithfully, writing in particular our feelings and hopes and plans for the future. Then we'll get together every Wednesday to talk about life and sort of brainstorm ideas for each other so we can be successful. A power group of sorts.

Everyone had a say in getting the club started. Tina Dayley coined the name, not surprising since her late husband was abusive; Evie McClaine asked to meet at her favorite restaurant, Mimi's Café; Rosalva Nolasco chose Wednesday because of her work schedule; and Bernice Stubbs, who's always spouting off about something we should be doing better, had the journal idea. I, of course, am the voice of experience and reason, the glue holding everyone together. We're a varied group of women but united in our determination to make our lives happy and complete. We all face challenges, some of us big challenges, but I won't go into all that right now. My cosmetic orders are waiting—I didn't get them finished because of the wedding reception.

That reminds me. Being at Kerrianne's wedding this morning and her reception tonight made me start thinking about Charles and the almost forty years we shared. I still love that man, and I still miss him. But there are some things about marriage that I don't miss—and those are exactly the reasons why I'm not marrying Harold Perry. For crying out loud, I'm not about to start having to take care of someone again at my age.

Not that I'm old, of course. Sixty-two is still very young, and people always say I don't look a day over fifty—probably a big exaggeration. I mean, I certainly don't look like Goldie Hawn or anything. No one could look like that at her age without serious medical intervention. Quite frankly, Goldie Hawn and others like her do all women a disservice. Sure, we can grow old gracefully, which is what I'm trying for and part of why I sell cosmetics, but that doesn't mean we must inject our faces with poison and let some bozo cut into us with a knife.

There I go, speaking my mind again. I get into more trouble that way, but I can't help myself. I've been around the block a time or two, and I'm beyond talking nice just so others will feel better about their mistakes. I call it like I see it. At least I'm only saying this now in my journal where it can't come back and bite me—until I'm dead, and then I won't care.

For the record, I'm not against widows remarrying, like my friend Bernice claims to be. Even Harold started to avoid her because she kept talking about his wife, who has been gone nearly *two years already. "Harold, what would your wife think? You know she'd never want you kissing another woman." It's enough to make me want to slit her tires.*

No. I'm kidding, really. When I think about it, she's doing me a favor. After all, she's just protecting me from Harold. I mean, if I were ever to get married again, which I'm not going to do, he'd have to be romantic enough to take my mind off all the cooking and cleaning and effort that goes along with marriage. Harold's only kissed me once for real, and that was months ago. No, I'm not going to write how I felt because . . . well, because I'm not sure myself.

Before the bell rang, the house had been hauntingly still. Maxine Madison was almost sure Harold was at the door—not that she was expecting him or anyone else this late on a Saturday night. All her close friends, members of the Independence Club, had been at their friend's wedding reception less than an hour ago and had no need to see each other so soon.

Harold had been there too, dashing and gentlemanly as usual.

Maxine took her baby blue sweater from the back of her chair and pulled it on. The first part of April had brought not showers but a snowstorm, and there was still a slushy layer on her lawn and driveway. That was why if Harold had any sense, he'd be home sleeping in a warm bed instead of standing in the cold on her doorstep.

The bell came again, insistently. Too insistently for an unexpected guest.

"I'm coming," grumbled Maxine. Despite her efforts to squelch the emotion, she felt a surge of . . . something . . . in her heart region at the idea of seeing Harold. *Nonsense,* she thought. *We're just friends. He hasn't asked me to marry him since January.*

She pulled open the door. Standing there, blinking in the sudden light was none other than Harold. "Hi," he said with a smile, looking as debonair and refined as always.

Maxine had to look upward at a fairly steep angle to meet his gaze. She never minded because the height was part of what made him remarkable. No matter how out of shape he might be, his frame didn't have the tendency to gain weight. His hair was dark gray with many bits of white, and his eyes, which today had taken on the color of his blue polo shirt, were topped by thick gray eyebrows. As usual, he wore dress pants and shiny black loafers. On Sundays and at dances, he would wear the suit she'd helped him pick out to replace the old one she suspected he'd bought years before his wife's death.

Maxine lowered her gaze. *Be strong,* she told herself. Aloud she said, "What are you doing here?"

"I've come to help you with the orders. I told you I would at the reception. Did you forget?" He reached for her hand, bringing it up to his mouth as if he were a character in an old movie.

The warmth from his touch spread through her in an astonishing wave, and she snatched her hand back. "Stop that! I've told you before, we don't live in those days."

"What days?" He lifted a brow.

"In the days when men kiss women on the hand."

"I'm old-fashioned."

"Well, that's fine and dandy, but it's not getting my orders done." Maxine felt flustered, but she did her level best not to show it.

Harold smiled knowingly, which infuriated her all the

more. "Then let me in." He stuck his hands in the pockets of his open jacket and leaned back on his heels.

"Oh." She stepped aside and opened the door the rest of the way, feeling unsettled all over again. "You know, I really don't think I need the computer to do the order." In fact, that was exactly why she hadn't responded to his offer to help. She'd even hoped he'd forgotten.

"You might feel differently once you see how much it can help you. At the reception Tina was telling me all about the bonus products you get when you sell a certain amount. She said on the website it's all written out so you know exactly what's what without having to add and re-add your products as you move them around in the different categories."

"Well, all that adding is a pain," she admitted, "but Tina's my upline, so maybe we should leave it to her."

"It's no problem." He flashed her another endearing smile. Maxine wondered if he'd always been so dashing, or if he'd just aged well. "Besides," he added, "Tina has four kids to take care of. I only have you."

Maxine bristled. "I can take care of myself, thank you very much."

"Well, I can't." He passed her in the direction of the kitchen. "Now where is this computer of yours?"

"In my office. Come on, I'll show you. And by the way, you are perfectly capable of taking care of yourself."

Harold stopped and turned toward her, taking entirely too much space in the narrow hallway. His face bent down to Maxine's and for a brief moment, she thought he was going to kiss her. "I certainly wouldn't be walking three miles a day if I hadn't met you," he said instead. "I could barely go down to my basement without breathing hard, before we met, let alone walk even one mile. I know I still have a long way to go, but you've changed my life."

Maxine didn't want that kind of responsibility. If you changed a life, you became responsible for it. Somehow for women that always seemed to mean washing clothes, cleaning up, making dinner, devising gourmet desserts such as hot apple pie served with ice cream. "Oh, no, you don't, I hate making pies." She squeezed by him, ignoring his puzzled stare.

"There's the computer," she said, jabbing a finger toward the desk.

"Where are your orders?"

"Oh, I left them in the kitchen. I'll be right back."

When she returned, he had her computer on and was logged onto the website. "I'll need a password."

"It's in my one of my e-mail folders." Maxine was happy she could say that. Now he'd know that she at least used e-mail. Never mind that it was only once a week to children. One e-mail sent to all five. It beat letter writing by a long shot.

"Okay, hmm." Harold clicked his way through several pages, finally coming to an order form. Since she was still on dial-up, the pages didn't load as quickly as they had when Tina had showed her the website at her house.

He eyed her stack of orders. "Want to read off the product numbers for me? Since you don't have high speed Internet, this quick form looks like it'll be easier than clicking on each product. Otherwise we'll be here all night, and what would the neighbors say?"

"Who cares?"

Harold chuckled. "Ready when you are." He didn't know how to type properly, but his pecking method moved things along nicely.

"So when have you been walking three miles?" Maxine asked when all the products were in and they had shifted to the shopping cart to see what bonus products she could qualify for.

"In the mornings. Like you."

Maxine narrowed her eyes. "Are you following me?"

"It's still mostly dark when you go. I wouldn't want anything to happen to you."

Maxine tried to be angry, but the idea of his wanting to protect her sent an odd shivering kind of feeling up her spine. "You might just go with me, instead of spying," she suggested.

"Okay." The quick response told her he'd been waiting for the invitation, and that made her feel set up somehow, though she wasn't sure why. Friends could walk together. Being friends with Harold meant no more than being friends with the women in the Independence Club.

She glanced over at him and saw that he was watching her. She knew the expression all too well. This couldn't be happening. He was going to do it again—ask her to marry him.

"Maxine," he began. Was she imagining the huskiness of his voice?

"What?"

"It's up to you, but I really think you ought to switch these three items down to your 'Host Special Products' section, since you can get all three of them for twenty bucks."

"Uh, um, yes. You're right. And I want those two travel kits I qualify for as well."

He started clicking, and Maxine's heart rate slowed. When it all boiled down to it, she was just an old fool. She wanted to laugh, but somehow she couldn't.

"There, all done. I'll need your credit card."

She handed it to him, but instead of grasping the card, his

thumb pressed down on the back of her hand, the thin piece of plastic caught between their fingers. "Maxine, I know you're happy with your life as it is, but did you ever think that together we could be even happier?"

She felt relieved that it was out in the open, instead of lurking between them like some fatal disease. Now she could set him straight once and for all. She opened her mouth to speak, but he rushed on. "Now, Maxine, don't start talking about apple pies. Or hand kissing. I know how to kiss for real."

She had her doubts about that. The one time he'd kissed her had been so long ago, she might have even imagined it.

Avoiding his eyes, she stared at the white eyelet curtains she'd put up four years ago when she'd changed the room from Charles's office into her own. He'd been dead a year at the time.

"I'm a practical woman," she told Harold. "I'm not going to pretend I don't like you because I do, but I'm—"

Her words were drowned out by a frantic pounding coming from the other room, accompanied by a voice calling something unintelligible. Harold looked at her expectantly.

Shrugging, she jumped to her feet and hurried down the short hall, with Harold on her heels, moving somewhat faster than his usual slow gait. She yanked open the front door.

"Sister Madison! I need your help!" A wet young boy stood on the porch, his eyes wild. It took Maxine a moment to realize that he was Skip Dayley, her friend Tina's thirteen-year-old son. He wasn't wearing a coat, though it was raining softly, and the night air was cold enough to bite Maxine's lungs as she took a breath.

"Come in, Skip. It's freezing out there!"

He shook his head. "My mother needs help."

"What's wrong with her?" Maxine was instantly alarmed. Tina was her closest friend in the Independence Club.

"I don't know. She just suddenly freaked out." Skip's eyes filled with tears, and his next words came in a jumbled rush. "Ashley and I were arguing in the kitchen, and I was mad at her so I pushed my book at her, but her glass was in the way and it fell off the counter. There was red juice and glass everywhere. Mom sort of froze. Then she started shaking and breathing funny. I thought she was going to yell at us, but she only stood there. The little boys came running in from their beds and started yelling, and Mom didn't even notice. She turned and ran down the hall to her room."

"And she won't come out?" Maxine prompted.

"She's not there! Ashley went to see what was wrong, but she was gone. We don't know where she went. We're scared because . . ." Whatever the reason, he couldn't finish the thought. "Well, we're just scared."

This didn't sound like Tina at all. "Did you hear a door shut?" Maxine asked. "Is her car gone?"

Skip's body convulsed with a suppressed sob. "I don't know. I didn't look. But she wouldn't leave us!" His eyes, so like Tina's hazel ones, were wide with fright.

"Of course not." Maxine touched his shoulder, which was stiff from cold or worry—or both. "Maybe she went to buy something to clean it up."

Skip didn't reply, and Harold looked at her as if to say, "That's it? That's all you can come up with?" Maxine ignored him.

"Look, Skip," she said, "let's go back to your house and take a look around. I can't believe you came all the way over here in this rain."

Skip gave a helpless shrug. "I ran. Ashley tried your phone number, but it was busy. Our neighbor wasn't home, and the other ones, well, I don't really know them. Ashley said I should get you. She's looking around the yard."

"Come on," Maxine urged. "Let's go through to the garage. I'll get my keys."

Harold stopped her with a touch on her arm. "I can drive you. My car's blocking your garage anyway."

"You don't have to come." Maxine felt bad as she said the words, but she didn't want to start depending on him too much.

"Tina's my friend, too."

Maxine couldn't exactly argue with that. He'd gone to enough LDS singles events to become well acquainted with all her friends. "Okay, but let me do the talking."

He grinned. "Don't I always?"

Maxine gave him a disgusted stare, but he was already heading to the door. She grabbed a lap quilt from her sofa and wrapped it around Skip's shoulders. "It's going to be all right," she told him. She hoped that was true. After spending most of his life with an abusive father, this boy had already suffered enough.

Tina lived only a few blocks away, the farthest of all her friends except Rosalva, but she wasn't in Maxine's stake. That was how it went in Utah, where sometimes the members across the street weren't even in the same ward.

When they arrived at the Dayleys', Tina's two younger boys and her teenage daughter, Ashley, were waiting in the living room. The bottoms of Ashley's pants were wet halfway to the knees, and her red hair hung in moist ropes around her face. "I didn't find her," she said, looking forlorn.

"Her car is out there." Maxine removed her coat. The heat

was always stifling in Tina's house, though the children didn't seem to mind. "I'm sure she didn't go far. Stay here, okay? I'm going to the bedroom." The children nodded, their faces tight with fear.

The house was small, but the master bedroom did have an adjoining bath. Maybe Tina had gone in there to recover from whatever had happened. When she didn't find Tina in the bathroom, uneasiness filled Maxine's heart. "Tina?" she called. "It's Maxine. Look, you have some very worried kids out there. If you're here, you might as well say something because I'll find you if I look."

Nothing.

Maxine thought about searching under the bed, but why would Tina be there? She had no reason to hide from her. More likely, she'd felt sick and gone to the neighbors, and they'd taken her to the doctor.

That's right. I'll call the emergency room.

She was almost to the door when she heard a small sob. Whirling on her feet, she scanned the room, her eyes searching and discarding every place except under the bed and the closet.

The closet.

The double folding doors were slightly ajar, and Maxine walked toward them with determination. She pushed the doors open. On the far right side, wrapped in a blanket, sat Tina, her strawberry blonde hair looking as though the blanket had at one point been over her head. Her thin face, normally made up to perfection, was streaked with tears and mascara.

Giving a little groan, Maxine fell to her knees and put her arms around her friend. "Oh, Tina, honey. What happened?"

Tina didn't speak, though her unfocused eyes said it all.

11

She was afraid—no, terrified. But of what? Her husband was a year dead in a car accident and couldn't hurt her anymore.

"It's okay," Maxine assured her. "Everything is okay. Skip came to get me, and that's why I'm here. Ashley stayed with the boys. They're all right as rain. And Harold's here. He was trying to ask me to marry him again when Skip came. Good thing, too. Anyway, I daresay Harold's telling your kids boring stories about when he was a dentist. That means he'll be at least an hour, so you just take your time. You know, I think he should have been a farmer, not a dentist. He takes a long time doing anything. It's like watching corn grow."

Tina's color was better now, and her eyes were more focused.

A movement in the hall caught Maxine's attention, and she spied Harold peeking around the door. She gave him a thumbs up to tell him she'd found Tina, and then she made a shooing motion so he'd know to keep all the children away. *Good thing he came along after all,* she thought.

Tina didn't notice Harold or Maxine's signal. She lowered her head onto Maxine's shoulder and let out a long breath. "That's it," Maxine said. "Breathe deeply. In and out. Everything else can wait." She breathed with Tina, and for a moment their breathing was their entire world. In and out. Slowly, evenly.

Maxine's knees felt stiff and her shoulder muscles ached by the time Tina finally spoke, her voice soft but steady. "I'm okay," she said. "I just . . . I just . . ."

Maxine shifted her weight and sat beside her. "Don't try to gloss over this, Tina. I know you like to look on the good side of things, but I want you to tell me what happened."

Tina's hazel eyes looked black in the darkness of the closet. She crossed her arms over her chest as though to protect herself, looking much younger than her thirty-nine years. "Ashley and Skip were fighting. The glass broke. There was blood—juice, I mean—everywhere. And suddenly I was back with him that day my arm broke. My nose bled a lot." She gave her head an abrupt shake as though to force the memory from her head. "All I wanted was to climb under the table and hide. It's a trigger, that's all. I see or hear something—and I need to get away. Usually, I'm okay if I sit on my bed for a while, or if I go into the bathroom. But today the kids were so . . . challenging, and everything happened just right—or just wrong, rather." She blinked and a mascara-laden tear slid down her right cheek. "But I didn't go under the table. I didn't do that in front of my kids."

Maxine reached out for her hand. "No, you didn't. You did fine. But I'm thinking that maybe you should see a counselor again. For a little while."

Tina shook her head. "I'm all right, really. I know how to deal with it. I took all the classes. It was just today. The kids were—I do still take them once a month to their counselor, in case you're wondering about that. They're all doing really well, and so am I. Everyone has days like this, right?" She gave Maxine a tentative smile. "Tomorrow will be better."

"I'm sure it will. Do you think you can get up? Would you like me to help you into bed?"

"I need to see my children, make sure they're okay." Tina arose unsteadily, but her smile was firmly in place.

Maxine wanted to shake her. Most of the time she was grateful for Tina's normally cheery outlook on life, but sometimes she wished Tina would get angry at how her husband had treated her and the children.

Tina touched her arm. "I'm okay, Maxine. I promise.

13

Thanks to you. I'm so lucky to have you as a friend. I have so many blessings in my life." She hugged Maxine.

Tina had firmly retreated behind her positive mask, and Maxine knew she had no choice but to bite her tongue. Of course that didn't mean she wasn't going to keep a good eye on Tina these next few weeks. "Okay, then. Do you need help with your makeup?"

Tina managed a laugh. "I'm the one who got you into selling cosmetics, remember? Go on, tell the kids I'll be right there." She gave Maxine's arm a gentle thrust.

When Tina emerged from her tiny bathroom ten minutes later, there was no trace of tears or upset. It was as though nothing unusual had happened.

CHAPTER

2

Tina

How embarrassing to have Maxine find me like that last night. I've tried so hard to be in control. I hate it when I can't take care of myself, when I let my children down. It reminds me of how I felt when Glen was alive.

Everyone thinks I'm so positive about life, but what they don't know is that being positive—or rather, pretending to be positive—is the only way I can survive. It's the only way I did survive all those years with Glen. But inside, where no one can see, I don't feel positive at all. I feel angry and depressed. I feel scared and cold. Yes, cold, even though I really haven't been cold for over a year.

If only people knew . . .

I never told anyone that Glen put a lock on our thermostat so that I couldn't turn up the heat when he was gone, no matter that my babies' lips were blue with cold. He lowered it each day before he left, claiming the sun would warm the house for us. But so many times the layers weren't enough, and the cold seeped into our very bones. We were all sick too often, but we tried to hide any sickness because it would make Glen angry to think we might have to go to the expense of a doctor.

Baking helped—especially if I closed off the kitchen doorway with sheets. No wonder I'm so good at baking. I soon discovered that ice cubes in a plastic sack taped on the thermostat did a decent job of getting the heat to kick on. I did it even after he discovered it that one time and sent me to the hospital with a bloody nose and a broken arm.

I am so glad to be free. I know now that I should have left him years and years ago, but I didn't know how. I thought he would kill me. Or maybe one of the children.

Well, I'm okay now. We're all okay.

I just have to figure out how not to react when the children raise their voices. They've had enough therapy, so I don't believe they're following in Glen's footsteps. They're simply teenagers who argue. I guess at least arguing implies that both are speaking and trying to work things out.

Ugh, there I go again trying to be positive when there is nothing positive about arguing. Then again, maybe there is. I know I wished for years that I could argue, but speaking back only made Glen more angry.

I wouldn't want anyone reading this journal in some future day to think that if Glen hadn't died I would still be with him. I had opened my own checking account, and I was saving the money I made selling cosmetics. I did everything online or in person so no bills came to the house. I'd saved up thousands of dollars, and as soon as I had a safe place, I was going to leave. He didn't even know

I was making money. He thought I sold barely enough to be able to buy my own makeup. He didn't mind that. He liked me looking pretty. Sometimes I think that was the only thing he liked about me.

At other times I remember the days when he looked at me with that certain something in his eyes, when I still felt that rush of love, the wondrous surprise that he was all mine. No, better not to dwell on that. He was sick, that's all there is to say about it. He missed out on what could have been a lot of joy.

He also wasted so much of my life. No, I wasted it. I was the one who chose to marry him. Looking back, I can see that I rushed to marry because I was trying to get away from my overbearing father. An abusive husband, an overly strict father—what is it about men these days? Yet I see my friends finding good men. Take Kerrianne's wedding yesterday. I was so happy for her and Ryan. He will make a good husband and be a good daddy for her children. I can see they're really in love. They've both been lucky to find love twice.

I'll be forty later this year, and I don't feel that I've ever known real love. Sometimes I think real love exists for everyone but me.

I wish I didn't have to go to church," grumbled Ashley, as she grabbed a pancake off the plate and headed for the door.

"Be careful what you wish for," Tina told her seventeen-year-old daughter. "It may come true. Believe me, if you were sick or your leg was broken and you couldn't do anything, you'd be happy enough to go to church. Going to church is a blessing."

Ashley bent to put on her shoes. "It's not that I don't like church. It's just so early."

"Early?" Skip looked at her, his hands in his pockets. "Uh, Ashley, it's eleven already. You've made us late again."

Ashley opened her mouth to retort but instead glanced worriedly at Tina.

"I'm okay," Tina said, feeling a strange pressure in her chest. She'd really blown it last night if Ashley was being so careful. "Don't worry, honey. Let's get out to the car." Tina turned to the little boys, Dallin and Ronnie. "Shoes, boys. Quick!"

Ashley shot Skip a deadly glare when she thought Tina's back was turned. Internally, Tina sighed. *It's okay,* she told herself. *Everything is okay.* The voice she heard in her mind wasn't her own but Maxine's—soothing and supportive. Tina felt a flood of gratitude toward the Lord for sending her this wonderful friend.

She'd met Maxine shortly after Glen died, and soon Maxine began selling cosmetics under her. Maxine was such a go-getter that her work had really helped Tina through the financial dearth she'd experienced as she waited for Glen's modest life insurance policy to be paid. Now Maxine was her dearest friend, and through her she'd met the other single women in the Independence Club.

Smiling, Tina went outside to where her car was parked on the slab of concrete next to the house. The Toyota had once been Glen's pride and joy, and Tina had never driven it until after he was gone. She liked it so much that she'd sold her ancient minivan and kept it instead.

The sun felt warm on her skin, and Tina lifted her face to better feel the heat. She breathed in the scent of clean air. Not a trace remained of last night's slushy rain. "What a beautiful day," she said. "Look at that blue sky. I bet winter is finally over. The flowers will be out soon."

Skip and Ashley both laughed, forgetting their argument. "You think everything's beautiful," Ashley said.

Tina put an arm around her daughter. "That's right, especially you. Now get in the car before those boys rip up the seat." Dallin and Ronnie had gone obediently to the car and were wrestling inside. Tina felt a convoluted sense of pleasure watching her young sons roll around in the car as they had been forbidden to do by their father. Was it wrong to be grateful that Glen had been driving to an electronics show with friends when the accident happened, instead of his own car?

"Can I drive?" Ashley asked.

Tina nodded and tossed her the keys. "Buckle up, boys."

At church her feeling of contentment continued. She made sure to put Ashley next to nine-year-old Dallin and six-year-old Ronnie next to Skip. That way they were less likely to make problems. The closer in age, the more they talked or poked at each other.

Ashley leaned in close to Tina over Dallin's head. "Mom, who's that?"

Their ward included a new subdivision a few streets over, and at seventeen, Ashley was always watching for new faces—particularly new guy faces.

Tina turned her head in the direction Ashley had indicated, and her eyes landed on one of the most handsome men she had ever seen. He was muscular, with thick, light brown hair cut short in the back and slightly longer on top—a cut most men her age seemed to wear these days. His face was handsome in a strong way, as though chiseled from the mountains, where he probably spent most of his time. Even though he was sitting, she could tell he was tall because his broad shoulders sat well above the line of the bench. At that moment he turned and caught her gaze, his deep brown eyes seeming to smile. Tina flushed.

"He's staring at you!" Ashley whispered.

He *was* staring, and Tina felt a rush of gladness that she'd taken time with her hair and makeup this morning. She looked her best, though perhaps a little on the thin side, a remnant from her time with Glen. When everything else had gone to pieces, when he had mandated even the brand of cereals she could buy, she'd at least had control over her weight.

"Mom, who is he? I've never seen that girl beside him."

Tina stared down at her hands. Girl. But of course he was married. What was she thinking? This was a family ward. A few single men with children had come and gone over the past year, but most quickly found their way to a singles ward.

"I'll probably find out in Young Women's."

Tina blinked and dared another look. Sure enough, the girl was far too young to be the man's wife. He had to be over forty. Inside her chest, her heart pumped overtime. She tried not to let herself find hope—she'd already met so many men who weren't what they'd seemed. Being single was a lot of fun when you weren't looking to settle down, that was true, but now that she thought she might be ready for love, dating had become complicated. Most important were her children and who they might like. She'd only brought two men to meet them—and neither of those had worked out.

Tina had difficulty paying attention to the speakers. Her eyes kept slipping to the brown-haired man and conjuring up all sorts of reasons why she shouldn't be interested—his wife was home with the flu, or she was still in another state packing up their old house. Possibly he was in the middle of an abusive divorce. That last thought chilled her long enough to allow her to listen to an entire talk.

Throughout the meeting Dallin held her hand, tracing the

veins with his finger. He didn't try to talk over her to Ronnie as he normally did or whisper to Ashley. *He's finally growing up,* Tina thought. *He's listening, like I should be doing.*

After the meeting the children scattered. Tina slowly picked up the paper Ronnie had been drawing on and the colored pencils he'd let drop to the floor. Skip had forgotten his scriptures, so she'd have to carry them as well. Tina followed the crowd down the aisles. Miriam, one of her friends and a former visiting teaching companion, stopped to whisper in her ear. "Did you see that new guy? You've got to meet him. He's gorgeous! Oh, and single, too."

Tina blinked. "Who are you talking about?"

But Miriam was gone, chasing after her four-year-old, who was running up to the podium. Tina watched them briefly and then turned and stumbled right into someone. The new man.

"Oh," she said, more from the impact than anything else. She tried to laugh it off, but his eyes were locked onto hers, and she felt disoriented. People streamed past them, the crowd thinning rapidly.

"I thought I should introduce myself," he said, sticking out a hand. "I'm Scott Manning. My daughter, Callie, and I moved into the ward over the weekend."

"Hi, I'm Tina Dayley." She let his hand engulf hers for a wonderful moment.

"Actually, I knew that. I've been told about you."

Tina stiffened. "Told about me?"

He grinned. "That you're single. Have you noticed how everyone always plays matchmaker?"

"Oh, that." She relaxed. Not many people knew that Glen had been abusive. Most would be shocked if they understood how his unexpected death had freed her and the children, giving them more relief than it had grief. "Yes, I've noticed."

"Well, I'm glad to meet you. Would you mind showing me to Sunday School? Someone already whisked my daughter away, thank goodness. I had no idea where to tell her to go. Come to think of it, she had red hair—redder than yours, though. Any relation?"

"I bet it was my daughter, Ashley. She was curious about your daughter during sacrament meeting. She's the president of the Laurel class."

"Callie's a Laurel, too."

"I'm sure they'll get along." Tina took a deep breath as she led him down the hall. "So, you're single," she began. She'd played this game enough over the past year, and usually it was fun and easy. It hadn't really mattered to her if they turned out to be tax evaders, ladies' men, still married, or not looking for a committed relationship. Once she realized the truth, she could always walk away because she wasn't involved. Yet already something was different about Scott. She could feel it—just as she had on the day she'd met Glen.

Look how that turned out. She shivered at the thought, both because she had suffered so much and because she'd do it all again if that was the only way she could have her children.

Scott flashed her a smile. "I've been single about eighteen months now. My wife left for good about two years ago." He shrugged and looked away, as though embarrassed.

"Callie chose to live with you?"

"Callie was with her for a while after she left, but it didn't work. It was a mess."

"I'm sorry," Tina offered.

He forced a laugh, and even Tina could tell it was fake.

How many times had she done the same thing? She sensed there was more to his story, but she would have to earn the rest, exactly as he would have to earn her story. At least the true one. She'd never shared it with any man before.

"Well, you've moved into the right ward," she said lightly, placing her hand on his arm as they stopped outside the Relief Society room where they held Sunday School. "The Young Women leaders are fabulous—all the youth leaders are. You'll see."

Their eyes met and held. Her hand was still on his arm, and through the material of his long-sleeved shirt she could feel the warmth of his skin. His smile made her stomach turn somersaults.

"Thanks," he said softly, pausing while a woman opened the door and went inside, leaving them alone again. Then he added, as she had known he would, "Now there's just one more thing—will you go out with me?"

She answered in the way she had planned to answer all along. "I would love to go out with you."

"We're still moving in, and I have to make several more trips from our old place in Fillmore, so we'll have to plan for Friday."

Tina wanted more. "I've got a better idea. You're probably all in disarray at home. Why don't you come over for dinner after church?"

His eyes widened for an instant before he masked his surprise. "Thank you. I think I'll take you up on that."

Could it be possible to fall in love in only a few moments? Tina didn't know. With Glen it had taken six months.

There was so much about this man she didn't know—practically everything—but all the dating experience she'd gained over the past year as a single adult told her there was something worth pursuing here. On the outside she might appear to be a widow eager to find a man—any man—to take care of her, but this was different. And she knew he felt the same. She *knew*.

She sat with Scott during Sunday School, heedless of the curious glances and knowing smiles cast her way. After Relief Society was over, she didn't see him again but knew he'd be over in less than an hour. She hurried the kids to the car, giving them assignments on the way. "Skip, you start the grill. Ashley, you set up the table on the patio. It's a beautiful day, so let's make the best of it." Her kitchen was small at best, and she didn't want to be crowded. "Ronnie, you set the table, and Dallin, you start washing vegetables for a tray. The others will help you when they're finished."

"I'm glad you invited them, Mom." Ashley backed carefully out of the parking space. "Callie seems really cool. But kind of sad."

"You mean sort of like Dallin?" Ronnie asked. "He's sad today."

Tina turned around and looked at Dallin, who was sitting in the middle between Skip and Ronnie in the backseat. Sure enough, he did look sad. "Are you feeling sick?" she asked.

He shook his head. "I feel fine." His gaze slid past hers.

Tina waited until they were home and the other children busy with their assignments before she approached Dallin again. He stood at the sink, a carrot peeler in his hand, but he wasn't moving.

"Honey, what's wrong?" Tina leaned on the counter next to him. "You've been quiet all day. What's bothering you? Is it because we're having people to dinner?"

Dallin stared down at his hands without answering, his brown hair falling forward to shield his eyes. A tear drop splashed onto his hands.

"Dallin," she prompted.

He looked up, brown eyes watery, eyes that reminded her of Glen's. "Promise you won't be mad?"

"Am I that scary?" She let her mouth drop in surprise. "Come on, when was the last time I was mad at you?"

"Last week when I didn't do my math."

"Did I beat you? Or lock you up in your room for a week? Did I feed you only bread and water?"

A tiny smile appeared on his thin face. "No. But you said it was a good opportunity for me to learn to wash the front door."

"There, you see?" She touched his arm. "I'm not going to be angry. And all the doors are already clean."

He looked down again at the carrot in his hand, pursing his lips in thought. Then, almost too quietly to be heard, he said, "I used to wish Daddy would die. Or go away, or something. Then he did."

Tina felt her heart crack a little. "Well, to tell you the truth, sometimes I used to wish he'd go away, too."

Dallin gazed at her, his brown eyes large in his round face. "You did?"

"Uh-huh. But I have to tell you a secret. Wishes like that never make things happen. You know that, don't you?"

He hesitated long enough to tell her that was exactly what he'd thought. "Are you sure?"

"Very sure." She pulled him close and smoothed his hair. "You are not responsible for your daddy's accident."

"You told Ashley to be careful what she wished for this morning."

Now Tina was beginning to understand. The scene she'd made last night had started Dallin thinking about his dad again, and her inadvertent comment to Ashley had only made things worse.

"Oh, that's because most people who wish for stuff work toward getting it," she told him. "You know, like people who want to be rich might work so hard they're always gone and end up missing seeing their kids grow up. That sort of thing. But wishes alone don't make things happen. Only actions. Neither of us would have done anything to hurt your daddy."

"He hurt you."

Tina swallowed hard. "He wasn't well."

He thought about that for a moment. "You were going to leave."

"Yes."

"I'm glad." Dallin nodded with satisfaction. "Because sometimes, when you weren't around, he'd grab my arm real hard, and he'd push me. He made Ronnie cry. That's why I wished he'd go away."

Tina's throat felt as swollen as it had the day Glen choked her, the day she'd finally decided to leave him. Because she'd been at many of her children's sessions with their counselor, she was mostly aware of what had happened between Glen and the children on the rare occasions when she hadn't been around to protect them, but every so often one of them would explode with a new memory that threatened the fragile web of sanity she had woven around what remained of their family.

She fought down the fury at Glen that threatened to overwhelm her each time she had a conversation like this. "That's why I was leaving. I wanted to keep all of you safe."

"I know," he said with a child's simple faith. "I'm glad he's gone, but I miss him, too." Tears gathered in his eyes.

"I know, honey." She blinked back her own tears. "I feel exactly the same way."

Dallin started peeling the carrot, the tension seeping from his body and the sadness from his face. Tina knew the moment was over. She had to make herself move on.

She went to the fridge and pulled out the pork chops she'd been marinating. She'd thaw a couple more in the microwave and add them to the others, making sure the guests received the tastier pieces.

"You-hoo!"

Tina turned to see her friend Evie McClaine coming in from the patio. "Evie, hi."

Evie's appearance at the back door wasn't exactly a surprise because she came over almost every weekday to work out on Tina's treadmill. Normally, she didn't come on Sundays unless she was having a hard day with her diet and needed emotional support. She'd lost fifteen pounds by exercising the past four months and, according to her doctor, needed to lose at least forty-five more to be healthy.

"Ashley told me to come on in." Evie had short, bluish black hair that curled slightly under at her jaw line, arresting blue eyes, shapely lips, beautiful cheek bones, and blemish-free skin. She had been a beauty queen in her youth—long before she'd gained seventy-five pounds. "I was hoping to find a walking partner because it's such a beautiful afternoon," Evie added, "but it looks like you're about ready to eat." She looked hopefully at Tina.

"Don't you usually walk with Maxine on the weekends?" Tina asked.

Evie frowned, a line appearing between her eyes. "Okay, I'll admit, Maxine did suggest that I ask you to walk with me today. She didn't say why. Is everything all right?"

"Yes, everything's just fine. Maybe she had her own plans." Tina couldn't bring herself to be really irritated at Maxine for checking up on her. At least she hadn't told Evie everything. Her secret was safe.

"Yeah, she's probably doing something with Harold. So . . ." Evie looked around the kitchen. "Hey, Dallin, looks like you're doing a fabulous job there."

"You're welcome to stay for dinner." Tina felt reluctant making the invitation. She'd wanted to get to know Scott, and Evie was so pretty and vivacious that she might just steal him for herself—never mind that she was at least several years older and carrying a few extra pounds. None of that would matter once he got to know her.

"We're having guests," Dallin volunteered. "A guy moved into the new subdivision."

Evie's eyes widened as she looked at Tina. "You're having a man over?"

"A guy and his daughter from the ward," Tina corrected her. "That's different."

"It is *so* not different! He's single, and that's that. Now for sure I'm staying, whether you want me or not. Wild horses or a case of raspberry-filled donuts couldn't drag me away. I've got to check out the man who gets to meet your children on a first date."

"Well, one thing's for sure," Tina said dryly, "we won't lack for conversation."

Evie moved around the table and reached in the drawer for another carrot peeler. "No, we won't. Not that it matters. You're

28

so beautiful that I'm sure he won't be able to take his eyes off you."

Suddenly, Tina was glad her friend was there. Everything with Scott seemed to be moving at light speed, and she'd learned too well that relationships were a bit like walking a tightrope. She might need someone to catch her if she fell.

CHAPTER

3

Evie

It wasn't as though Cecilia was prettier than I am, though she was thinner—like I was at her age—but she was enough like me to be me ten years earlier, the professional version of me, I mean. All I ever wanted to do was to stay home and be a good wife and mother. I wanted to raise a whole bunch of kids. Jason wanted only three, so that was what we had. Cecilia was a teacher, a woman who always had her makeup on and her hair just right. She wore suits to teach in and worked out at the gym. She took her own car in when it needed to be fixed (as I learned to do after Jason left). Cecilia was mother to a roomful of children that she didn't have to feed and tuck in at night.

Jason met her when she went into the bank for investment advice. They hit it off immediately, but instead of leaving the relationship as an acquaintanceship, she came in again and again. They went out to lunch.

That's all I know, really. And most of that I gleaned from people who used to be my friends but who really weren't anymore after the breakup. We could divide up the money and the belongings, but how do you divide up friends? They had to choose sides, and I think I lost more than he did. I remember running into our old neighbors a few months after they were married. I hadn't seen them since I'd moved out of the house six months before. The wife let it slip that they'd been to dinner with Jason and Cecilia. She said Cecilia reminded her of me, that it was almost like I hadn't left at all.

Hearing that hurt a lot—both that Cecilia was like me and that she had so completely been absorbed into my old life. My old friends weren't my friends any longer but were hers instead. How could Jason have traded our future and our eternal family for a younger, thinner wife? How could he have simply stopped loving me? Was it because I gained too much weight? Sometimes I think so.

Maxine says if he were any kind of a man, he would have honored his vows, that he would have tried to fix what was wrong and not walked away. She says if he'd been bothered by the weight, it should have been only out of concern for my health and that he should have joined a gym with me and hired a personal trainer. He could have easily afforded it.

I know men do care a lot about appearance, and I admit that I could have done better at keeping myself fit, and better as well in tending to my marriage. I took him and the permanence of our relationship for granted. Even so, I didn't deserve to lose everything. I didn't deserve any of what he and Cecilia did to me. I blame them both, but I blame him more than her because after the children left home, he really was my whole world.

Now I see him only at functions where our children invite both *of us. Cecilia is always at his side. By unspoken agreement, I come late to the events, and they leave early. I guess I can be grateful he waited until Julia graduated from high school before telling me our marriage was over. Julia was only seventeen, but she went right to college that summer so it wasn't really hard on her. It was weird, though, when she got married last year and Jason and Cecilia were at the temple ceremony. It's very difficult to get those blessings restored when you've been unfaithful, and I suspect he lied during his interviews to gain what he wanted. Seeing them there, I felt a wave of betrayal as though I had lost everything all over again. How could he be in the temple with another woman when he'd made promises there with me?*

To be wholly truthful, I didn't lose everything, like some of my divorced friends did. I got more than half the money, which was a lot. I don't have to wait for alimony because of the settlement but can live off the interest of my investments. I also bought a new house and a car. I like being in control of my own finances. I'm glad I got the killer lawyer everyone recommended.

Sometimes, though, I wonder if I should have stayed in the old house and kept my old friends. It hurt too much at the time to see their pity, to feel their stares. I kept wondering what they might be saying behind my back, if they blamed everything on my weight. I've since learned that weight isn't who you are; it's only the suit you're in. Now I suspect many of them would have helped me. I just didn't know how to ask. I felt so alone.

I have a new life now and good friends. Maxine and the rest of the Independence Club are my mainstays. I love them so much. I'm exercising and finally losing a bit of weight, though it's not coming off as fast as I'd hoped. Rosalva says that's because I'm forty-five. Well, she's three years behind me, and she doesn't have a problem. Not that I'm jealous. Besides Maxine, Rosalva is my dearest friend in the Independence Club. I thank my Heavenly Father for them every single day. I can't wait for Wednesday to meet them for brunch at Mimi's. Two more days.

So what will I do today? Truthfully, I'd like to sit down and eat an entire box of Hostess raspberry-filled donuts. They're my absolute favorites. But eating when you're depressed is like an addiction, and I don't want to let myself be controlled. Still, it's hard.

That's why I walk with Maxine or go to Tina's to walk on her treadmill—the top-of-the-line model that she inherited from her husband when he died. I know I should buy my own, and I can well afford it, but I'm afraid I won't use it if I have to stay home. I'm here alone so much as it is. Besides, I don't know if I could endure the looks I'd get at the store where I'd have to buy it. A fat woman buying a treadmill, the poor thing. Don't people know it's rude to stare? Maybe I'll buy a treadmill after I lose fifteen more pounds.

The shrill ring of the phone cut through the silence of the late morning. Evie McClaine set down her pen and shut her new journal. It felt good to write again after all these years. Before her divorce six years ago, she'd written at least once a week. She couldn't bear to read those journals now. The emotions they held were still far too hurtful.

She picked up the phone. "Hello?"

"Hi, Evie. It's me, Cecilia."

Evie blinked, her mind unable to process the information. Cecilia, the woman who had stolen her husband. The woman who had accepted his attention even while knowing he was married.

"What do you want?" The effort to be marginally civil made Evie's voice husky.

"I—I . . . I don't know. I need someone to talk to, and I just . . . There's no one else. No one who will understand."

Icy fingers inched up Evie's back and down her arms. There had been a time when she'd felt that way, a time when not even she understood the insanity that had become her life. "Understand what?" she managed.

"Please. Will you meet me somewhere? A restaurant maybe? We could have lunch."

At least Cecilia didn't want her to go back to the old house, to be a guest in what had once been her own domain.

She still wanted to say no. Justice demanded that she say no. But the heartache in Cecilia's voice could have been her own all those years ago. "All right," she said tightly. "How about that pancake restaurant by Wal-Mart?" Since Cecilia lived in Lehi and she lived in Pleasant Grove, it would be a good location for both of them. Besides, Evie loved pancakes—any time of the day—and she might as well get something out of the deal.

"Can you come right now?"

"Well . . ." Evie really didn't have anything else to do. She should have gone to Tina's to exercise, but yesterday at dinner she'd heard Tina make plans to drive somewhere with Scott to pick up a load of his possessions. Tina wasn't due home before her kids' school let out, so there was nothing really stopping her from meeting Cecilia. "I guess I can work it in."

"I really appreciate it. I just—I just . . ." Cecilia trailed off. "I can be there in ten minutes."

"Make it twenty. It'll take me fifteen minutes just to drive there."

"Okay. I'll see you then." A click signaled the disconnection of the phone.

Evie went to her bedroom to change into her black pants and brown suit jacket that she'd had specially tailored. The outfit made her feel confident, which was exactly what she needed for this meeting. Then she brought out her cosmetics, purchased from Maxine, and made sure her face was perfect, smiling at the mirror when she was finished. She looked good.

Strange how sometimes when she looked in a half mirror like this one, she could see that she was pretty and didn't even feel overweight. It was only the full-length mirrors that made her want to hide away. "But I'll do it," she said, lifting her chin. She no longer had visions of being slender but of losing enough to be healthy, enough to feel good. And she would do it for herself, not for any man.

Evie was five minutes late to the restaurant, and Cecilia was already waiting for her at a table, twirling a lock of short light brown hair and staring out the window at something only she could see. Cecilia had gained weight in the last year since they'd seen each other at Julia's wedding—a lot of weight. Her face hadn't fared well in the transition, and Evie felt a shock at seeing her. This was the woman who'd come between her and Jason? If Cecilia hadn't looked so worn and miserable, Evie might have experienced pleasure at this unsought revenge. As it was, her heart went out to the other woman.

"Sorry I'm late." She slid onto the bench seat opposite Cecilia.

"I haven't been here long." Cecilia's blue eyes ran over her face. "You look good, Evie, but then you always do. You've lost weight, too, haven't you?"

Evie nodded once, still taking in the transformation of her enemy.

"I'll be right with you!" sang a cheery-looking waitress as she sailed past their table.

Cecilia ran a finger down the side of her menu. "Well, as you can see, I've gained a lot lately. I've been too upset to exercise, and all I want to do is eat. My face is all puffy."

"I know what that's like," Evie ventured.

"I doubt you ever reached this low. I feel like I'm living in a nightmare!"

A burst of anger shot through Evie. "How would you know how I ever felt," she spat. "You didn't exactly bother to ask me before you stole my husband."

Cecilia's face collapsed, becoming red and blotchy, and her voice wobbled as she replied. "I deserve that. I know I do. And if anyone understands how I feel, it's probably you. I'm just so confused, and it hurts so bad." She fell silent as a pregnant waitress passed their table.

"I'll be right with you," the girl told them with a bright smile that filled her whole face and made Evie's heart ache. They nodded, and she was gone.

"What happened?" Evie asked.

"I did everything I could to make our marriage work—everything." Cecilia swallowed with apparent difficulty, her voice rising as she continued. "But he keeps betraying me. Most of the time I feel he's not really part of the relationship at all. I finally realized he's never going to change."

Evie reeled with the news. All these years she'd wondered if she had only done this or that, would he have stayed? Yet here he was again, breaking the heart of a woman with his inability to keep his promises. "I'm sorry," she told Cecilia. "For you, I mean, not for him."

The first waitress passed by again. "I'll be with you in a

minute," she said cheerfully. "Or I'll get someone else. I'm sorry it's taking so long."

"Okay," Evie said, barely looking at her.

"I didn't want you to come here only to tell you that." Cecilia dabbed at her eyes with a crumpled tissue. "I also wanted to tell you that I'm really, really sorry. I had no idea of the pain you must have gone through—the pain that I caused. I thought only of what I felt. I believed the things he told me about you."

"What, that I wasn't a good wife? That I wasn't loving enough? That I let myself go?"

Cecilia didn't meet her gaze but stared at her finger as it traced tight circles on the table. "Something like that. But I'm sorry now. I regret . . . so much. I can't believe I was so stupid. What made me think he would treat me any better than a woman he'd been married to for more than twenty years?"

Evie could tell she was ready to dissolve into tears, despite any observers in the restaurant. "So," she said briskly, steering Cecilia away from self-pity, "what next? Counseling? Separation?"

"We did counseling. It helped for a few months, and then it didn't help anymore." She shrugged. "Honestly, I don't know where to go from here, but I can't stay with him. It'd be different if he wanted to make it work. To tell the truth, I don't think he even cares. It's too easy to walk away if he doesn't get what he wants. I do know that I can't live like this. I've still got my job, though I'm only teaching part time now—I got a substitute today—and I can't afford to keep up that house by myself. I guess I should move out, get an apartment."

Evie shook her head. "No. Don't leave. He's the one who should go. You have to stand your ground and get everything you can from him so that you can take care of the future. Just think of it. That house with no more toenail clippings on the sink. You can always sell it later."

Cecilia managed a strangled laugh. "I won't miss those clippings, that's for sure. Or the way he leaves the hose strung out over the lawn."

"Or the peanut butter on his pancakes." Evie wrinkled her nose.

"Or the TV in the bedroom."

"Actually, I kind of like it there now," Evie said, "but if I was married, I'd definitely take it out." They both laughed. "I'm sorry it's taking so long to order," Evie added. "They aren't usually so slow. And there's no one even really here."

"That's okay. I'm not hungry, anyway. It's still early for lunch—and the last thing I need is food." Cecilia's eyes shimmered again with tears.

"Look, I'll give you my lawyer's number." Evie put her hand over Cecilia's. "She'll walk you through everything. But are you really sure? I mean really, really sure."

Cecilia nodded, a tear slipping down her swollen cheeks. "There's nothing left." In her voice Evie heard the truth. It was over. Strangely, the knowledge didn't give her any pleasure but rather a feeling of compassion.

The pregnant waitress stopped by their table. "Did anyone get your order?" she asked.

"No."

"Well, I'll be right ba—"

Evie arose. "You know what? Don't worry about it. We're finished here. But thanks."

Ceclia arose, too, and under a flurry of apologies from the waitress, they left the restaurant.

"I have the number somewhere at home," Evie said as they went down the sidewalk. "I haven't needed to use it for a while. I'll look for it and call you."

"I wouldn't mind coming over and helping you find it," Cecilia said. Then she hurried to add, "That is, if you don't mind and if you don't have other plans."

"I was only going to exercise. I can do it later." Oddly enough, Evie was enjoying Cecilia's company.

"Oh, do you go to a gym?"

"No. Usually, I go to my friend's house and use her treadmill. I like the company. On the weekend I sometimes walk outside with a friend."

"You should really try my gym. It has water aerobics, weights, treadmills—all sorts of programs. The people there are really nice."

Evie made a face. "Yeah, nice and skinny."

Cecilia laughed. "Well, there are a lot of people there who are really into fitness, but there are also a lot who're trying to lose a few pounds or to maintain."

"My doctor says I need to lose at least forty-five more pounds," Evie confessed. "That's just to be healthy. I still wouldn't be thin."

"I'm in the same boat." They smiled at each other.

"You want to follow me to my house?" Evie asked.

"Sure."

When Evie pulled into her garage in Pleasant Grove, an old red sports car was sitting at the curb. Her friend Rosalva paced on the sidewalk, wearing high heels, snug jeans, and a red top that set off her nice figure. Her long dark brown hair was styled becomingly around her face, highlighted slightly with glints of lighter brown. Her full lips gleamed a moist red, and her olive skin, a legacy of her exotic Mexican heritage, was beautiful in the morning sun. Evie knew Rosalva had turned forty-two last year, but she looked better than ever.

Evie climbed from her car and walked down the driveway. "Rosalva, what are you doing here?"

"I just wanted to talk. How about going for a walk?" Her accent was thick this morning, and that told Evie something was bothering her.

"In those shoes?" Evie glanced down at Rosalva's feet.

"We don't have to go far. I'm used to heels."

"Well, I can't right this minute." Evie motioned her chin to where Cecilia was parking her sleek new car behind Rosalva's old one. "If you'll come in and wait a minute while I get her a phone number, then we can talk. Are you working today?" Rosalva was a new assistant manager at the Sizzler restaurant in Orem and would need to leave soon if she was working.

"Not till afternoon. I'm training new girls tonight. But who's she?" Rosalva looked with interest at Cecilia, who was standing uncertainly on the sidewalk.

"That's Cecilia."

Rosalva's eyes grew big. "*The* Cecilia?"

"Afraid so. I think she's leaving him."

"Strange, but she looks like you. Except your hair's darker and your face is, well"—she lowered her voice—"pretty."

"She looked more like me when they got married. She was thinner then. Now she weighs as much as I do. Come on, I'll introduce you."

"Cecilia," Evie said, as they reached her. "I want you to meet Rosalva. She's my best friend."

"Nice to meet you," Cecilia stuck out her hand awkwardly.

Rosalva touched her fingers briefly and then put her hands

on her hips. "So you're the other woman." There was a challenge in her voice, and Evie knew she was trying to protect her.

Cecilia colored. "I guess I am."

"Well, I knew it was only a matter of time till you came to your senses." Rosalva flipped her hair behind her shoulder. "Any man who could leave Evie obviously has serious problems."

"I, uh, yeah," Cecilia floundered.

"Come on." Evie turned and started up the drive. "Don't mind her, Cecilia. Rosalva is divorced, too. Her husband was twice the jerk that ours was—is." Weird, saying it that way. "I'll get you your phone number, and then we'll all sit down for a snack. It's nearly lunchtime, and I feel like cheating a bit on my diet."

Cecilia hurried to catch up. "Actually, I was thinking we could go to my gym. I'm allowed to take visitors. I always have my gym bag in my car so I can go after work. What about it?"

"That's a great idea." Rosalva was smiling.

"You can come, too," Cecilia offered with an eagerness both pathetic and charming.

Rosalva shook her head. "No. I've got to work later. I actually came by to ask Evie's advice about something."

"About a guy, I bet."

"How did you know?"

"It's the same reason I called her."

They had reached the sitting room, and Evie turned to face them. "And we all know I'm the voice of experience. I should open a clinic." The others laughed. "Sheesh, I'm as clueless as either of you. Have a seat."

As she settled on the brown leather sofa, Cecilia looked

around in appreciation. "Wow, this is a nice place. I like the vaulted ceilings, yet it's still kind of cozy, isn't it?"

"That's why I bought it." Evie should have known Cecilia would like it. After all, she lived in Evie's old house, and this was simply a scaled-down version of that one. She'd even used the maple wood motifs similar to those she'd had built into the bigger house. "Make yourselves comfortable, and I'll go find the number."

When she returned, Rosalva was sitting in her favorite arm charm, spilling her guts. "So basically, we met at the wedding reception on Saturday night. When I found out he was our friend's new brother-in-law, I was leery because she hadn't told us good things about him. Turns out I really liked him. Still, I've already had one jerk of a husband. This time I want to find Mr. Right. I want someone who will fight to make it work, no matter what."

Cecilia nodded sympathetically. "Well, I say go out with him a couple times, test him a little. See how he is around his family. But don't let your heart get involved until you see what you're up against."

"Oh, tell me you're not talking about Willard Oakman," Evie groaned.

Rosalva looked up at her sheepishly, and her accent was thicker as she continued. "Yeah. Silly, huh? But you got to figure that Kerrianne—that's our friend's name who got married, Cecilia. Anyway, Kerrianne married his brother, so he can't be all that bad, right? They had the same upbringing."

"Well, Willard's a lawyer." Evie settled on the couch near Cecilia. "He followed in his father's footsteps, and his brother didn't. From what I heard, their father never had much time for either of them."

Rosalva sighed. "His being a lawyer is probably most of his attraction. I'm tired of working so hard to make ends meet. I don't know how I'm going to pay for Jaime's mission."

"You know I'll help." Evie would be glad to put her money for good use. While only two of her children were married, all three were independent. Besides, if they needed money or someone to co-sign a loan, they usually went to their father, who was only too glad to buy his way into their good graces. Evie liked to think they came to her out of love.

Rosalva stood. "I'd better get going. I'll see myself out. Nice to meet you, Cecilia."

"You, too."

"Hey," Evie called after her, "for what it's worth, I agree with Cecilia. Go ahead and date him a time or two, but don't start liking him too much until you know what's what."

"Thanks!" Rosalva's voice drifted back to them. "See you at brunch on Wednesday."

"She's nice," Cecilia said into the abrupt silence. Without Rosalva in the room, everything seemed to have lost both color and sound.

Evie handed her the paper with the lawyer's phone number. "Rosalva's been my biggest support since . . ." She trailed off. How had she forgotten that the woman in front of her had been partly responsible for all her pain? "Well, there you have it." She stood, hoping Cecilia would get the hint and leave. It wasn't like they could really be friends or anything, not with the actions of the past wedged between them.

Cecilia's brow furrowed. "But aren't we going to the gym? This is a great time of day because it's mostly housewives. I don't get to go this early that often because I work, but I thought—well, don't you want to give it a try? Or if you're getting hungry, we could go out for lunch first and then head over. That's a great time, too. Businessmen come in after their lunches, or people who work earlier shifts." She looked so vulnerable standing there, with her beautifully styled brown hair and nice suit contrasting with her puffy face and sad, sad blue eyes.

Evie's heart lurched. Almost, she was seeing herself after Jason had left and she'd been so alone. "Okay, why not?" she said. "The worst that can happen is we can make all those skinny minnies there grateful for what they've got. Tell me, why is it that the skinny ones always complain about how much they weigh?"

Cecilia laughed. "When I understand that, I'll probably be smart enough to understand all the other mysteries of the universe—including men."

"That will never happen."

An hour and a half later, after a light lunch at the Sizzler, Evie was puffing on a treadmill, a book on the stand before her. She might not be as thin as she'd like, but at least she would appear intellectual—not that anyone was noticing. She scanned the room subtly to make sure.

A large guy two treadmills over gave her a warm, if timid, smile. He had kind brown eyes and short, curly blond hair. Too fleshy, really, to be handsome but apparently good-natured. Someone she'd like to meet. She smiled back—and then her jaw nearly hit the moving belt under her feet.

Beyond the smiling guy on the treadmill, a new man had come into the large room. He was a fine specimen of the male gender, enough to be any woman's Mr. Perfect. He had vibrant blue eyes, and his chiseled face was so good looking that Evie actually felt weak looking at him. He was taller than her five foot seven by a couple of inches and walked with an air of confidence that drew every eye. Even his hair was extraordinary, the top bleached whiter than the rest and worn slightly long.

Evie's treadmill stopped as her time came to an end. She almost tripped but grabbed the support bars just in time. She couldn't take her eyes off the newcomer. He was about her age—would it be possible for him to ever notice her as a woman? *Probably not,* she thought as her ever-constant insecurities roared to life inside her—insecurities that had been born on the day her husband told her he was leaving. She'd been rejected by her own husband; why should this perfect man even look twice at her?

"That's Christopher," Cecilia said in her ear. "He's one of the sweetest, kindest men alive. He's usually here between this time and an hour or so later. I was just thinking that you two might get along."

He was coming her way—and he was smiling!

Involuntarily, Evie stepped toward the end of her treadmill. She took another step and another.

"Oh, excuse me," he said, bumping into her. "I didn't see you there." His gaze flicked over her body, and she regretted wearing the black spandex that left none of her bulk hidden.

He smiled again, but it was at someone behind her. A leggy blonde stepped off a treadmill and came to meet him.

Cecilia sighed and watched him as he moved away. "He's beautiful."

"Christopher." Evie liked the sound of the name.

"Oh, that's not Christopher," Cecilia said. "That's Jack. Come on. I'll introduce you to Christopher." With an arm on her elbow, Cecelia took Evie to meet the smiling, heavyset man two treadmills over.

CHAPTER

4

Rosalva

I've seen Willard Oakman twice since Saturday—and it's only Tuesday. The first time was when he came over to my house on Sunday and we talked on the porch. Jaime had gone to pick up Lucas from their dad's, so I didn't worry about what the boys would think. Jaime hates having Lucas over there a minute longer than necessary.

Anyway, I was a little worried about the boys coming back, so I hurried Willard off. Besides, I got to wondering why he is even interested in me. I know his parents never got along with his brother's first wife because her grandmother was Mexican. They didn't even help out much when Ryan's wife was diagnosed with cancer and died. Such a sad story. I wonder what motivates Willard to have a relationship with me, a native of Mexico through and through. Won't it cause problems in his family?

The second time I saw him was when he came to see me at work last night. After talking to Evie and Cecilia yesterday, I made sure not to come across too interested. I can't make a mistake again. I won't. But I don't mind going out, having my dinner paid for. Hmm, I wonder if he knows how to fix a transmission. I think mine's about ready to break.

I can tell he likes me—a lot. I don't trust myself, though, about being a good judge of character. He admits his divorce was his fault but says he's come a long way since then. What if he's lying?

It's hard to know. I've dated a lot of men in the past four years, but I haven't found anyone I want to spend eternity with. Funny how the gospel wasn't that important to me when I first married Enrique. After all, none of my family here or in Mexico was active, so I didn't care that he wasn't a member. All that changed when my babies were born—and when I saw how Enrique and I were drifting apart. More than anything I began to want an eternal family, but Enrique wasn't interested in that. He was only interested in whether I had his dinner ready and the bills paid. He wanted me home, though he could stay out all night. He said it was the way men were and that I should accept it. He laughed when I asked him to come to church. Why should he waste three hours of his time going to my church when the Catholic church service was only forty-five minutes?

I remember quite vividly the day I realized it would make my life—and the boys' lives—much easier if he were gone. I did it all anyway, from the dentist bills to paying for groceries. Home was only a place he came to eat and shower. How can you be married and be so completely separate? The loneliness I felt was larger than at any other time in my life. It didn't make sense to continue on that way. At the divorce hearing, he actually tried to sue for alimony. I was frightened, but the judge just laughed and told him to pay me. Of course it was only a small amount because he managed to hide most of his true income, and I never saw a penny until we had his wages garnished last year. It's made things a little easier.

Jaime is still so angry with his father. A lot of that's probably my fault. He was only fourteen when Enrique left, and I know I said things I shouldn't have—I never can seem to keep my mouth shut. Yet in a way I'm glad I've said things because he hasn't let his father's lifestyle change him the way Lucas has.

Last week I found cigarettes in Lucas's drawer, and I grounded him for a month. Now, suddenly, after refusing to go for the past three months, he wants to visit his father. He thinks he'll get away with anything there. Sadly, he's right. Enrique has promised not to let him do anything I wouldn't, but he's a liar, and I can't trust that he'll follow through. I wish Lucas had a good role model to follow. I put him in drum lessons six months ago to keep him busy, but he still has way too much free time. Jaime's with him a lot, but once he goes on his mission later this year, then what? Lucas will be turning sixteen soon and will want to drive. I can't imagine what trouble he'll get into then.

Why do I keep hoping Willard will help? He doesn't even have children. He couldn't possibly know how to treat them. I think I'm making a mistake by agreeing to let him come see me again after I get off work tonight. But then why do I feel so happy when I think about being with him?

Tuesday afternoon dragged by. Rosalva was glad she didn't have to stay for the dinner shift. That was the best thing about being an assistant manager—she could pick her shifts. When the boys had plans, she could work, and when they didn't, she could arrange to spend time with them. She often found herself working six shorter shifts instead of five longer ones.

At five, Willard came in and sat at one of the tables. After changing from her uniform, putting on high heels, and touching up her face, she went to meet him.

He stood up halfway as she sat down. "Hi."

"Hi." She felt strangely breathless, an unpleasant feeling for a woman who wanted to maintain control. *He is just a man.* The words came to her mind in Spanish as they always did when she was trying to think clearly. Though she had lived in the United States for more than twenty years and always made herself speak English, some things were still clearer in her first tongue. *He is a man like all the other men I've dated. He is nothing to me. Nothing but perhaps a new transmission for my car.*

He stared at her for a long moment before adding, "You look amazing."

"Thank you." Rosalva was accustomed to men admiring her looks. They loved her long brown hair, heart-shaped face, and trim figure. English-speakers also loved her accent, which thickened when she was nervous. She hated that about herself and vowed to speak carefully in front of Willard.

Truth was, he was looking good himself. His hair was almost as dark as hers and his eyes a steel gray that seemed to melt when they focused on her. He was handsome, though in a slightly round, baby-faced way. His clothes were of the finest make, but they sagged on him more than she would have expected for a successful lawyer. Maybe that meant he'd recently lost a few extra pounds. Or maybe he didn't know how to shop.

He shifted uncomfortably under her stare. "I thought we could go out for dinner. That is"—he scanned the restaurant—"if you haven't already eaten."

"I haven't. But I do need to take dinner home to my

children. I—I'm not sure why I said for you to come here. I have to get home pretty soon."

Jaime was at his after-school job at a grocery store, but Lucas would be getting a ride home from guitar lessons right about now. If she didn't hurry, he'd be there too long on his own. She had to make sure he did his homework.

Willard blinked. "I thought you wanted to see me."

"I do. It's just, well, I have a lot on my mind right now. I have my two boys at home, and now my car's giving me trouble. Every day I worry about making it to work."

"Why don't you take it to a mechanic?" The comment was casual and almost a little condescending.

This isn't going to work, Rosalva thought. *He has no clue.* She stood. "Because I have to pay my rent next month. Getting my transmission fixed is going to take all the money I've saved to buy my son clothes for his mission. It's not easy being a single parent."

He blinked, remorse apparent on his face.

He's so easy to read, she mused. Not like Enrique, who could say he'd been fired and his money withheld when in his wallet he concealed all the cash from his paycheck.

"Please," Willard said, "I didn't think. I guess I figured your ex-husband helped out more."

Rosalva laughed. "His contribution wouldn't even pay for food for my two boys. And it's less now that Jaime has turned eighteen."

Willard shook his head. "I've made a lot of mistakes in my life, but that was never one of them. I'd never desert my children."

There was something of a wounded animal about him, something that tugged at Rosalva's heart. She pushed the emotions away. "How do you really know how you'll act until you have a child?"

He frowned. "I guess I don't. But I've spent a lot of time with my brother's children in the past few months. I'm thinking it's training me for my own kids someday."

A laugh tumbled from her lips. If he wanted children, he was looking in the wrong place. At forty-two, she was too old to begin a new family, never mind that a few neighbors her age were still having children. Having young children meant always worrying about them. It meant juggling baby-sitters. It meant sleepless nights while still somehow managing to keep a full-time job to pay the bills. Oh, no. She'd been down that road before. If that's what he hoped for, he had the wrong woman. She laughed again.

"What?" he asked, puzzled at her amusement.

She was about to ask him how old he thought she was. Hadn't she told him? No, she didn't remember doing so. Maybe it was better not to mention it now. "Nothing," she said. "It's nice that you're a good uncle." She walked toward the door, with Willard keeping pace. "So," she asked, "do you know anyone who's good with cars—someone who's cheap?"

He shook his head. "I'll ask my brother, though. He should know."

At her beat-up red convertible, he opened the door for her and then crouched down beside the car until he was even with her face. "So when are you really going out with me? I'm not giving up, you know. I want to get to know you."

Warmth filled Rosalva's heart. He wasn't at all like she'd expected. Kerrianne, who'd married Willard's brother on Saturday, had hinted that Willard was a snob, that Willard cared only for himself. But she'd also said that he'd made good progress in the past months and that her children had grown to love him.

His eyes pinned hers until she felt faint. *No, I can't feel this way about him—not until I know if he's* . . . She couldn't even complete the thought. She'd been on her own so long now. Even when she'd been married to Enrique, she'd been alone.

"Well, if I get my car fixed, I might be able to go out this weekend."

"Saturday, then?"

She shrugged casually, denying the flutters in her stomach. "Maybe."

He seemed satisfied with the response. Was that because he could see in her eyes how much she liked him? Or was he a glutton for punishment? "I'll call you tomorrow. Or stop by. What time do you get off?"

"Same time, more or less." She gave him a smile, and his response was immediate. He swiftly bent down and placed a quick kiss on her cheek. She caught the aroma of aftershave. Her cheek tingled. He shut the door before she could respond.

Be calm, she told herself in Spanish. *He's just a man. You can handle it.*

She turned on her car and put it into gear, hearing the usual clunk that made her worry that the transmission was about to fall apart. Willard was still watching her, and she lifted her hand in farewell. The car revved but didn't move. She tried to shift again. The car died.

"Great, just great," she muttered. She tried again, but it soon became apparent that her car was going nowhere. Tears bit at her eyes. Oh, how she sometimes hated life! Now she would have to borrow money from Evie to pay for a tow truck and likely pay an outrageous repair bill. Why couldn't she have dated a mechanic? She'd dated a roofer who'd repaired her roof and a cement layer who'd had helped her pour a slab in the back for basketball and barbecues, but there was no mechanic when she needed one. Not even her home teachers were skilled in that area.

There was a tapping at the window, and Rosalva looked up, almost surprised to see Willard still standing there. "I'll give you a ride," he said, his voice muffled by the glass between them. "We can go see if a shop is still open."

She opened the door. "It's five-thirty already. No one's going to be open. Besides, my son is home alone—I should be there already."

"I'll take you home, then."

Rosalva was relieved. "I appreciate it." But for some reason she felt uneasy letting him drive her home. Lucas didn't like meeting her dates. She wondered if part of him still hoped she'd get back with his father.

As they walked to his BMW, his hand on her elbow, Rosalva spied her friend Bernice emerging from a gold sedan. "Hey, Bernice!" she called.

Bernice had gray, chin-length hair that had been styled straight, so different from her old permed look. She wasn't even wearing her normal gray clothing but a peach outfit that made her seem almost cheery. "Hi," Bernice answered, flushing a deep red. Only then did Rosalva notice the white-haired man next to her. He was slightly barrel-chested, and he had a teasing look about him that made Rosalva wonder what he was doing with the grumpy Bernice.

Bernice and her companion took a step toward them, and the couples shook hands. Rosalva caught the aroma of mints from Bernice's date, who seemed slightly familiar. Had he been at some of the LDS singles events?

"This is Clay Bates," Bernice said. Clay smiled and put an arm around Bernice, who looked extremely uncomfortable.

Rosalva knew why. Bernice had made no secret of how much she loved her deceased husband, and more than once she had hinted that women who dated or remarried didn't love their husbands as purely as she had. Rosalva grinned. She'd heard rumors about Bernice dating, but from the looks of these two, things were much more serious than anyone had known.

"I'm sure we'll be seeing a lot of each other," Rosalva said to Clay with a mischievous glance at Bernice, who paled and was uncustomarily silent. "Well, see you tomorrow, Bernice. At Mimi's. I'm sure all us girls will have tons to talk about, won't we?"

Bernice's brown eyes, her best feature, grew wide in her round face. She shook her head, and Rosalva knew she was asking her not to say anything about her relationship with Clay. Rosalva had no intention of telling the others about Bernice's date, but that wouldn't stop her from teasing Bernice right now, especially with the hard time she'd so often given Maxine for dating Harold.

Pretending not to see Bernice's distress, Rosalva stepped away, smilingly merrily. "Bye. See you tomorrow. I can't wait to hear about everything!"

"Uh, yeah. See you tomorrow." Bernice's voice was faint, and Rosalva was sure she was two shades paler than before.

Clay pulled his arm tighter around Bernice and led her into the restaurant. The minute they were out of earshot, Rosalva burst into laughter.

"What?" Willard asked, his gray eyes twinkling. "Something was definitely going on there, but I'm not sure what."

"It's Bernice." Rosalva began walking again toward Willard's car. "She's given some of my friends no end of grief about dating and remarrying after their husbands died. Bernice, of course, loved her husband way too much to do something like that. She planned to remain faithful to him until she died. Yet here she is with a date."

"And now she's afraid you're going to say something to your friends." Willard chuckled. "I almost feel sorry for her."

"Well, don't. Believe me, she's put a guilt trip on more poor widows than you can possibly imagine. It's good for the shoe to be on the other foot."

"What about you?" Willard opened the car door for her. "How do you feel about remarriage?"

Rosalva's smile died on her face. More than anything in the whole world she wanted to find a man to take her to the temple. She wanted to have someone be so in love with her that he was willing to sacrifice everything to make her happy. She wanted an eternal family. But she couldn't say any of this to Willard. He was a man who had, by his own admission, thrown away an eternal relationship. In all the years he'd been married, his wife hadn't been able to change him. What made Rosalva think she could?

"I would like to get married again," she said softly, hating the way her increased accent betrayed her deep emotion. "But I would have to be very, very sure." She sat down in the passenger seat, not looking at him even when she felt his hand on her shoulder. It was a strong hand, one that made her feel small and protected. *I don't need him,* she told herself. Yet the truth was she did need someone. She just knew it couldn't be him.

CHAPTER

5

Bernice

I just about died when I saw Rosalva in the Sizzler parking lot. I knew she worked there, of course, but I was sure she'd be gone before we arrived. She would have been, apparently, but for her car trouble. I guess that's what happens when you hide things. They come back to haunt you. How am I going to tell the Independence Club that I was wrong? Then again, maybe I wasn't wrong. Maybe I've stopped loving my husband, just like some of them have. But how could I? He was my whole life for thirty-five years. Sometimes I feel like a completely different person from who I was then. Maybe I should tell Clay to go away, but when I'm not with him, the loneliness is so very profound and I start thinking that I would sooner die than not see him again.

Last night he was such a dear. After dinner he took me up to the mountains where we could see the valley below—all the beautiful blinking lights that seemed to stretch forever. When he pulled out the ring . . . well, I had no idea he really cared for me that deeply. I was stunned, shocked, amazed, scared, excited, flattered. I know he was disappointed that I couldn't give him an answer right away. I feel bad about that. Am I leading him on?

I'm embarrassed now to think that I once went to see the bishop to tell him to keep a better eye on Maxine because she was dating Harold. I guess it serves me right to be in the bind I am. Now I understand how she feels and why she didn't tell Harold to get lost. I even understand why Harold wasn't happy when I asked him if he thought his wife would like him dating another woman. What is it about Clay that makes me see these things? It wasn't that I was miserable being a widow before I met him. I was just fine. Really.

Maybe it was a good thing, me seeing Rosalva last night. It reminded me firmly of where my loyalties should lie. I have six children and a husband I dearly loved. I'm fifty-seven years old—do I really need anything more? I think the answer is clear. After the brunch at Mimi's today, I'm going to tell Clay that I can't marry him or see him anymore. I'm perfectly fine with that decision. It's the only correct one.

Everyone except Rosalva was gathered at Mimi's at ten o'clock when Bernice arrived at the restaurant. She felt relieved that Rosalva's tardiness meant that she had not already recounted their meeting in the Sizzler parking lot last night. Despite her worry, the pleasure of meeting her friends made her feel content.

"Hi!" Tina stood up and waved her over, never mind that a restaurant worker was already showing Bernice the way. Tina looked happier than ever, and her thin face held an uncharacteristic glow.

"Welcome, Bernice," Maxine said, beautiful and elegant as usual in a yellow suit that reminded Bernice of daffodils. "Glad you made it. I called last night to invite you to carpool, but you weren't home."

Was that some sort of broad hint? Did she know about Clay's proposal? But how could she? Bernice herself had been surprised. Still, she searched Maxine's face for any hidden knowledge—and found nothing.

"Did you hear?" Evie leaned forward, her smooth face bursting with excitement. "Tina's met someone, haven't you, Tina?" Without waiting for a response, she tumbled eagerly on. "He's a new guy from her ward. I went over to her house, and she was barbecuing for him. Oh, and he's a dream! You should see him around her. He's completely smitten. Completely!" She made a show of patting her heart.

Tina grinned. "I've seen him every day this week. We've been helping him move in. Honestly, he's the most gorgeous man I've ever seen. Things are moving rather fast, though. Not that fast is a bad thing." Her bright tone belied the worry in her eyes.

"I'd better meet this guy," Maxine said a little grumpily, reaching for a piece of the dark sweet bread the waitress had set in several baskets on the table.

"What about Harold?" asked Tina. "He was such a dear to come over with you the other night. My boys really liked him. They said he's a hoot."

"He's a hoot, all right," Maxine said dryly. "I've been walking with him, that's what's been going on with Harold. That's why I sent Evie over to your house on Sunday instead of coming myself. I can't believe he's been following me on my morning walks without my knowing it."

"I think it's sweet he's been worried about you," Tina gushed. "Simply sweet. It's something I imagine Scott might do." She stared dreamily into the air.

Maxine hid a smile behind her napkin. "He sounds too good to be true. Ask him if he expects you to cook dinner every night."

"He's cooking Friday night for us at his place," Tina replied.

"Well, ask him about laundry."

Evie laughed. "Maxine! What is it about you?" Then her eyes grew wide. "Oh, Harold's asked you to marry him again, hasn't he?"

Maxine flushed, not the horrible red that Bernice knew came over her own face but a delicate color that made her seem more beautiful and enticing. "Well, yeah, but the answer's still no—or would have been if Tina's son hadn't interrupted us Saturday night."

Tina's smile faltered. "I'm so sorry about that."

Maxine put a hand on her arm. "Don't worry, dear. Believe me, I was glad."

Bernice wanted to ask what was going on, but she was too afraid of drawing attention to herself. She had to protect her secret or these women would never let her hear the end of it. Maxine would laugh herself silly if she knew how much Bernice *wanted* to take care of Clay—even if it meant cooking and cleaning. She had loved it the first time around, too. Besides, Clay made everything fun.

"Bernice, are you okay?" Evie asked, her forked poised over a salad the waitress had set before her. "You look a little distracted. Is there anything you want to talk about?"

If only they knew. They'd tease her, ridicule her even. She couldn't allow that. "Nothing," she said. "I've nothing new to share. I am writing in my journal, though. I hope all of you are. It's a commandment, you know."

"We've all been doing it. Well, we don't know about Rosalva yet, since she's not here." Evie's beautifully sculpted eyebrows gathered in concern. "Where is she, anyway? I'm giving her another five minutes, and then I'm calling her cell. I would have called her this morning to see if she wanted a ride, but . . ." Evie's face dissolved in a big grin. "Guess what I did this morning! I joined a gym. Yes, me!"

"I'm so proud of you!" Tina leaned over and hugged her.

"Not only that but I met someone. Well," Evie frowned briefly, "he doesn't exactly know I'm alive yet, but he will. I'm sure he'll look at me once I lose a bit more weight. We're perfect for each other."

Bernice scowled. She didn't like that kind of thinking. It was one thing for Evie to lose weight for herself but to do it to get the attention of a specific man was ludicrous. He either liked you or he didn't. Take Clay. He was a bit overweight around the middle, and she still liked him. And he certainly didn't expect her to have the figure of a teenager. After all, she'd borne six children. He respected that. They didn't see the need to change each other, and that was exactly how relationships should be. Of course she couldn't say any of this because then they'd know how serious she was about Clay. Or had been, rather.

"So my goal this week is to talk to him," Evie continued. "You know, get him to notice me. That and lose five more pounds."

"I thought you weren't supposed to lose more than two or three a week," Maxine said.

"Well, I've been on a plateau for a while now, so I could lose more this time. In fact, it's been two weeks since I've lost more than a few ounces. I think the different exercises will really help."

Maxine shrugged. "No cheating with chocolate is what will really help."

"Oh, you're right." Evie snapped her fingers. "You know what, that's what I'll do—go on a no-sugar thing. Just for a couple of weeks to get me jump-started."

"It'll sure cut your sugar craving," Tina put in.

Evie bounced a bit in her chair, which Bernice thought a bit excessive. "Oh, I'm so excited," she said. "Any other ideas?"

"I think new exercise outfits," Tina said.

"What a great idea! They have a lot of choices out there. I'm really liking this power group idea. I'll work on both these things this week—no sugar and new outfits." Evie looked at Tina, as though eager to let her have a share of the attention. "So what about you? How can we help you?"

Tina shook her head. "This week has been absolutely perfect. I don't want to change anything."

"Anything?" Maxine was looking at her with a frown. "I'm thinking that if you're going to enter a new relationship, maybe it would be a good idea to make sure—"

Tina held up a hand. "No, really, Maxine. It's good. I'm fine. Perfectly fine."

Evie asked the question Bernice burned to voice, "What are you two talking about? Did something happen that you haven't told us?"

Tina and Maxine exchanged an unreadable look. Tina was

the first to drop her gaze. She took a deep breath. "Nothing, really. I was a little down the other night, and Maxine came and cheered me up. But everything is wonderful now." She looked so happy that Bernice believed her.

Maxine gave a little sigh. "Okay, but you know we're here if you need us."

The conversation paused as the waitress took their orders. When she was gone, Tina beamed at Maxine. "So what about you? How can we help you? What's your response to Harold going to be? He'll ask you to marry him again, you know."

"Harold's a nice man, and I really care for him, but I guess I'm with Bernice in the marriage thing—though for different reasons. I feel pretty content where I am. I don't want to go back to washing clothes and feeding a man."

"It isn't all work," Tina said, picking up a roll.

"No, you're right. If I were your age and had young children, I would definitely remarry. Not a question."

"Provided you had the opportunity." Evie gave them a glum look before taking a long sip of water.

"Actually, I've been thinking that I'd like to travel more," Maxine said. "I've never been to England or France, and I'd like to go. So that's going to be what I want to work on. I want to save money, learn a little French, and be brave enough to go on a trip."

"Why go alone?" Evie asked. "I'll go with you." It was a nice gesture. With her comfortable divorce settlement, Evie was in the best position to afford such a trip.

"Would you?" Maxine asked. "That would make it a lot more fun."

"I couldn't leave the kids," Tina said, "even if I had the

money. But I'll help in the planning. I love to plan trips. I have an e-mail friend in London. Maybe she has some suggestions."

After sharing a few more ideas about Maxine's dream trip, the conversation wound to its end. Bernice knew it was only a matter of seconds before someone asked her about her goal for the future. She certainly couldn't tell them she was planning on breaking up with Clay. But neither did she want to lose weight or go on a trip. What could she tell them?

"Look, there's Rosalva!" Tina's exclamation pulled Bernice from her thoughts.

Rosalva was waving to them from across the room. As usual, she looked fantastic, though a little too flamboyant for Bernice's taste. She wore a red, fitted dress that made her dark skin beautiful. Her brown locks were swept up in a clip at the back, with the graduated bangs loose as though she were ready for a formal dance. Her makeup was muted, but her eyelashes were so long that even Bernice felt a little jealous. Eyes from around the restaurant followed her as she gracefully walked to the table.

"What a morning!" Rosalva sank into the last vacant seat with a drawn-out sigh. "My car broke down last night, so I borrowed Jaime's to go see if I could get it towed this morning, and it's not even there! I didn't know what to do, so I called the police. That's why I'm late. I had to fill out a report. But what I can't figure is who would want to steal that old broken-down piece of junk?"

"You got me," Evie said with a shrug. "That thing barely runs."

"Well, I need it. Jaime's going to find a way to get to work today, but we can't keep doing that. If he's late or misses work, he could get fired, and we need the money to save for his mission."

"Maybe nobody stole it," Tina said thoughtfully. "Maybe someone decided to help you."

"Ha!" Rosalva rolled her eyes. "Tina, that is too positive even for you. I wonder if Enrique has something to do with this. He always needs money. My ex is the king of scams."

"It'll show up." Evie passed her the breadbasket. "Try one of these. It'll make you feel better. Tell me how it tastes."

Rosalva pushed the basket away. "I'm too upset to eat sweet bread. Taste it yourself."

"I can't. I'm on a very special diet now."

Tina giggled. "It's the Get Mr. Right Diet."

"Not Mr. Right—Mr. Perfect," Evie said with a sigh. "I met him at the gym."

Rosalva looked interested. "The one Cecilia took you to?"

Evie nodded.

"Tell me all about it."

Bernice was glad when the waitress brought her sandwich. Chewing would keep her from saying anything that might draw attention to herself. But after Evie was finished recounting her first "almost" meeting with Mr. Perfect and her plans to go out and buy several chic exercise outfits to impress him, Bernice couldn't help herself. "That's all wrong, Evie. True love can't be based on weight." She patted her own ample girth. "I thought you learned that already and that you were working on losing the weight for yourself."

Evie blinked in surprise. "Well, yeah. *Of course* I'm doing it for me. But it doesn't hurt to have a little more of an incentive—not to mention a gorgeous incentive."

"A *perfect* incentive," Tina added with a giggle.

Bernice pursed her lips. "I don't like the sound of this guy at all."

"Well, that's not news," Maxine said. "You haven't liked the idea of any of us getting remarried, Bernice. But that reminds me. Whatever happened to that guy, the one who smells like mints all the time? Rumor had it he was dating seriously, and the only woman we ever saw him with was you. So are you still dating him, or not?"

Bernice was afraid of this. Maxine always dug right to the root, never mind if she destroyed the plant while she was at it. "His name was Clay," she replied shortly. She hoped using his name with the past tense would help the conversation move on, and after all, she had decided not to date him anymore, so it was true. At the same time she felt an unsettling disloyalty toward Clay. He was a marvelous person. She liked it that he knew so much about politics and the world, that he had spent years studying the scriptures and had so much insight to share. She herself studied an hour every day, and they could talk for an afternoon about a single chapter. He was so much like her first husband that it was almost uncanny.

First husband? Had she actually thought that? First husband implied there would be a second—and that wasn't happening. These ladies would never let her hear the end of it.

"Was, huh?" Maxine didn't miss anything.

Rosalva's eyes dug into Bernice's, and her mouth opened as though she might speak. Bernice held her breath, but then Rosalva smiled and reached for the breadbasket. "Maybe I'll try some now."

Relief coursed through her. Rosalva wasn't going to spill her secret, and after today there would be no secret.

"So what about your goals, Bernice?" Tina put down her fork and folded her hands in front of her plate.

Bernice had her answer ready. "Well, I guess I'd like to become more spiritual. I figure my husband's doing that in heaven, and I'd like to be a fit partner for him when we're together again." There, that would stop all the questions about another man. Everyone fell silent.

"That's a wonderful, fabulous goal," Tina finally said.

"Yeah," Evie agreed. "I think you should start by studying the Old Testament. I never noticed before we studied it in Sunday School a while back, but it's really full of fascinating events."

"You should definitely read some of the commentaries," Maxine offered.

"You can share what you learn with us," Tina said brightly. "That would help all of us."

Only Rosalva remained silent.

"Okay, I'll do that," Bernice agreed quickly—anything to turn the attention from herself. Besides, she did have a lot of experience and wisdom to share. After she broke up with Clay, of course. "Rosalva, it's your turn. What's your goal?"

"I've got a whole bunch of goals to work on," Rosalva said. "You know, mostly making sure Jaime gets out on his mission and keeping Lucas out of trouble. Unfortunately, that means keeping him away from his father. He needs a good role model, so that should be my first priority. Except that right now all I can think about is my car. I have to get it back."

"The police will find it," Tina said. "You'll see."

Evie set down her water glass, which she had emptied. "What about Willard? Have you been seeing him?"

"Yeah, but I'm not getting my heart involved, just like you told me."

Bernice thought she detected sadness in Rosalva's voice. "So wouldn't he make a good role model?" she asked.

Rosalva shrugged. "I don't know, really. I mean, he's successful, but he has little experience with children."

"I think you ought to give him a try," Maxine said. "You might be surprised."

Evie's eyes sparkled. "There's no better way to test a man's mettle than to throw him to the children!" The women all laughed.

"But you don't want your children hurt." Tina's face was unsmiling, making her look almost like another person altogether. "Just be sure of that."

"Of course," Rosalva said, placing a hand over Tina's. "I promise, I'll be careful."

They talked a bit more before calling it quits. As they left the restaurant together, Rosalva held back to walk with Bernice instead of going with Evie as she usually did when the group was together. "I think Clay seems like a nice guy," Rosalva said quietly, holding the door for her. "I'm glad to know he has a name other than Mint Breath."

Bernice smiled. "He likes mints. He carries this little tin in h—" Her smile froze, and she shook her head. "Never mind. It's over, you know."

Rosalva tilted her pretty head. "I'm sorry."

The others were waiting outside for them, so Bernice couldn't reply. She was sorry, too. Very sorry.

"Come on," Bernice," Maxine said, jingling her keys. "If we hurry, we'll just get back in time to see if FedEx has brought your makeup order."

Bernice followed Maxine and Tina to the parking lot, wondering how she would find the courage to tell Clay she couldn't see him anymore.

CHAPTER

6

Maxine

I am a woman on a mission. I want to help Tina get married. She deserves to know what it's like to have a good husband, one who doesn't hit or belittle his wife. I think she may have met a potential husband already, that new guy in her ward. In the past year and a half, I've never seen her so happy and dreamy. I will have to meet him, of course, before I decide to throw in and help him win her. Still, I can't help but feel a little bit of worry as I think about Tina huddled in her closet. That was not normal behavior, and I'm not sure you can build a new relationship if you are still caught up in a past one.

Oddly, I see nearly the same thing in Bernice—only the opposite. Was her husband so good and kind that he simply can't be replaced? I was sad today when she implied she was no longer going out with Mint Breath. But she's lonely—I can see it, and she really is at her best while she's ordering someone arou—I mean, taking care of someone else. I still don't know why she thinks it's wrong for two old people to buoy each other up in their last few years of life. Heck, I'd get married if I was looking for what I'd had before. For crying out loud, it's too bad I can't put her and Tina in a bag and shake up their past lives so that their futures could proceed more smoothly. Tina wouldn't be so damaged and Bernice wouldn't be so self-righteous when it comes to remarrying. They could be normal.

Of course, what is normal? Me? I think so, yet at the same time I don't want to be normal. I like being young for my sixty-two years, in charge of my life, outspoken, and considered good-looking. Yes, I know I'm attractive—not in the way of younger women, but in my own way. I don't ever feel lonely the way I did when Charles first died. I like my life. I loved my husband, and we had a good life. This life I have now is just different. I wish I could make Harold under-stand that I don't want what I had before. I'm enjoying being me right now. I feel content.

Well, I guess if I were really honest, I would say that I'd like Harold to kiss me. I'd like it a lot. Yet then where would we go from there?

I hate making pies.

That reminds me. I told Tina at Mimi's this morning that I sent Evie over there on Sunday because I wanted to walk with Harold instead of Evie, and that was true, but I was also making sure to check up on her. I didn't know Tina would meet a man. I hope that works out for her. She deserves someone good.

Well, I'd better get changed—I'm going to work out in the yard later today. But first Tina and Bernice are coming over to help me sort orders. I really hate that part of selling cosmetics, mostly because my eyesight isn't what it used to be.

I wonder what Harold is doing. I bet he'll call soon. Maybe he'll even come over. He's a good friend.

Maxine had barely finished changing when the doorbell rang. Smoothing her pants over her hips, Maxine hurried to the front door, glancing at her image in the living room mirror to be sure her fitted top hid certain curves on her stomach. Sure, she was only going to work outside later, but it was important to always look your best. You never knew who might stop by. Her friends always commented that she was trim, and she walked daily to make sure she stayed fit, but the truth was her stomach was inches bigger than it had been even ten years ago. But that was life, and she didn't dwell on it. Not everyone could look like Rosalva.

"I thought you got lost," she said as she ushered Tina and Bernice into the house.

"I watched out my window until I saw Tina arrive," Bernice said, motioning across the street at her house.

"I walked over instead of driving, so it took me longer." Tina breathed deeply. "Spring is a wonderful time of year. Don't you think, Maxine? All the wonderful smells, the birds coming back, the plants coming alive."

"What's wonderful is you sorting my orders."

"Oh, Maxine, that's easy." Tina gave her a bright smile. "Now where are the orders? I can't wait to show Bernice that personalizer. She will absolutely love how it controls shine on her face. I use mine every day."

"Right this way." Maxine led them into the kitchen.

"This really works," Bernice said a few minutes later, peering into a table mirror Maxine used at her makeup parties. "There's no shine, and I only put on a little bit."

Tina laughed. "Of course it works."

"And this new lipstick color is nice," added Bernice.

Tina leaned over to take a look. "It makes you look springy."

"Springy?" Bernice made a face, but Tina had already returned to sorting.

Within a half hour Tina had everything organized and ready for Maxine to drop off to clients. She looked at her watch. "I think I'd better get home. I'm meeting Scott in a few minutes for lunch."

"For lunch?" Bernice asked. "But we just ate."

Tina flushed. "I know but he . . . well, he . . . I just . . ."

"Oh, leave her alone, Bernice." Maxine went to sit by Tina. "So when do I get to meet him?"

Tina shrugged, a secret smile on her lips. "Soon. It's just—oh, Maxine, I'm happy and scared all at once. He seems so wonderful, but what if . . ." She stood abruptly. "Never mind. I won't borrow trouble. See you later, ladies."

"Do you want a ride?" Maxine offered.

"No, I have time to walk, if I hurry. It's only a mile or so. Keep smiling." Tina waved and was gone.

Bernice stared after her. "I hope he's a good man."

"Me, too."

Maxine smiled. "There's one way we can find out."

"How?"

"I need a shovel."

"Don't you have one?"

"Yes, but I need to borrow Tina's."

Bernice grinned, and the action changed her sour face, making it appear relaxed and happy. "Fine, let's go."

"We'll have to drive, or we'll never make it in time. She has a good start on us."

They hurried to the car, but as the garage door opened, a blue sedan pulled in behind them. "It's Harold!" Maxine said, squelching the sudden flutter in her stomach. She walked toward him.

Harold unfolded his tall frame from the sedan. "Are you going somewhere?" The color of his eyes leaned toward green today, like his spring sweater. They took in her black pants with a quirk of his left eyebrow.

"To Tina's to borrow a shovel."

"I can lend you mine."

She shook her head. "I need Tina's."

He chuckled and raised his hands. "Don't tell me. I don't want to know. Well, I do, but only if you want to tell me. Look, I came because I was feeling like some pie."

Hands on her hips, she retorted, "You know I don't make pie."

"Not for you to make. I want to take you out to eat some."

"But you haven't had lunch."

"We can do that, too."

"I just ate."

"Well, then in an hour or so."

"That would give me time to get Tina's shovel," she conceded.

He smiled. "Good. Shall I drive you there?"

Maxine considered a moment. She didn't really need Harold to come, but it might be nice to have a male perspective on Tina's date, and besides, he had offered so gallantly. "Okay." Then she remembered Bernice. The other woman was already walking toward them, and Maxine wondered what she would say—probably something to push Harold away from her.

Bernice opened her mouth. "If we're going to get there before Tina leaves, we'd better hurry." She nodded at Harold. "Hi, Harold."

"Good to see you again, Bernice. You're looking nice today. Whatever you're doing must agree with you."

Bernice turned a shade of unbecoming red. "Thanks," she muttered.

"Harold said he'd drive us," Maxine said. "If that's okay with you."

"Fine by me. But I'll need to get home right after."

"You could go out for pie with us," offered Harold, ever the gentleman. Maxine wanted to strangle him. Her coming with them would only give Bernice more time to talk about how they shouldn't be dating at all.

"Thanks, but I have an appointment." Bernice's face was pale now, as though something had made her ill.

Maxine felt immediately repentant. "Are you all right, Bernice?"

"Fine."

Maxine wasn't too sure—Bernice had been quieter than normal all day. "You aren't going to see a doctor, are you? Do you need someone to drive you? Because all you have to do is ask."

"I'm not going to the doctor." Bernice's voice warned her not to delve further, but that only whetted Maxine's curiosity.

"So where are you going, then?" Maxine settled in the front seat. Harold shut the door behind her and opened the back door for Bernice.

"To see a friend," Bernice said shortly.

"Oh, a friend." Maxine waited for more, but nothing more was forthcoming. When Harold started the engine, she said, "Anyone I know?"

"I don't think so."

"Well, you really are welcome to come with us if you change your mind. In fact, we could double date sometime." She steeled herself for the inevitable lecture on staying true to their deceased husbands, but Bernice stared quietly out the window and said nothing.

Harold shook his head at her, and Maxine fell into silence—not because of Harold but because she was so amazed that Bernice hadn't taken the opportunity to point out how disappointed Charles would be with her—as if Charles wasn't busy enough in the Afterlife. *Something is definitely up with Bernice,* Maxine decided. *But what?*

They made the rest of the drive to Tina's in silence, arriving at the same time a red truck pulled up at the curb. "That must be Scott." Maxine opened her door and slid out, hurrying across the lawn and into the path of the man from the red truck. He regarded her curiously, pausing on his way to the door.

"Are you Scott?" Maxine asked.

He smiled. "Scott Manning," he said, offering a hand. "You must be Maxine."

"I am."

Harold and Bernice arrived, and Maxine made the introductions. "We're going to lunch," Scott said, looking up at the house. "Uh, are you all coming? Tina didn't mention it."

"No, no. We came to borrow a shovel." Bernice shifted uncomfortably.

"Well, that was our excuse," Maxine put in. Scott really was a handsome man, so for that part at least she could see why Tina was smitten. "We really came to meet you. We're Tina's friends. Her good friends."

Bernice's face was flaming again, but Harold was grinning, hands in his pockets. He shrugged as if to say to Scott, "Just go with it."

"I bet you want to know my intentions," Scott said.

"Actually, yeah." Maxine stared at him.

"Well, we just met on Sunday, you know, and it's—"

The door opened and Tina stepped onto the porch. She made an exclamation of surprise. "Maxine, what are you doing here?"

"I came to borrow a shovel, of course." Maxine looked down at her pants. "I'm in my working clothes, can't you see?"

Tina's brow furrowed. "No, they look like any other clothes. You always look nice."

"Well, can we? Borrow the shovel, that is? Bernice, will you go with her to get it?" Now that she'd come this far, Maxine wanted to finish her conversation with Scott.

With an apologetic smile at Scott, Tina went to find her shovel. When she was gone, Maxine looked at Scott. "Now listen, young man, I want no messing around with Tina's heart. There's things going on here that you've no idea about, and I'll tell you right now it's not going to be easy. You'd better decide up front if you are strong enough to be in this for the long haul."

"What do you mean?" Scott's eyes narrowed in confusion.

"That's all you need to know. Tina's the best friend I have, and she's great, but she's been through a lot."

Harold took a step forward. "Now, Maxine, don't frighten him. Look, Scott, there's nothing love can't solve. That's my belief. No, don't ask me what Maxine's talking about. Ask Tina."

Maxine was grateful for the suggestion. "Yes, ask her about her husband."

Tina and Bernice were coming from around the back of the house, so Maxine shook Scott's hand. "Nice to meet you. Remember what I said." She took the shovel from Tina, whose eyes were locked on Scott's. Maxine could almost feel the intensity of the emotion between them. "I'll bring it back after my work is done, okay?"

Tina barely glanced at her. "Keep it as long as you like."

Scott took Tina's hand and led her to his truck.

Maxine watched them go. "I'm so afraid for her," she whispered. Then she shook her head. "No one was there to help her the first time, but I'm here now."

"Seems like a really nice boy," Harold said.

"He looks patient," Bernice agreed.

"I hope so. Come on. Let's go home."

They dropped Bernice at her house before parking in Maxine's driveway. Harold carried Tina's shovel into the garage. "Do you really need this?"

"Well, I am going to work in my yard. I have some new rose bushes to plant. But I do have my own shovel."

Harold grinned. "I guess this one's for me. You're bound and determined to get me in shape, aren't you?"

Maxine laughed.

Harold watched her for a moment, a gentle smile on his face. Maxine stopped laughing. He took her hand, and his skin felt warm against hers. "Maxine," he said softly.

Her heart pounded in her ears. Funny how she could still

feel this way. Funny how the body didn't forget what it was like to care for another person.

He brought her hand to his lips and kissed it once. That broke the spell for Maxine. *Silly man,* she thought. *I'm not dead and buried yet. I want real kisses.*

She pulled her hand away and took the shovel. "Are you going to help me or not?"

Harold took the shovel away from her and put it firmly to the side. "Maxine." His voice was low but compelling, and she had to look at him. His arms went around her, pulling her close. "What if I do this . . ." He came closer, inch by inch until Maxine wanted to either grab him or push him away. His lips met hers, sending warm shivers throughout her body. He kissed her for a long moment, and Maxine was amazed at how she remembered this, too. Kissing—it was like riding a bike. A person didn't forget—not even after almost six years.

At last they drew away, both of them breathless. "And now what?" he asked.

The same question I asked myself, Maxine thought. Understanding flooded her. Harold had held back, not because he was too old for romance but because he didn't know where it would lead, not with her so adamant against taking care of another man.

I like my life exactly as it is! she thought. Aloud she said, "Aw, Harold, just shut up and do it again."

This time it was Harold who picked up the shovel. "I don't think so, Maxine. If I start kissing you, it'll just be that much harder to stop." With a reluctant chuckle, he moved toward the door leading to her backyard.

Maxine watched him go, exasperated but knowing he was

right. She'd wanted him to kiss her. She'd wanted to feel alive. But then what?

She asked herself the question while they planted the flowers and then again while she changed to go to the restaurant for a late lunch. She was still asking it over the piece of pie they shared for dessert.

Harold was his normal agreeable self, but there was something different in his eyes, in the way he watched her face. Maxine couldn't remember when she had felt so loved, though she knew she'd been looked at that way by her husband many, many times before. Yet the years had erased so many of the poignant moments of her past. The brain could only hold so much. What did that mean for her future? Why was she holding out? Was it really the cooking and cleaning and taking care of Harold that frightened her?

I like my life. I don't want it to change. Yet she remembered Harold's touch. She couldn't have both.

Harold stood and offered a hand to help her rise from the table. Maxine allowed the courtesy. Harold knew the old ways, and he was always a gentleman. That's why it surprised her when outside he didn't open her car door. He walked halfway to his side and stood there, a blank look coming over his face.

"Harold? Is something wrong?"

He still didn't move. His eyes were open, looking bluer now against the backdrop of the cloudless blue sky. His mouth moved slightly but without sound.

"Harold." Maxine ran to his side, fear gripping her heart. "Harold!"

His face had drained of color, and the muscles were relaxed as though at rest. She half expected him to crumple and fall to the earth, but he simply stood there, completely immobile except for his mouth, which she thought might be trying to tell her something. What was happening?

Tears started down his face. That was all. One tear, two. Then three more. His mouth stilled. His eyes were fixed at a point beyond her, but they seemed to beg for help.

Maxine reached for her cell phone and dialed 911. "Hang on, Harold," she said, putting an arm around his tall frame. "I'm getting help."

CHAPTER

7

Evie

I hope Jack is at the gym today, yet I'm nervous about seeing
him. Of course he might not even be there, so I could be getting all
worked up for nothing. Anyway, I'm determined to keep losing and
toning. Most of all I want to officially meet Jack. I'm so compelled
by him that I keep thinking surely there's a reason I feel this way.
Maybe it's meant to be. He's not exactly thin himself (though well-
built), so maybe he will see me and not my extra weight. I figure I
can probably lose the forty-five pounds the doctor wants me to by
summer's end. I know I've tried so many times before, but with the
support of my friends and this gym membership, I'm really going to
do it this time.

Cecilia is going to meet me at the gym right after she gets out of *class. Strange, but I'm looking forward to seeing her. I hope Jason hasn't been an idiot to her again.*

Evie pulled up at the gym, butterflies filling her stomach. She was later arriving than she'd hoped because she'd been trying to help Rosalva find her car. *I can't believe someone actually stole that piece of junk,* she thought. The only thing nice about the car was the paint job Rosalva had paid a hundred bucks for. Still, Rosalva needed the car, and Evie hoped the police would find it soon. Right now they were following a lead given them by a man from a neighboring business who'd seen a tow truck in the area late the previous evening.

After helping Rosalva, Evie had driven to the nearby mall to pick up two new exercise outfits. Though they couldn't hide her weight, the outfits made the best of what she had. Evie was both excited and nervous to put them on. Would Jack approve, or would he see only her flab?

Courage, courage. I can do this, she told herself as she emerged from her car. *I will talk to Jack today!*

In the locker room, Evie changed into the sleekest of her new outfits—navy blue crop pants with two white stripes down the sides and a white top with navy stripes on the sleeves—trying not to think about the fact that she hadn't been able to wash the clothes before wearing them. It was more important to look good today than to worry about who else might have tried them on.

She went first to the treadmills, looking for Jack. Had she missed him altogether? Cecilia had mentioned that he was an executive at a company, and rumor had it that he came to the gym daily on an extended lunch hour, often conducting work from the gym. Yesterday, he'd been on his cell throughout his entire treadmill time.

At last she spied him at the weights and breathed a sigh of relief. Maybe she should give the weights a try herself. That way she could be there when he finished. "Excuse me," she said to one of the gym employees. "Can you show me how these work?"

After what seemed like hours but had only been thirty torturous minutes, all she had were sore muscles and no more clues into Jack's life. She didn't even know his full name. At least the possibility of his seeing her weight lifting made her try harder.

Finally he was finished. She arose as gracefully as she could from her machine and walked in the direction he was going, careful to angle toward him so they'd meet at the narrow opening which led to another part of the gym. She timed it perfectly.

"Oh," she paused, looking up in false surprise as their arms brushed. "I'm sorry. We keep running into each other." His blue eyes seemed even bluer today, and his face carved by a skilled artist's hand. Strong, handsome—everything she remembered. Her knees felt weak, and her stomach held an entire swarm of butterflies.

He rubbed his neck with a towel and stared at her with a smile that held no recognition. "Uh, were you going in there?" He indicated a sign with his head: *Men's Locker Room.*

"Uh, I guess not," she said, flushing. "I'm new here—I must have gotten turned around. I need to get to the treadmills." Not too bad a save. Didn't men like being helpful?

"Back that way." He thumbed over his shoulder.

"Thank you." She gave him a smile that had always melted all her dates—and even Jason near the end of their marriage.

Jack returned her smile and took a step forward.

Evie wasn't ready for it to be over. She shoved a hand in his direction. "I'm Evie, by the way. Evie McClaine."

He had to turn or ignore her completely. She was relieved when he turned and briefly shook her hand. "Jack Riley."

"Nice to meet you," she said.

He dipped his head slightly in acknowledgment or perhaps agreement. "See you around."

Evie was glad that he walked away without looking back because she felt so weak she could only stand there outside the men's locker room like a starstruck teenager, her heart pounding overtime. "Get a grip," she told herself. Her hand still felt warm where he had touched her. She gave a long sigh.

"Is everything all right?"

She looked up to see a vaguely familiar man who had emerged from the locker room. He was big and tall, with curly blond hair cut very short, and his brown eyes were concerned. Evie found her voice. "Oh, I'm fine, thanks."

He gave her a wide, friendly smile. "I remember you. You're Cecilia's friend. We met briefly on Monday. I was in early that day. Usually I'm just waking up at that time. I work the night shift at the police department."

"How interesting."

He chuckled. "You'd think. And sometimes it is. But a lot of nights it's pretty quiet."

"So this is morning for you." They walked together in what Evie recognized was the direction of the treadmills.

"Basically. I get up and come here. After working out, I go shopping or do whatever and then go to work at midnight. I get off work, go home, and go to sleep."

Evie pondered for a moment what it might be like to have a life so opposite that of most people.

"I used to stay up in the mornings and then sleep in the afternoons until it was time to go to work," he added. "But I didn't have much of a social life. It works better this way."

"Don't you get tired before work?"

He shook his head. "Not anymore. Especially since I started coming here." He patted his wide chest. "Exercising has given me more energy."

"I hear you there."

"You look great." He smile again as he said it—a genuine smile that made her feel happy.

It had been years since any man said something like that to her, and Evie felt a compelling desire to thank him. Instead, she said dryly, "Not according to my doctor."

A blush tinged his ears at the allusion to her weight, and Evie almost laughed aloud. He was so transparent, almost like a boy. It was hard to imagine him as a police officer.

"How far do you walk?" he asked. They'd reached the treadmills now.

"Well, I'm up to four miles a day, but I'd like to make it six. My ankles hurt, though."

"When I talked to a personal trainer, he said mixing exercises is important. So maybe try something else that's just as good for you."

Evie smiled. "I did weight lifting today."

"They have bicycles, too." He punched a few buttons on the nearest treadmill. "I keep thinking I'll use my real bike at home one of these days, but I want to get in better shape first."

At that Evie really looked at him. He was quite a bit overweight. Almost as much as she was, in fact. But hadn't she read something in the paper months or even years ago that police officers had to fit certain guidelines? Probably that was the reason he was here in the first place. At least being tall would help him meet his goal. "Well, it's nice to see you again," she said, inching away.

"Oh, in case you forgot, I'm Christopher. Christopher Fletcher."

"Evie McClaine." They both smiled.

He was nice, but Evie was glad to get on her treadmill to dream in private about her encounter with Jack. She was almost glad she'd forgotten her book to read. Reading right now would only get in the way of her imagination. Besides, Jack wasn't around to look intellectual for.

Tomorrow, she thought. *Tomorrow I'll see him again.* It really wasn't like her to be this infatuated, so something must be meant to exist between them, something special and lasting.

She looked past Christopher on the next treadmill and saw Cecilia enter the room. She waved, and Evie smiled. She couldn't wait to tell Cecilia about her encounter with Jack.

CHAPTER

8

Rosalva

I can't believe someone stole my car. What if the police never find it? I'll have to get a loan to buy a new one. I can't use Jaime's mission money. I just can't! Tomorrow I'm going to have to use Jaime's car again or ask one of the ladies for a ride. I'm so grateful to have them in my life. I don't know where I'd be without them—especially Evie. She has such a great head on her shoulders. Well, except for right now, when she seems to have gone a bit crazy over this guy she doesn't even know. But who's to say it won't work out? Usually, she's a pretty good judge of character. She's saved me from some real jerks in the past. I hope she has the same judgment for herself.

As for my car, I keep waiting to hear that the police have found it, but so far nothing. Where could it be? Who'd want it anyway? I barely want it. I keep thinking Enrique is somehow involved.

I finally decided to write some of my feelings down. Bernice claims writing soothes the soul. I think she's right. I am feeling better. I know I have friends who will help me, and I know my Heavenly Father is aware of me and my family and our needs. It's going to be all right.

I wonder if Willard will show up after work today. When he brought me home yesterday, he was very gentlemanly and opened the door for me to get out of the car and walked me to the house. I knew he wanted to stay, but Lucas was home and he would hate seeing Willard there with me. I think he still hopes that even after four years I'll get back with Enrique.

Rosalva sighed when she heard a crash come from the back of the restaurant. With her car missing, she'd had a hard time keeping her thoughts on work, and her nervousness and foul mood had apparently transferred to her staff. Two workers had already dropped a stack of glasses each, and she'd had to resolve two arguments. Fortunately, the restaurant wasn't busy at the moment.

Her cell phone rang, and she fished it out of her bra where she always kept it in case her boys needed to contact her urgently. Sometimes she wouldn't hear or feel it in her pocket. "Hello?"

"Mrs. Nolasco?" a voice asked.

"Yes."

"This is Ted Cornell calling from the Orem police department. We've found your car."

Relief flooded through her. "You did? Great! Where?"

"Well, it's at a local garage, which is actually how we

tracked it down since you said it wasn't working. But the man who took it there says he knows you, and he's sure you won't press charges."

Enrique! Rosalva thought. *He was probably trying to sell it!* Rosalva's rage burned so hot she didn't hear the rest of what the policeman was saying. She thought only of the years of humiliation and hurt that had resulted in the end of her marriage to Enrique.

"I want to press charges," she said, cutting through the officer's babble. She would show Enrique that she wasn't going to be pushed around a moment longer, that he couldn't consider her stuff his anymore. They might share two children, but that was it.

"Ma'am, are you sure? Really, it seems—"

"Yes, I'm sure. The snake took my car, and I'm pressing charges." Her accent was thick again, and she forced herself to calm down and speak slowly and correctly as Evie had coached her since the beginning of their friendship. "How do I go about pressing charges?"

"You'll have to come down to the station. When can you come?"

Rosalva considered. It wasn't busy today at the restaurant, and she could make up her time later. "Right now would actually be the best. But when will I get my car?"

"You can pick it up any time from the garage. Apparently, it's fixed. But that's what I was trying to say. If this guy was going to pay for it, why not let him?"

"Because he never pays for anything. He never has. Look, I'll be there in a while. Can you give me the address?" Rosalva wrote it down, tears springing behind her eyes. Why did Enrique still have the power to hurt her?

Fifteen minutes later, Rosalva pulled into the parking lot at the police station. Inside, she was ushered to a room where a police officer waited. Behind him, studying a painting on the wall, was Willard.

Rosalva experienced a sinking feeling in her chest. Where was Enrique?

Willard turned, his face brightening at seeing her, but he quickly squelched the emotion, replacing it with what she assumed was his lawyer face.

"What is he doing here?" she asked. "Where's my ex-husband?"

The police officer, a thin, wiry man, stared at her in confusion. "Willard Oakman is the man who had your car towed, ma'am. He said he was a friend and wanted to get it fixed for you. I told you all this on the phone."

He probably had, but he didn't know what it was like speaking English as a second language. She had to speak a lot of Spanish with customers and employees during the day, and it was still all too easy to tune out English when she was focusing on something so intently—like being angry at Enrique for stealing her car. Only he hadn't, and if she had listened better to the officer instead of letting herself be consumed with fury, she would have known that.

"Are you really pressing charges?" Willard's eyes dug into her. "Because I was doing it to help you, and I think I can prove it in front of any judge. That is, if I still have my job after having to leave in the middle of a crisis to come down here."

"No," Rosalva said faintly, reaching for the back of a chair. "I didn't realize it was you."

"Well, you should have found out!"

There was enough anger in his voice to make her retaliate.

She glared at him, hands on her hips. "Who gave you permission to move my car in the first place? Do you know the worry I've gone through all day because of it? No, you have no idea, because you're some hotshot lawyer who could buy a new car more easily than I can buy a pair of jeans for my son. Who said I needed your help?"

"I thought I'd surprise you, that's all." He approached, pushing a chair aside as he came, sending it skidding into the table.

Rosalva's chin came up. "Yeah, you surprised me, that's for sure. I've spent all day trying to track down my ex, thinking he stole my car. I haven't been able to work. My sons are upset, and—"

"Look," the police officer said. "I'm just going to step out in the hall and let you two discuss this. No throwing chairs, though." This last to Willard, whose face was flushed.

Willard nodded. "Sorry about that."

"I'll be outside if you need me." The man hurried out the door.

Rosalva glared at Willard, who met her eyes without flinching. She recalled their conversation about marriage last night with a pang. She'd been right about him. Look at how mad he was. His next words took her by surprise.

"You thought your ex-husband took your car?"

"It wouldn't be the first time he tried to get money from me. Once he took my TV and all my DVDs."

Willard pulled out the chair and sat down, the color leaving his face. "I'm sorry," he said softly. "I didn't realize. I thought I was helping."

"You should have told me." Rosalva forced herself to speak calmly, though she was still angry—far more angry than she knew she had a right to be. "I would have been thankful. It's just . . . I don't like that kind of surprise."

"I've always trusted my judgment." Willard looked up at her, his gray eyes like liquid metal that seared her heart. "But I didn't take into account your life before, the baggage we all carry. I'm really sorry." Abruptly, he stood. "Let me make it up to you. I'll take you to get your car. Please?"

I don't need you! Rosalva wanted to say, but instead she said, "I have to go back to work. Besides, I'm driving my son's car right now."

He nodded. "Do you get off at five again?"

"Not until six today. I was late to work this morning because of this mess."

"I'll call and see how late the garage is open. Then you can follow me there. We'll at least be able to pay for the work and leave the car where we can pick it up whenever we please. Come on, let's get out of here." He took her elbow and steered her to the door. The officer was waiting and accompanied them from the restricted area.

Willard walked with Rosalva to her son's beat-up Ford Tempo. "Look," she began.

"I'm really sorry," he said at the same time.

She stared miserably at the ground. "I'm sorry, too. I should have listened to the policeman. I was just so sure it was Enrique. I was angry."

He touched her chin, drawing her eyes up to meet his. "We'll laugh about this later. You'll see. In a year or so."

Her heart thudded in her chest. She had felt so strong and in control of her attraction to him while she was angry, but now she felt young and afraid . . . vulnerable. She'd never expected to feel this way at forty-two. "What makes you think you'll know me in a year?"

"Because I want to. Won't you give me a chance?" He was looking at her, just as so many of her dates had before, but this time was different. She knew he really cared, even after she'd screamed at him—and, yes, because she felt something for him, too. That made everything different. But it still didn't mean she could trust him.

"What do you want?" she asked, forcing her voice to be hard. "A family? Wasn't that what you had with your wife? Or could have had? You just gave it up, didn't you? So what makes everything different now? Or do you like me because I'm different, a challenge? I know your parents didn't like your brother's wife because her grandmother was Mexican. Are you trying to hurt them?"

"Rosalva." Nothing more, just her name, but she knew she'd wounded him.

"What?" she snapped, irritated at the sympathy she felt.

"My parents have nothing to do with this. I like you because you're beautiful, smart, confident, outspoken. As for my ex-wife, I know I blew it, but does that mean I'll never get another chance? Ever? I've changed. Really, I have. I hope you'll let yourself see that." He gave her a wistful smile and then started to walk away.

Rosalva swallowed the lump in her throat. "Willard!"

He turned a hopeful face in her direction.

"It's just . . . I—I don't have any money to pay for the car. I'll need time to get a loan."

"No," he shook his head, "it was my surprise, remember? You don't need to pay me back. No strings attached. I promise."

The relief she felt must have shown on her face because he gave her a bigger smile this time. She walked over to him and reached up, taking his face between her hands. "Thank you, Willard. Thank you." She stretched to kiss his cheek, as she would have done to a close friend, but a car honked in the parking lot, and at the last moment he turned to look. Their lips met.

Rosalva pulled away quickly, but not before he responded and not before her own emotions piled inside her chest. She waited, wondering what would happen next. Could she really love this man? The idea was inconceivable to her.

"You're welcome," he said, his voice crackling with warmth. "I'll see you at six."

She watched him drive away.

On the way back to work, her phone rang. Retrieving it from its customary spot, she answered, one hand on the wheel. "Hello?" She hoped it was Willard, though she knew that he was on his way to work to deal with whatever crisis he had left.

"Rosalva, it's Tina. Look, something terrible has happened. It's Harold. He and Maxine were out, and he had a stroke. No, don't come now. I know you're working. I'm here with Maxine, and when I have to go home, Evie will come. I was just hoping you could come later tonight. Maxine refuses to leave, and I don't want her to be alone. I thought we all could pitch in."

"Sure, I'll come."

"I know you'll need to check on your boys. I thought maybe once Lucas was in bed . . . Maybe you can talk Maxine into leaving."

"Poor Maxine."

"I know." Tina's voice sounded choked. "We just have to hope that he'll be all right."

CHAPTER

9

Maxine

We shouldn't care so much about people as we get older. Age makes your friends too fragile. One minute they're proposing, and the next minute they're having a stroke. But the truth is that you become more sentimental as you get older. It's plain not fair. Take movies, for instance. Things that wouldn't have caused a second thought in my younger years now make me weep for the beauty or sadness of them.

Maybe Bernice is right about dating and remarriage. Noninvolvement would be easier in moments like this.

Harold's had some kind of stroke. They say it happens sometimes that the person can't move or speak, though inside they are trying so hard to tell you something is wrong. One of the nurses said it happened to her father, and the only way he could tell them something had happened was by crying. I think that's what happened to Harold. His tears certainly weren't delayed reaction to my refusal to answer his proposal.

I've been at the hospital for the better part of the past two days, despite the fact that visitors aren't allowed to stay long. I've spent much of that time in the waiting room. For the first hours I was the only one there for him, and that's why they let me in the ICU, even though I'm not family. The first time he awoke, he said my name—or tried to. I assured him I was there and not to worry. He said something else, and it took three tries before I realized he was saying "thank you." It was all I could do not to cry.

His daughter, who lives in Provo, has been there a lot, and it was nice meeting her. The first time she had a bunch of kids with her, so I watched them in the waiting room while she went in with him. Then she actually had to give the hospital permission to let me see him. I'm glad she managed that because I'm the best friend he's got. This became really important because suddenly a lot of ladies were showing up with cards, flowers, and cookies and stuff that he isn't even allowed to have. Many of them I recognize from when we used to attend the singles dances more, but some I didn't know. Guess Harold's a popular guy when he's not chasing me.

I feel numb inside. It reminds me of how I felt when Charles was sick. Four months from his diagnosis with brain cancer to his death. Too fast.

I keep asking if Harold's going to be all right, but they don't know much. Apparently the stroke affected the right side of his brain, meaning the left side of his body. The right side of the brain controls perceptual skills, vision, and who knows what else. Two of his sons from Salt Lake stopped by, and they gave him a blessing. They said they thought he would be all right, but what these youngsters sometimes fail to understand is that you're all right when you die. You're *just not here anymore. Maybe I should be happy that Harold might join his wife. But I have to confess, I'm just the slightest bit jealous.*

I miss having Harold to talk to. I hope today when I go see him he's a little more alert. I keep praying for him. I still can't believe this is happening. Did I push him too hard with the walking and gardening? Is this my fault?

Maxine sat miserably in the waiting room at the Utah Valley Regional Medical Center. She hated waiting. As a young wife and mother of five she had spent what used to seem an eternity waiting for this or for that. A simple dash to the grocery store became an afternoon production with the children. At the time it had been enough to make her want to give up eating altogether. Waiting for her teens to come home from dates had been even worse, and when Charles had forgotten to tell her he was working late, the waiting was the worst of all, as she conjured up all sorts of things that might have kept him.

Now that she was a mature woman living alone, she didn't have to wait. She arose when she wanted, went to sleep whenever she was tired, and ate whatever she was in the mood for. In fact, she almost always ate dessert first these days, because she had no children to force broccoli down. It was one of the best aspects of aging. She had sworn she'd never wait again unless she wanted to, but here she was. The minutes on the clock ticked by.

Maxine was relieved when Janette, Harold's daughter, came from the ICU. "Any news?" Maxine asked brightly.

"Well, they think they'll be able to move him from the ICU."

"That's good news," Maxine said, although that meant he

was going to be able to receive the other female visitors who had been coming to leave cards in what seemed like streams, all anxious for what she had twice refused.

Janette shook her head, and for the first time Maxine noticed how pale she was, her face contrasting sharply with her short, dark brown hair. "Well, it means they don't think he's going to die this minute at least, but they have no idea of the permanent damage he's sustained, and they won't for a few weeks. He may never walk again. He can't even move his left side—it still seems weird that a right-brain stroke affects the left side of the body." She blinked back tears. "The worst is, they've just told me he seems to be having a hard time understanding things. There's no doubt someone will have to take care of him, at least for a while."

Tears clogged Maxine's throat. "But he could get better."

"You're right." Janette smiled and her eyes, so like her father's when he wore a blue shirt, brightened. "Thank you, Maxine. I should be more positive."

Maxine had spoken more for herself than for Janette, but she was happy her words had comforted Harold's child. "He's a fighter, you'll see. At least he doesn't seem to have memory loss, and since the stroke isn't on the left side on his brain, his speech should be all right."

"I know there are good things. It's just . . . well, I love my dad so much, but I worry, you know, about taking care of him and keeping up with all my children. My brothers' wives are older, and they're working, so I'm really the only one. Besides, my dad wouldn't feel comfortable at their houses anyway." She sighed. "I don't how it's all going to work out."

"I know it seems overwhelming right now, but maybe we

should wait to see what happens." Maxine put a motherly arm around her and squeezed her shoulder.

"One day at a time, right?" Janette smiled again, though tears gathered in her eyes. "It's nice to know you're here with him. It makes me feel better somehow, knowing he's not all alone. I know I should probably get a baby-sitter and—"

"You've been here a lot," Maxine said. "He understands. Believe me."

Giving her a look of utter relief, Janette nodded. "Thanks, Maxine. Oh, and you can go in now if you want to. He was awake but not very coherent."

"Thank you. I think I will. You go on home with your family. I'll stay here for a while."

Minutes later, Maxine entered Harold's room, feeling nervous. He was lying flat on the bed, eyes closed, looking pale and old, though he was only sixty-six. She bit her lip to keep from crying. Had he really kissed her on Wednesday? Looking at him now, it seemed impossible. The realization that he might never be the same came to her with astonishing clarity. Her heart ached.

"Oh, Harold," she murmured. Sinking into the chair by the bed, she reached for his left hand, the one without the IV. She leaned forward and held his hand to her lips, tears stinging her eyes. "You're too ornery to give up," she whispered. "You have to fight! I know it's going to be work, but you have to. I'll miss you if you . . ." She stopped then because it sounded so selfish of her and because, as her friends were constantly telling her, Harold wasn't ornery at all. He was stubborn, persistent, methodical, and downright annoying with his attention at times, but he wasn't ornery. She wished he had really been ornery because then maybe she wouldn't care so much.

"Now who's kissing whose hand?" His voice came hoarsely and unexpectedly, the words slow but understandable. His eyes were open now, studying her. They were almost colorless, as though the white sheets had soaked up any pigment they'd once held. But there was amusement in those eyes, and his face looked more alive, though the muscles on the left side drooped slightly.

"Hi, Harold. How do you feel?"

"Ornery." A slight upraising on the right side of his mouth—a smile, she presumed.

His reply irritated her. Here she was trying to be helpful and serious, and he was joking around. "I mean, really. Have they told you what to expect? How serious is it? Your daughter is so worried. They don't seem to give her information."

He shook his head, apparently too exhausted to attempt speech, and Maxine didn't have the heart to push.

"Well, let's not talk about that now," she said. "You just rest. I'll sit here and keep you company. I can read to you, if you want, or tell you the news in the neighborhood."

But his eyes had already closed, again leaving him frail-looking and old. Maxine's heart hurt, and she felt like weeping. This wasn't her Harold at all. She kept holding his limp hand until her muscles cried out for release.

Stretching her legs, Maxine decided to take a walk around the hospital. She was grateful for the respite, but she worried about Harold waking up alone.

"Maxine!" Bernice was coming toward her, dressed in a gray skirt that exactly matched the gray in her hair.

"Oh, Bernice." Maxine was grateful to see a friendly face, even one that always looked a bit disapproving.

Bernice took her hands. "How is he?"

"Not well, I'm afraid. It's basically just wait and see at this point. See how much damage"—her voice rose to a squeak on the word—"there is and how much he'll get back."

"Some people recover fully."

"Some don't."

Bernice frowned and gave a tight laugh. "Funny, but I feel suddenly that I don't know what to say to you. I never expected . . . I mean you've always been so strong, so sure."

Maxine made a face. "I think it's this place. Reminds me of Charles, how he died."

Bernice's face looked sour, but Maxine knew her well enough to know it was really an expression of sympathy. "Have you eaten lunch?" Bernice asked.

"I thought I might stop by the cafeteria."

"Let's go somewhere else. You need to get away from here."

"I have to be here for him. The nurse promised to page me if he wakes."

"I'll go with you to the cafeteria, then."

By the time they'd ordered their food and found a place to sit, Maxine had made up her mind. "I have to marry him," she said. "That way I can be close enough to help him recover. He won't have to convalesce at his daughter's at all."

Bernice choked on her drink. "You said you didn't want that responsibility. You've said it at least a dozen times in the last month—no laundry, no schedule, no meals to make."

"I know. But I feel . . . Oh, Bernice, I've been horribly, horribly wrong. Look at how much time I've wasted! Harold and I could have been happy together all these months."

"You haven't been happy?"

Maxine thought for a moment. "Yes, but a different kind of happiness. This has made me realize how much I love Harold."

She replayed the kiss of Wednesday in her mind and how she had responded to his touch. Their hearts had been one.

Now she knew exactly what came after "and then what?" Marriage. It was a simple realization, without bells and whistles, but accompanied by a rush of love so tender that her heart felt ready to burst with the emotion.

She held her breath, expecting Bernice to go off on her usual lecture about how remarrying meant that she hadn't loved Charles. No, better that Maxine bring it up first. "And don't talk about Charles," she said as Bernice opened her mouth. "He's not here, and he has no say in this. Harold needs me now."

Bernice pursed her lips sourly. "I was going to say that maybe you're right. But are you up to taking care of an invalid? Think about it, Maxine. You have the rest of your life ahead of you."

"I love him," Maxine said. It was all so clear to her now. Was that the way Harold had always seen it?

"But what if he, you know, never recovers? Are you willing to take care of him then?"

"He'd still be Harold, wouldn't he?" But Maxine was less certain now. She'd heard that strokes often changed people. If Harold no longer was the same man, if he no longer loved her, well, that would make a difference in her plans. She couldn't believe that would happen. Not now, not when she finally understood what he meant to her. Not when she would will-ingly give up all her so-called freedom to have his companion-ship and love. "I'm going to do it, Bernice," she said, lifting her bagel sandwich, "and there's nothing you can do to stop me."

"I don't want to stop you." Bernice sniffed loudly, her brown eyes sincere. "It's just all so irrevocable. Sometimes I think it would be much easier if our first marriages hadn't been as good as they were."

The way she said it made Maxine looked sharply at her. "Is this about me or about you, Bernice?"

"It's not about either of us." Bernice studied her untouched sandwich.

Normally Maxine would try to get to the bottom of such cryptic remarks, but she was suddenly eager to talk to Harold. She couldn't exactly spring her surprise on him until he was a little more aware, but she would prove to him that she was going to be there for him. She would be with him every single step of the way. *If only love could always mean healing,* she thought, but she knew that love sometimes meant saying good-bye.

Not this time.

Maxine quickly ate her sandwich. Harold was waiting.

CHAPTER

10

Tina

I haven't felt this way since . . . well, I'm not sure I ever felt this way in all my thirty-nine years. Looking back I see that I married Glen more to get away from my father than because I loved Glen. I was more in love with the idea of marriage. But I still believe we would have made it work because I did grow to love him very much.

That's what frightens me now. How can I trust my opinion? Scott seems absolutely perfect. I mean, he's gorgeous and he has a good job as a salesman at a software firm. He's good with my kids. He seems crazy about me. True, he does love the outdoors a little more than I do, but I'm learning to enjoy things I never did before. I actually wore shorts for the first time since my marriage when Scott took me and the kids hiking in the foothills this morning. I had no bruises to hide. Pleasant Grove has beautiful foothills, and the day was so warm.

Scott is strong and smart and fun to be with. The kids went with us because it's Saturday, and they're getting along fabulously well with him, though Skip and Dallin are a bit reserved. I guess at thirteen and ten, they remember only too well the life we had with their father. It's only been a year since he died—well, almost a year and a half now, I guess. Sometimes I find them watching Scott with longing but also with fear. It makes me furious at Glen. So darn furious! Ronnie, however, seems unaffected. I guess he was too little to really understand—only four and a half when Glen died. Besides, we all protected him.

Scott's daughter, Callie, and my Ashley have become great friends this week. They're together every second. I have to admit that I haven't discouraged it, because with Callie showing up at my house all the time, I know Scott will be there soon after. I think about him almost every second of the day.

As if to prove that, I've written four whole paragraphs and haven't even mentioned Maxine and Harold. Harold's not going to die, at least, but we don't know how damaged his body is. Maxine was heartbroken during those first days, and all the Independence Club members took turns staying with her at the hospital whenever we could.

Yesterday when Maxine came home from the hospital, she was looking better. She said Bernice had come to eat lunch with her and had helped her decide to marry Harold. That's really weird. I mean, sometimes Bernice's sour comments can be quite funny, but I never imagined her encouraging Maxine to marry Harold!

Anyway, it's all pretty much up in the air. Harold is too sick right now to be involved in Maxine's plan. The truth is, we don't even know if he's going to be the same man he was before. I looked it up *on the Net, and besides all the physical problems, people who have right-brain strokes have a tendency to act more rashly than they did before. Maybe that wouldn't be all bad if it's not too pronounced—I mean, Harold's always been a bit too deliberate for my taste. But maybe that's part of what made Maxine love him. What if that person is gone forever? That makes me really sad. I looked up to him a lot, almost like a father. I wish he had been my father. Maybe then my life would have been different.*

No, I can't wish that. If I hadn't married Glen, I wouldn't have my children. I wouldn't have met Scott. And here I am back to thinking about him again. Is it wrong for me to be so happy when Maxine is so miserable?

Tina hummed as she looked in her freezer to check the contents. Scott was taking her out again for dinner tonight, but she had invited him and Callie for dinner after church tomorrow. It would be their one-week anniversary.

Ashley came into the kitchen, brushing her long strawberry blonde hair. She always brushed it a lot, trying to rid it of the natural curl. "Mom, can I go to the mall with Callie? I really want to see if they have those jeans on sale."

"I don't have any money for jeans. Maybe after I get paid. I haven't sold as many products as I normally do, but Maxine and some of my other ladies have been selling like crazy."

"That's okay. I have enough money of my own."

"Even after you bought that IPod?" Ashley worked at a pizza restaurant ten hours a week, which was all Tina allowed because she felt school was more important than the clothes and the other things Ashley always wanted now that she was older. Putting four children through college was a daunting thought, and any scholarships Ashley could earn would be welcome.

"If they're on sale."

"What did Scott say?"

"I don't know, but Callie is the one who called to ask me if I could go, so it should be all right. Can I use the car?"

Tina considered. "Only if you'll stop off for some spareribs. I want to have them for dinner tomorrow."

"All right."

"And some lettuce, onions, and french bread."

Ashley laughed. "Make me a list, okay? I'll call Callie back and tell her I can go." She gave Tina a hug on her way out, and Tina felt contentment spread through her. She was lucky, very, very lucky.

"I'll make the list," Dallin said, his brown eyes eager.

"You can use my pencil." Ronnie went to get his bendable pencil that Ashley had won at school during a class contest of some sort. He'd admired it so much that she'd given it to him on the spot.

The boys bent over their paper. "How do you spell *onions*?" asked Dallin.

Tina smiled and spelled it out, enjoying the moment with her children. Only Skip was missing, having gone to a friend's after they'd returned from their hike that morning. Since he'd done his chores, Tina hadn't minded, but she missed him all the same.

After Ashley was gone and the younger boys were outside playing, Tina tried to focus on what she was supposed to be doing around the house. There were the boys' clothes to be folded, the curtain in Skip's window to fix, and she'd been considering taking off the wallpaper and painting the kitchen. It wasn't something she ordinarily thought she could do, but since Glen's death, she'd discovered she was handy at many things. *If he could see me now,* she thought. Would he be surprised at how capable she was? Not that it mattered; she didn't suppose death had changed him any. Such drastic alterations would take a lot more than eighteen months on either side of the veil.

"Mom, Scott's here!" Dallin called, coming in from outside. Scott was behind him, his footsteps heavy on the linoleum.

Surprised, Tina looked up from the strip of paper she was pulling from the wall. Scott wasn't supposed to pick her up for at least two more hours. Ashley had promised to be home by then to watch the boys.

"Hi," she said, greeting Scott with a smile. She hoped she looked all right. There wasn't time to check a mirror.

He nodded and returned her smile, but he didn't kiss her cheek as he sometimes did, even with the children watching. His body was taut and his expression serious. "Have you seen Callie?" he asked.

"Well, not seen her exactly, but I know she went to the mall with Ashley. Is something wrong?" The hair on Tina's head prickled, and a sudden dread felt heavy in her stomach.

Scott ran his hand through his hair. Tina noticed how strong his arm looked—maybe twice the size of hers. So much available power. He was much stronger than Glen, who had been on the underdeveloped side.

"She was supposed to be studying," Scott told her. "She has a biology test on Monday, and she knows it's not good to study on Sunday."

"I never study on Sunday." Dallin was standing near Scott,

very much aware of their conversation. Tina felt a too-familiar urge to protect him. But from what?

"I took a shower," Scott continued, "and then ran down to the hardware store. When I got back, she was gone. There was a note saying she'd tried to call me and that she was with Ashley. My cell phone doesn't get great reception at Home Depot, but she knows better than to leave without permission."

"Well, they're together. I let Ashley take my car to the mall." Years of instinct kicked in, and she found herself withholding the information that Callie had called to instigate the outing. Saying she had allowed it would direct his attention toward her and away from the children. Tina swallowed hard.

He frowned. "Looks like I'm going to have to crack down on her. She's not answering her phone." He grinned at her suddenly. "She thinks I'm too wrapped up in you to notice anything she does. And the truth is, she's almost right."

Tina felt her tenseness ease. What was she afraid of, anyway? This was Scott, a man she believed was falling in love with her. "Well, they'll be back in a few hours."

"I've got to find her now. She has to study—plus she's disobeyed. Any idea what store in the mall they went to?"

"No, but I gave Ashley my cell phone. We can call her. She always answers, or she knows I'll call the police."

He flashed another smile at that, but there was anger in his eyes—not directed toward her but frightening all the same. "May I use your phone, then? That way they won't know it's me calling."

"Sure. It's right there." She pointed to the counter.

"I just don't understand why she's acting this way. When do they ever grow up and start being responsible?" He threw out his hands in a helpless gesture, nearly hitting Dallin. The boy

cringed and stared up at Scott, his eyes huge and his face growing suddenly pale.

Scott, heading for the phone, didn't notice. Tina stepped
over to her son and set a hand on his shoulder, kneading the
muscles softly. He still looked shaken, and though she gave him
an encouraging smile, she couldn't blame him. Her own nerves
were so tense that she wanted to retreat to her room.

"Where's Ronnie?" she asked Dallin.

"Outside in the sand box."

"Will you go check on him for me?" She knew if she could
get him outside, he would likely start playing and forget everything else.

Dallin cast a nervous glance at Scott but nodded slowly.

"It's okay," she urged. "Really." Tina was relieved when he
left. She walked over to Scott. "Maybe I should talk with
Ashley."

"It's okay. I'll do it." He listened for a minute. "Ashley? Hi,
it's Scott. I'm here with your mom, and she said Callie went to
the mall with you. I need to talk to her. Thanks." There was a
pause and then his voice became stern. "Callie, you are in big
trouble. No, I don't care what excuse you have. You had better
get home right this instant. What? No, you can't go to the grocery store." He listened for a long moment and then burst out
in fury. "No, Callie! You get home right now!"

Tina watched from a place outside herself. She knew he
was right to be upset at Callie, but at the same time terror rose
in her heart. What if that anger were someday directed at her
or her children? What if those strong hands tried to choke her?

Stop it! she told herself. *Stop right now. Or leave the room.
That's it. Go down the hall.* But she was rooted to the spot. Her

heart pounded, and she felt a compelling urge to scurry under the table to hide.

Scott was still speaking heatedly with his daughter, but Tina couldn't understand the words. Her breath came quickly, and her whole body tingled with fear.

"Ashley?" Scott's voice was calmer now. Bits of the words began to register in Tina's brain, but even those didn't have much meaning for her. "Thanks . . . yeah. . . . drive safely . . . no hurry . . . don't tell her that, though. Good-bye."

He turned to her, and Tina took a step back.

"Tina?" His voice came from far away. "Are you okay? Tina? The girls are fine. Ashley found her jeans, and they're coming home." He reached out to touch her, but she shrank from his hand. "Tina, did I do something?" There was hurt in his voice now. On some level Tina knew she wasn't in danger, and yet . . .

"Tina?"

She'd loved the sound of her name on his lips, but now it brought no comfort.

"Tina, answer me." It was a plea, but for so many years any request from Glen had been a veiled demand, and it frightened her. She shook her head.

"Mommy?" Dallin came in from outside. He hadn't forgotten her.

She held out her arms, and he ran to her, burying his face in her embrace. "It's okay," she soothed. She was feeling steadier herself now, her normal hearing returned, and her heartbeat was slowing.

Scott shook his head. "Tina, I don't understand. What just happened here? And why is Dallin upset?"

She opened her mouth, wanting to tell him, wanting it to

all be okay. *It is okay,* she told herself. "It's nothing," she said aloud. "Dallin gets a little nervous when people sound angry. We all do." She smiled up at him, willing nothing to give her away.

Scott's eyes wandered over her face, as though searching for the truth. "Are you sure?" he said a little huskily. "Because your friend Maxine told me I should ask you about your husband. What did she mean?"

Tina waved the words away. "Oh, Maxine's just an old busybody. You know that. Don't mind her."

Scott stepped toward her, eyes going to where Dallin still clung to her side. "You know I'm crazy about you," he said in a low voice. "I want—"

"Dallin, go play with your brother," she said. When Dallin looked up, she gave him a big smile. "Go on. And you can both have a popsicle from the freezer, okay?"

He grinned and ran to get the treat.

Scott took her in his arms when Dallin was gone. "I want to make you happy," he finished.

She hugged him back. "I am happy. Everything is perfect."

He kissed her, and they laughed.

"I'd better go finish putting on the doorjambs," he said reluctantly. "If I don't do that, Callie will put another hole in the wall. She opens the doors with way too much force. A sumo wrestler in disguise."

Smiling, Tina followed him to the door. "Don't be too hard on her," she said. "Remember, she's still very young."

Scott tilted his head, looking up at her from the bottom of the steps. "Don't worry, I'm a nice man—and probably too much of a pushover where my daughter's concerned.

Everything will be all right. See you tonight. You're going to love the restaurant."

She watched him get into his truck to drive the block to his home. "Everything *is* all right," she said quietly. "I'll make it all right."

CHAPTER

11

Bernice

I know I said I'd break it off with Clay, but I haven't been able to. I've seen him every day except Wednesday. I was supposed to go out with him that night, but I went to the hospital to be with Maxine, and I used that as an excuse. I've gone down there every day, but usually in the afternoons. In the evenings I've been with Clay. He hasn't said anything more about marriage, but he's still waiting for my response. I can feel a sadness in him that hurts my heart.

Today after church he's coming over to look at a passage in the Old Testament with me. It's kind of confusing, and it's nice to have his opinion. The weather is warm enough for us to be on the back patio, so I can be sure and keep distance between us. I need to tell him that I can't see him anymore, but how can I? What if I'm wrong? What if women should remarry even though they loved their husbands? What if I had died first? Would I have wanted David to remarry?

No. That's my gut answer, but when I think of Clay all alone, making all his food, trying to keep house . . . No fun at all, though he's gone back to working part time at Home Depot—quite different from his old job as an accountant. I know he started that because he was lonely. He wanted to get out and see people. He's so friendly, it's no wonder he's good at the job. The other day he said he could tile my kitchen if I wanted. I've wanted that for years, but it's so expensive to have it done, and letting Clay do it . . . well, it's not right, feeling the way I do.

Yet how do I feel? That's what the journals are for, writing how we feel. But I don't know how I feel really. Except that when I'm with Clay, I'm happier than when I'm not with him. I think I know at least a little how Tina feels about the new man she's met. I don't remember ever being giddy before—so high in spirits that I want to sing—though I probably was, at some point or another in my life. Why does everything feel new with Clay?

I wonder what my children would say if I told them I was getting married. I think they'd accept it about as well as the ladies in the Independence Club. I wish now that I hadn't spouted off so much with my big mouth. Funny how your perspective can change so quickly.

Speaking of the Independence Club (because I really don't want to investigate my feelings further), Maxine worries me. She's decided to dedicate the rest of her life to Harold. I worry she'll give up too much, that she's only doing it for guilt. I mean, if they'd already been married, that would have been one thing, but she didn't even want to get married. I don't like seeing women coerced into difficult situations. What can I do to help her? Maybe I'll ask Clay when he comes over.

I'm making strawberry shortcake to give him. I know it's his favorite. It's such a pleasure to bake for someone who appreciates it.

Bernice watched as Clay dug into the mound of whipped cream on his dessert, pushing the fork through the strawberries and the shortcake, still warm from the oven.

"This is the best strawberry shortcake I've ever tasted. Mmm." Clay savored the mouthful.

Bernice knew it was the bit of sugar she'd put into the strawberries that pulled out the juices and made the not-quite-ripe ones taste sweet. The berries had to be chilled afterward, to complement the warm cake, and the cream had to be fresh and whipped with two spoonfuls of powdered sugar. Tina, who was the best cook Bernice knew, had given her the recipe for the cake, and it was heavy enough to hold its own next to the strawberries. She hated how regular cake mixes were so light it felt like you were eating sweetened air.

"I think it's nice your friend wants to take care of her boyfriend," Clay commented, taking another bite.

"But what if he's a vegetable? What kind of marriage would that be?"

"Well, he'll probably recover. Didn't you say they moved him from the ICU?"

"Yes, and he's been more alert. Maxine says he starts working with the therapists on Monday."

"What does he say about all this?"

Bernice shrugged, pursing her lips with concentration. "Last I heard she hadn't let him in on the plan yet. He might be doing better, but he had so much family and other visitors yesterday that she was never alone with him. Likely things will be the same today."

Clay set down his fork and reached a hand to her face, gently smoothing it. "Don't look so worried. I'm sure it'll be all right."

Knowing that worrying made her face looked pinched, she forced her face to relax. "I just wish I could think of some way to help her."

"Maybe being her friend is enough."

"I hope so." She was trying to be a better friend, especially after how blunt and cruel she had been in the past with her views on remarrying.

Clay continued to stare at her, the teasing expression he normally wore replaced by seriousness. "In the midst of all this thinking, have you thought at all about us?"

She was tempted to say she'd been too occupied, that her worry for her friend overshadowed all, but she had never lied to anyone that she could remember. At least not directly or intentionally. No, she had to look at this as an opportunity to break things off. To have him become the "was" that she had reported to the Independence Club. She opened her mouth. "Actually, I've thought of little else."

He smiled, and it made her heart jump a little. He had a beautiful smile, a friendly one like the roundness of his chest and the smell of the mints he so enjoyed. Even his brown eyes smiled. "And what have you decided?" Tenderness showed in his voice and in the lines of his face. Bernice felt happy and sad all at once. Happy for herself that she was loved but also sad for both of them because of what she had to do. "So are you going to marry me?"

For the space of three heartbeats she didn't reply, and then she said, "Yes, I'll marry you."

He gave a glad exclamation and leaned over to hug her, tears of happiness coming to his eyes but quickly laughed away. Bernice was too shocked at her response to return the hug.

"I love you," he mumbled in her hair.

He loved her despite the fact that she was fifty-seven, had a thick waist, and would never dye her gray hair. Maybe he even loved her partly because of all that.

"I love you, too," she answered. The feeling was different from the feeling she'd had with David, but it was still love, and her heart knew it. With Clay she didn't feel dried up and sour. She felt like singing and dancing and loving everyone, and suddenly she couldn't imagine a future without him.

Clay pulled the ring box from his pocket. "I brought it with me, just in case." He opened it, and she stared again at the ring he'd shown her on Tuesday night. The band had three equal-sized diamonds, so different from the plain wedding band she still wore on her left hand, even after three years. She touched the diamonds with a forefinger.

"Let me." He didn't ask her to take off her other ring before placing his on her finger, as though content to let her decide what she would do with it. Or maybe he was content to share her feelings.

She looked down at her hand with a rush of joy. Yet as he kissed her, she realized that the ring wasn't something she could wear—not if she wanted to keep face with her friends. Unless she told them, and didn't honesty demand that she tell them? The thought made her wince.

"Did I hurt you?" he asked.

"No, not at all. I was just thinking that maybe I should move to a new house."

"I thought you loved it here. I don't mind selling my house—after we're married, of course."

If she couldn't explain it to him, maybe she had no right agreeing to the marriage. She drew in a deep breath, tasting the lingering smell of the mints that were always on his breath. "It's just that . . . well, you know I never thought I would marry again. No, to be honest, I really didn't think a woman should remarry after her husband died."

"Your husband wouldn't want you to be alone. I know if it had been my wife who survived, I'd want someone to take care of her." He cleared his throat gently. "Like I want to take care of you."

His sincerity made her feel cherished, the way David had cherished her. "I see that now," she said, staring at his chest instead of his face. "But I told all my single friends that if they'd really loved their husbands, they wouldn't remarry. I was so vocal about it." With a rush of shame, she knew her actions now for what they were: idiocy and self-righteousness.

"And now you're worried about eating crow." Amusement tinged his voice, and she raised her eyes to his, frowning. Was he enjoying her dilemma? Maybe a little, but there was also concern in his expression. "I'm sure your friends will be all right with it," he said. "And I would love to meet them. I used to see them around at the singles dances, but of course we haven't been there for months."

"They haven't gone much, either."

"Oh?" He gave a hearty chuckle. "Maybe they're taking your advice."

Bernice felt worse, though it wasn't true. Everyone in the

Independence Club was dating or trying to find someone to date.

"So when do I get an official introduction to these friends of yours?"

"Well," she hedged, "with Harold in the hospital and some of the ladies dating now, it's difficult."

She felt more than saw his body tense. "Are you ashamed of me, Bernice? I mean, if you'd rather move than tell your friends about us, what kind of a relationship is that?"

Bernice let her eyes run over him—the white hair, congenial face, large chest, and polyester pants that she loved because they would never wrinkle. "I'm not ashamed of you." She took his hand in hers. "I need a little time, that's all. Maybe I can fix the damage I started with my big mouth." She could begin with Maxine and Harold. Now that Maxine had decided to marry him, it would be a simple matter to get them together. As a side benefit, Maxine's marrying would take some of the attention from Bernice's situation when she finally told them about her engagement. Of course, that wasn't the reason she would try to help. *It's because I want Maxine to be happy,* she thought.

"Okay, then. Take the time you need. Only please don't let it be too long." He kissed her fingers and wrist and then pulled her closer, ending with a kiss on her lips.

"I'll try," she promised, "but for now you'd better eat the rest of your shortcake before the strawberries make the cake soggy."

With an amiable sigh, Clay released her, picked up his fork, and went to work.

———

Bernice walked down the hospital hallway toward Harold's room. The door was slightly ajar, and she would have to knock. As she approached, the door swung open wider, and two ladies her age, both with their hair dyed a youthful dark blonde, emerged from the depths. One was Bernice's own build, stocky but not obese; the other slightly thinner and shaped like a pear. After a few steps, the pear-shaped woman said loud enough for Bernice to hear, "It's really too bad. He was such a nice-looking man. And kind."

"Maybe he'll recover," the other woman suggested.

"I wouldn't have baked him cookies if I hadn't any hope." The women chuckled, but their smiles vanished as they noticed Bernice. She had the distinct impression that they were sizing her up as a potential rival. No wonder Maxine had suddenly changed her tune; the competition was certainly taking advantage of Harold's being in the hospital.

Bernice purposefully brought her left hand up to her chest so they could see her ring. She'd taken off her old wedding band, knowing it would please Clay, but the ring was big enough to attract their attention. "Were you visiting Harold Perry?" she asked.

"Right in there," answered the pear-shaped woman, smiling now. "He's with his daughter."

"Thank you."

With a forced smile, Bernice stepped past them, pausing before the half-open door. She could see the bed and Harold in it. He was pale and old-looking, and she could see what the women had been talking about. Harold was definitely a shadow of his former self. But he was getting better, apparently, or they never would have moved him from the ICU.

Harold detected her movement and said something she

couldn't hear. A slender woman Bernice judged to be in her thirties appeared in the opening. She had short brown hair that looked as if it had been carefully sculpted to follow the shape of her head. "May I help you?"

"I'm here to see Harold."

The woman glanced back at the bed and then at Bernice. "My father's a little tired now. He's had a lot of visitors." She peered briefly down the hall where she could still see the other women, who had paused to talk with a nurse. Without another word passing between them, Bernice understood that Harold was tired of being visited by women who had romantic intentions.

"I won't be long," she said. "Tell him Bernice is here. Tell him it's about Maxine. I'm sure he'll want to see me." Bernice didn't understand why Harold couldn't see her standing out there himself. As far as she knew, he didn't wear glasses or contacts.

The woman went back into the room and talked with Harold, her body obscuring Bernice's view of him. She was back in seconds. "Come on in." And then to her father, "I'm going to stretch my legs a bit. Have a nice chat." She left, closing the door behind her.

Bernice was glad. What she wanted to say was best done in private. Slowly, she approached the bed, turning the new ring on her finger so the diamonds were inward. She wasn't ready for Harold to notice it and spread the word of her engagement.

Engagement? Could she really be engaged? She'd come so far in a matter of months.

"Bernice," Harold said so faintly she had to strain to hear. "I'm surprised to see you." His voice wasn't slurred, though tired and halting as though he'd been ill for a long time.

She stood next to the bed, not planning to stay long enough for the nearby chair. "You shouldn't be," she said. "I've been here every day except yesterday. Wasn't my fault they wouldn't let me see you. Glad to see they think you're well enough now."

He tried to laugh, but the sound was forced. "Sometimes I wish I was still in the ICU." He glanced at the flowers and a plate of cookies on the small nightstand.

"From your fan club?"

He nodded but didn't try to speak.

"What's the use of cookies?" she asked. "I bet they don't even let you eat them."

He started to say something and then thought the better of it. Perhaps the effort was too great.

Bernice decided to get right to the reason she was there. "Did you see Maxine today?"

"She was here earlier. My sons, too." His left arm slid off his stomach where it had been resting, and frustration filled his face as he picked it up with his right hand and pulled it back into place.

"She'll be back."

He smiled, but it was sadly lopsided as the left side of his mouth refused to do his bidding.

"Well, she's what I came to talk about. I don't know if she's said anything, but I think this accident has made her look at your relationship differently. Have you talked to her about that?"

He shook his head, his pale eyes looking in her direction but somehow they were different from before—a difference Bernice couldn't pinpoint.

"Too many visitors, huh? I thought as much. Or maybe

Maxine's suddenly shy. That happens sometimes when a woman wants to talk about something dear to her heart." She paused, thinking of Clay and his proposal. "Anyway, I know in the past, I've said a lot of things I shouldn't have to Maxine and the others—about not getting remarried. But I was wrong. Really wrong."

Harold nodded encouragingly, no doubt hoping she would get to the part that had to do with Maxine.

"I think most of my old ideas came from the fact that if I'd been the one to die, I wouldn't have wanted David to forget me and go on. But now I find that I'm not so sure. I hope that at least in heaven I'd be the kind of person to wish him happiness again—even if for a time it would be without me." Her legs felt weak, and she gave in to the urge to sit down on the chair. Harold's eyes followed her downward movement. "Anyway, I'm sorry for all the things I said to you and Maxine. I think you two are meant to be with each other for the rest of your time here on earth. That's why I'm here. I want to help."

"How?" The right side of his face looked interested, but the left remained without expression. Pity tightened Bernice's chest.

"Well, on Friday, Maxine told me she wanted to marry you. She's angry at herself for all the wasted time." She paused, but when Harold didn't immediately speak, she hurried on. "Don't you see? All that bit about not wanting to care for a man and doing things her own way—that means nothing when compared to how she feels about you. You'll need someone to do all those things, and she wants to be the one. Oh, Harold, tell me you'll forget about her pushing you away. She loves you, and that's what's important." Her voice lowered. "And please forgive me for what I did."

"You didn't do anything," he said. "Maxine makes her own choices."

"Well, my attitude couldn't have helped. Anyway, she's changed her mind now. Isn't that great news? That's why I'm here, to help you prepare to sweep her off her feet when she comes to tell you herself."

Harold turned his head on the pillow and stared upwards, contemplating the ceiling.

"Harold?" Bernice was starting to worry. Was this another attack? Maxine had said he'd simply tuned out the last time; maybe it was happening again. She stood and stepped closer to the bed, peering more closely at him. "Are you okay? Should I get a nurse?"

His face moved again, this time in her direction. "My eyes are damaged. I have no . . ." His last words were garbled, as though the muscles in the left side of his face refused to cooperate.

"What?"

He tried again. "Depth perception. I might not be able to drive."

"Can they fix it?"

He shrugged. "Maybe not."

"Well, so what? Maxine drives."

"I can't walk, not even to the bathroom." He gestured to a tall blue bottle near the bed that Bernice recognized with embarrassment.

"Don't worry, Harold. You'll get better, and even if you don't, Maxine will be there for you. You'll see. She'll take care of you, no matter what it takes. That's what love's all about."

Harold watched her for a minute and then offered a weak

smile. "Thanks, Bernice." Or at least that's what she thought he said.

"See?" Bernice felt happier. "If you want, you could even beat her to the punch and ask her to marry you again—first. She'll say yes this time, I guarantee it. Don't worry about anything. Remember, we're all here for you." She reached out to pat his leg under the blanket but thought better of it. "Well, I'll leave you to your rest. I'm sure your daughter will be back soon, or maybe one of your admirers." She laughed at his grimace. "As soon as you tell them you're getting married, I bet you'll get less traffic in here. And believe me, Maxine would rest better too. I don't care how confident a woman is, it does her no good to see other women chasing her man."

Harold chuckled, but it was a sluggish thing that made Bernice glad she was leaving.

"Take care," she called from the door.

There, that should do it, she thought as she strode down the hallway. Now when Maxine went to visit Harold, he would propose again and Maxine would say yes. She would help him recover from the stroke, and they would be happy together. If only everything in life were always so well mapped out.

Bernice went to her car, pushing her diamond ring back the way it belonged. Maybe it wasn't too late to stop by Clay's on her way home.

12

Maxine

I swear, since they put Harold in a regular room, it's been like Grand Central Station in there. Flowers, cards, candy, cookies—don't these women know he's a sick man? He needs nourishing foods, rest, and therapy, not chocolates and hints about asking them out.

I am glad his children and grandchildren came to see him so much this weekend—even his son from Arizona was here. Honestly, they are such a nice bunch, and they seem to accept me as part of the family. I'm sorry I didn't get to know them before. I wonder if that was somewhat like Harold's kisses—he didn't want to share them until he knew I'd stick around.

Well, he's not getting rid of me now. I've been so impatient to tell him my news—our news, really. Knowing Harold, it'll have to be done just right. I want to make sure he knows my change of heart didn't come because of pity or jealousy (well, maybe just a tiny bit from jealousy), but from the realization that I do love him and want to be with him. And as more than just as friends. There's nothing like a stroke to give people a wake-up call.

I've been thinking that my trip to Europe would make a good honeymoon. I know Evie said she'd go with me, but truthfully, I'd rather be with Harold. He should be well enough by the fall, and if not, I'll put it off. I know Evie will understand. I'll tell her at brunch on Wednesday. It's weird to think of how much has happened since our last brunch. Seemingly a lifetime.

Though I'm still very worried about Harold, I'm full of excitement about our future together. It's different from when I married Charles. We were both so young then, not really formed in opinions or anything. We grew together. Harold and I are who we are already. It's takes more adjustment, but there is more wisdom there as well, a knowing when to let the other have space and the understanding that problems do eventually get resolved—mostly by patience (well, at least on Harold's part, as we can see by this marriage thing).

I'm going to see him today. I went twice yesterday, once right after church and then again after having dinner with Evie at her house. She hates eating alone because she's afraid she'll eat too much and get off her diet, or so she says. But I think it was more for me because she had her friend Cecilia there as well. How odd that they should be friends after all that's happened.

When I got to the hospital after dinner, Harold's daughter Janette was there, and later her husband came with all their children. Harold was tired out, so I decided I should leave to make less stress for him. I hope Janette got the kids out of there before too long.

One bad thing that happened is that Harold's eyes seem to be damaged by the stroke. He can't tell how close things are anymore, or if something's moving forward or backwards. He won't be able to drive. The doctor says he may heal, but it's just as likely that he won't. Also, the doctor says he may have to use a wheelchair for the rest of his life, but I can't believe that. He's a fighter. It's not even been a week. I say give it more time.

Maxine tapped on the door, and after hearing a grunt from within, turned the knob. Harold watched her enter. He looked pale, but not anywhere near as lifeless as he had while in the ICU. Today he was propped up with pillows and had the TV on, though he hadn't appeared to be watching it when she came in.

"Hello," she said brightly,

His eyes, a pale blue followed her eagerly, but his smile seemed forced. Or was that because the left side drooped a bit? Even that was getting better, or so she thought.

"What? Cat got your tongue?"

He shook his head, but she knew why he didn't speak. Though the stroke had occurred on the right side of his brain, leaving his speech center on the left side of the brain intact, the resulting paralysis on the left side of his face still made speech more of an effort than before.

"Don't tell me," she went on. "I bet you've already had three visitors this morning and none of them related to you. I didn't realize you were such a ladies' man, Harold." She sat in the chair on his right side, but on the edge so she could be closer to him. She wanted to be close to him all the time now, a difficult desire as they had been rarely left alone.

The TV blared a commercial, and Harold glanced at it in annoyance. He pushed the mute button with his good hand. He looked at Maxine and then away again. There was something in his eyes that sent a shiver up her spine.

"What's happened?" she asked, the playfulness gone from her voice. "Bad news?" She knew he'd had some tests done this morning, but surely the results wouldn't be in yet.

"I'm fine." Though the words weren't enunciated perfectly, she felt a comfort in the rich bass of his voice. He was still her Harold.

She put her hand on his. "You seem a little depressed. Do you want to go for a stroll? Janette said the nurses will let me push you around in a wheelchair. Or you could even try a bit of walking. It might be fun."

His jaw clenched and unclenched. "You've been here a lot."

"Of course. Where else would I be? I've abandoned selling makeup until you get out of here and can order it for me on the Internet. I'm too impatient waiting for the pages to load."

"You need DSL."

"Well, once you're out of here, you can tell me how to go about it." Maxine figured that making him feel needed was a good thing.

He studied the door and said nothing.

"Harold, what is it? Come on, cough it up. After all, if we're planning on spending the rest of our mortal lives together, we should communicate."

He looked at her then, his eyes troubled and his forehead creased.

"Oh, I know this isn't the most romantic setting to give you an answer, but I do want to marry you, Harold. I'm sorry I've been such an idiot. I really want to be with you. I need you. I'm sorry for wasting so much time."

No response. She'd hoped for a smile, an exclamation of joy—anything but the stoic stare he gave her.

"What, don't you want to marry me now, Harold?" Fear

shot through her. What was wrong with him? "Look, together we'll conquer this. Before you know it we'll be out walking again."

He took his hand out from under hers. "No, Maxine."

"What do you mean?" She arose and stood so close to the high bed that it touched her hips.

He took a deep breath. "I have to do this alone."

"Nonsense! Harold, I want to help you."

"You hate making pies."

She knew exactly what he meant. So many times she'd said she didn't want to take care of someone, that her life was hers to live. But couldn't he see that she hadn't known what she was talking about? She understood now that taking care of someone wasn't such a burden where there was love. She'd expected him to be delighted with her acceptance, maybe even a little grateful, but now he was being plain stupid.

"So, we'll order out for pie."

"Go home, Maxine." He met her stare without flinching.

"I'm not going anywhere."

With his right hand he picked up his left and let it plop lifelessly back to the bed. "I don't know if I'm even going to walk again. Three miles . . ." He shook his head as if it was too much to finish the statement. "There will be laundry, food . . . Like taking care of a baby. Please leave."

If he had slapped her, he couldn't have hurt her more. She placed her hands on her hips. "So that's what kind of a friend you think I am? For crying out loud, Harold, you don't have any idea."

"Yes, I do." He gazed pointedly around the room. "This is my life now. Good-bye, Maxine."

"I was right last week. You are ornery. Too darn ornery to

sit there in that bed. I don't know why I was even worried!" She glared at him, but he didn't take the bait. "Whether or not you start seeing well again, you'll get up and back to normal. You already have some feeling in your left side—you can't deny that. Once you're up, then we'll see how you feel about this. Now, I'm going down to the cafeteria for a late breakfast, but you haven't seen the end of me yet. I'll expect you to be more gentlemanly when I return." She whirled away from him, finally allowing her face to crumple with her sadness. Was it the stroke that made him act so rashly? Before, his deliberate plodding had sometimes irritated her, but she'd give anything to have that part of him back now.

"Maxine."

She paused at the door, composing her face before turning to him. "Yes?"

"The walking was good for me. They say it might have been more serious if I had been in worse shape. Thank you."

Relief flooded her. She hadn't worked him to death after all! Yet neither had she paid attention to the rest of his health. Of course, that was just the kind of thing she hadn't wanted to spend the rest of her life doing. She'd believed she'd had her share of raising children and husband-tending. None of that mattered now. With Harold lying there, all she wanted to do was love him and care for him and make sure he was all right.

She retraced her steps and bent swiftly, planting a kiss on his lips, pleased to see that he was startled into a response. She drew slowly away. "See?" she whispered. "Everything is going to be fine, Harold. You'll see."

Harold met her stare, his eyes searching her face hungrily.

The nurse came into the room. "The doctor wants to talk to you," she told Harold. "He'll be by in a minute."

"I'll see you later." Giving him an encouraging smile, Maxine left the room and went to the cafeteria.

It's going to be okay, she thought, but now she started worrying about what news the doctor might want to discuss with Harold. She dawdled over her egg and muffin sandwich to give them time to finish.

When she returned to Harold's room near the nurses' station, a nurse stopped her from going inside.

"Did he have a relapse?" Maxine asked, her heart straining with fear.

"I'm not allowed to give out that information. But you can't see him. I'm sorry."

"Please," Maxine begged.

"Oh, just tell her," another nurse said, looking up from her computer screen.

The first nurse nodded. "Mr. Perry's condition is the same, but he's asked not to be visited by anyone but family."

"You've got to be kidding!"

"No, ma'am. I'm not."

Swallowing the bitterness rising in her throat, Maxine walked slowly out to her car and drove home.

CHAPTER

13

Evie

A whole week has gone by, and I've only had two brief conver-
sations with Jack. I'm not giving up. He doesn't seem to have a girl-
friend, though a lot of women are attracted to him, so it's just a
matter of time before he settles on someone—hopefully me. The good
news is that I've lost seven more pounds in the past nine days. I'm
so excited! That brings me up to a total of twenty-two if I include the
other fifteen I lost before going to the doctor. Of course that means
I've still got thirty-eight pounds to lose to make my doctor happy (for
a total of sixty in all, including that first fifteen). I actually want to
lose more than that, but if I think beyond the doctor's recommenda-
tion I get depressed, so for now I'm not going there.

I'm still not eating sugar, but it's been really hard since I have a
decided sweet tooth. On the other hand, exercising is becoming easier

and easier. In fact, it's become an integral part of my life. Since I've read dozens of books while I'm walking on the treadmill, I feel like my mind is exercising as well. Sometimes after working out at the gym, I'll go walk by the canal. I feel good in my new clothes, and the people I meet along the path are friendly. I bought a heart rate monitor on the Internet to make sure I'm pushing myself enough. If I do push myself, I feel a kind of rush that keeps me going. I love that feeling!

Rosalva has been preoccupied with Willard since learning he fixed her car, and I haven't seen her as much as I used to. I can't wait to catch up on her life today at our brunch—and to see what the others have been up to as well. That reminds me, the strangest thing happened the other day. I thought I passed Bernice in a car with the man she is supposedly not seeing anymore. I think it would be fabulous if they got together, but it was probably someone else. Too bad.

Cecilia always comes to my house after we go to the gym, and we have dinner together. She is so fun to be with! I always thought she was a lot like me—the professional version of me—so I guess I shouldn't be too surprised to see we have so much in common. But I am. It's amazing.

A few times when she's been fighting with Jason about the terms of their divorce, she has actually slept over at my house because he has so far refused to move out, though he doesn't spend every night there. I can't express how fun it was to tell him she was here when he called but that he couldn't talk to her. She certainly doesn't deserve how badly he's been treating her, no more than I deserved it all those years ago. Seeing her situation makes me understand even more clearly that it wasn't my fault my marriage failed. He's doing the same things to her as he did to me, and I know she didn't make the same mistakes I did (well, except for gaining weight, but so has he). Cecilia sees him as he really is now. I do, too. I've come to

*believe there was nothing I could have done to prevent what hap-
pened in our marriage. It truly wasn't my fault. I couldn't force him
to stay and love me.*

*I told Christopher from the gym about Jason and Cecilia just in
case there is a problem. He doesn't work in Pleasant Grove, but it's
nice to have a policeman as a friend. He says he's lost five pounds in
two weeks but has twenty more to go before he'll be within police
regulations. I guess I was right about having to be within a certain
weight to be a police officer. Must be so they can be healthy enough
to chase bad guys. Seems weird. It's nice to have Christopher to chat
with on the days Cecilia can't make it to the gym. He's a nice guy.*

Mimi's Café was more crowded than on the last morning they'd met. As Evie made her way to their customary table, Rosalva hurried up behind her. "I only
have an hour," she said, out of breath. "I'm working earlier
today so I can be sure to be home for Lucas." As usual, Rosalva
looked eye-catching in a bright blue blouse, black pants, and
high heels. Though Evie was also wearing black pants—
complete with a tummy net—she felt a pang knowing she
would never look like her friend. Even when she'd been thinner, she hadn't looked like Rosalva.

Jack will just like me as I am, she consoled herself. Evie had
begun to think of things a lot in relation to how Jack might act
or respond. She had watched him covertly for minutes on end
and felt she knew him—at least enough to know that he would
like her if he would give her a chance.

"Wow, Evie, you look great!" Tina smiled her usual upbeat
smile, one that practically screamed sunshine.

Evie's heart lifted as she slid into a chair. "Do you really
think so?"

"Fabulous," Tina gushed, while the others nodded in agreement.

"I'm glad I'm tall," Evie said. "Cecilia's having a harder time, you know, being a bit shorter than I am."

"Well, I'm sure the divorce isn't helping her," Rosalva added. "So how much more have you lost?"

"Seven pounds in nine days. That no-sugar thing is really helping. I might even decide to do it longer than two weeks."

"Great!"

"Wonderful."

"Congratulations!"

Evie basked in their approval, deciding not to tell them how much she still craved sugar after an entire week of not having any. "Well, I feel better. Lighter."

"Just don't take it off too fast," Bernice added. Leave it to her to say something negative. But Evie wasn't going to let Bernice bother her. It only meant she cared.

The waitress arrived to take their orders, so the personal conversation died away. After she left, Rosalva grabbed a roll from the breadbasket and asked, "Well, who's first?"

Tina giggled. "You, I guess."

Rosalva sighed. "Well, you all know that Willard fixed my car."

"I can't believe you almost had him arrested," Bernice said with a sniff.

"He should have told me. It's my car, and he nearly caused me a heart attack. But anyway, he's done more since then. I let him come over and introduced him to the boys. Before I knew it, he'd fixed a leak in my sink and helped Jaime change his oil—though that was rather funny since I don't think he's ever changed his own oil before." She chuckled and shook her head.

"You should have seen him all covered in black. Anyway, he and Jaime are getting along great. They talked a lot."

"And Lucas?"

Rosalva's smiled faltered. "Well, he's coming along. He's going to his dad's this weekend, though, so next week will probably be tough."

"Maybe having Willard around will make a difference," Tina offered. "Are you going to keep on dating him? Do you think he's *the one?*"

Rosalva propped her elbow on the table and rested her chin on her hand. "No, I don't, so I'm trying to keep my heart out of this. Besides, I found out he wants more children."

Everyone fell silent as they digested the information. "That's ridiculous," Evie said finally. "You've already raised your family."

"I think it's sweet," Tina put in.

Bernice frowned. "That's what you get for dating a younger man."

"He's only five years younger than me," Rosalva said. "But you're right. I should probably stop seeing him so he can find someone who wants to start over with a family."

Evie toyed with her fork. "See if you can get your lawn re-sodded first. Your yard looks terrible."

Rosalva's only reaction was a long sigh.

Maxine glanced up with vacant eyes from her water glass where she had been swirling her ice. "From where I'm standing, forty-two doesn't seem all that old. I bet most of our mothers had babies past that age."

Everyone was more surprised at this than at Rosalva's announcement. Rosalva arched a brow. "Hey, you're the one who always says that you finally get to do what you want *after* the kids are all gone. I'd be starting completely over. And I couldn't have only one or it would be lonely for him or her. I'd probably have to have fertility treatments." She lowered her voice. "My cycle's been a bit, well, irregular."

"Well, whatever you decide, just don't make your decision too late." Maxine went back to swirling her cup.

"And whatever you do, be up front about it," Bernice added.

Rosalva nodded. "You're right. I'll tell Willard this week and then decide what to do from there. But meanwhile, what do I do with Lucas?"

"More lessons," Evie said immediately. She'd been thinking a lot about this during her walks. "Something to occupy his time. What does he like to do?"

"Well, he takes drum lessons. I heard him say something once about horseback riding, but that costs a fortune, doesn't it?"

"I think it's like any other lesson." Evie took a sip of water. She hoped her salad would arrive soon because she was ravenous. "What about a computer class? Kids these days love computers."

"That's a good idea. I'll talk to him about it. Though how I'm going to afford it . . ." Rosalva trailed off. "What about the rest of you?"

Tina sighed dreamily. "Well, things with Scott and me are going really well. The only problem is his daughter."

"Doesn't she like you?"

"Oh, that's not it. In fact, she practically lives at my house. But she's not doing as well as she used to in school, and Scott's worried about her GPA. They've been fighting."

Evie thought Tina's voice grew fainter. Or was that just her imagination?

"Fighting how?" Maxine asked, her shrewd eyes on Tina.

Tina visibly flinched. "Just yelling. He's not the kind of man to hit or anything." She didn't sound convinced.

Bernice slapped her hand down on the table, startling them. "You should make him really mad. Then you'll know for sure what kind of guy he is."

Tina shook her head. "I'm not in a hurry. Anyway, I think this week my goal will be to work on finding another makeup consultant to sign up. Bernice, what about you? You could be a consultant."

"And take away my best customer?" Maxine said with a delicate snort.

Bernice gave them a sour smile. "I've got too much on my mind. Besides, I'm not a sales person." No one contradicted her.

"That reminds me," Evie said. "Bernice, I thought I saw you driving down State Street last Monday in a gold sedan. Was that you?"

Bernice sniffed. "I don't remember being on State Street."

"Must have been someone else. The guy in the car was nice-looking. He seemed familiar." When Bernice didn't respond, Evie turned to Tina. "Cecilia might be interested in becoming a consultant. I'll ask her. Or she may know some others who would be interested. I bet she'd throw a party. We could have it at my house."

Tina grinned. "Thank you, Evie!" There was no trace of the faintness of voice Evie had detected before.

"I think it's weird," Bernice said. "Going around with your husband's new wife."

Evie grinned. "Soon to be ex-wife. Don't forget that. Truthfully, I can see why he likes her so much. I wish now that I had been nicer to her these past years."

"Well, she wasn't exactly nice to you," Rosalva countered. "There was that little matter of her marrying your Jason."

"I know, but he can be charming, so I don't blame her, not anymore." Evie was amazed herself that it was true. "Anyway, she's certainly learned her lesson, and it's really nice to talk to her about it all. She knows exactly what I went through—every little bit. It helps to talk to her."

There was a brief awkwardness as if no one knew how to respond to Evie's confession, but the waitress arrived with their food and the moment passed as everyone began to eat.

"Okay," Tina said after swallowing a mouthful of her pasta. "Rosalva's going to work on getting Lucas into more lessons and telling Willard she doesn't plan on raising another family. I'm going to talk to Evie's friend about being a consultant or at least throwing a party. I'm also going to continue dating my fabulous new boyfriend. Bernice, how's your Bible reading coming along?"

"I haven't gotten the guide yet," Bernice said, "but the reading is really fascinating. I've been looking up all the footnotes."

"Have you discussed them with anyone knowledgeable?" Maxine wanted to know. "That was one of the ideas we came up with, wasn't it?"

Bernice was now a bright crimson. "Yeah, I did talk to someone."

"Who?" Tina asked.

"No one you know. Just a friend. But anyway, what is so fascinating about Genesis is that . . ."

Evie didn't mean to tune out Bernice and her report, but

Jack had just walked in the restaurant with two other men. They were all wearing business suits, which looked nice but didn't show off Jack's build to its best advantage. He was smiling and laughing, and Evie was glad she'd worn her peach shirt, a color that was supposed to be attractive to men.

"It's your turn, Evie," came a voice.

Startled, Evie looked up at Maxine, realizing that Bernice had finished her spiel about Genesis and had probably mentioned a goal for the week as well. She grimaced. "No, you go first, Maxine. Tell us about the trip we're going to take. Did you look into the French classes yet? And are we only going to France?"

"I think you should go to England, too," Tina put in. "You simply can't miss that."

"What about Spain?" Rosalva said. "I could teach you some Spanish."

To their surprise, Maxine's blue eyes filled with tears. "I—I don't want to go on a trip."

For the second time that morning everyone stared at Maxine in surprise—not because of what she'd said but because of the tears. Maxine simply didn't cry. She was always the strong one, the supporter.

"What happened?" Evie said, ready to do battle. Rosalva also looked angry and Tina concerned. Even Bernice looked more troubled than sour for a change.

Maxine blinked furiously. "It's Harold. He won't see me. Left word at the hospital not to allow visitors except family."

"Well, that's because of all those women who keep visiting," Bernice said. "That's all."

"No. He did it right after I told him I'd marry him." Maxine dabbed under her eyes with her napkin. "I went to the cafeteria, and when I came back, they wouldn't let me in."

"Why would he do a stupid thing like that?" Evie blurted out.

"I'll kill him," growled Rosalva.

Tina shook her head at Rosalva. "I'm sure there's an explanation. Harold's a reasonable man."

"He *was* a reasonable man," Evie said. "This is not reasonable."

Maxine shrugged. "He's worried that he'll never drive or walk again and that I'll have to take care of him."

"So he's trying to protect you," Tina said. "That's a good thing. His heart's in the right place."

"But he doesn't know for sure any of that's really going to happen!" Maxine's color heightened, making her look alive and vibrant. "I don't know—it was like he knew I was going to agree to marry him and then he'd spent too much time thinking about how bad that would be for me. So basically, he's throwing us away. Oh, I should never have put him off! I've been a fool. A terrible fool."

"Truthfully, I think it's kind of romantic." That came from Tina, of course. Sometimes Evie wished she could dull the chirpiness.

Maxine sighed. "It doesn't feel romantic."

"I agree with Maxine." Bernice looked two shades paler than normal. "He's jumping the gun—and it's him who's the fool. I'm going to kill him myself, if Rosalva doesn't beat me to it!"

Maxine allowed herself a small smile. "I know I could make him see the light if I could just talk to him."

"You could talk to his daughter," Evie suggested. "She likes you."

"No." Rosalva leaned back in her chair and folded her arms. "We break in and find him."

Tina wrinkled her thin nose. "Uh, Rosalva, the hospital is open to everyone. It's just his room that's not."

"They can't protect it all the time. It's not like he's still in the ICU."

Bernice had regained some of her color. "That's right. The nurses are way too overworked to hide him. It's only if you ask that you won't be allowed in. So we'll just waltz right in!" She looked triumphant.

"I tried already yesterday," Maxine admitted. "They've moved him to a new room. I don't know where he is, and they won't tell me."

"Don't worry—we'll help." Rosalva smiled and rubbed her hands together so craftily that the others had to laugh.

Evie recovered first. "That's right, we'll help. Maxine, you go home and stop worrying about it. We'll make a plan, and when we find him, we'll take you down there and make a commotion while you slip inside."

Maxine looked at them. "You'd do that for me?"

"Well, you'd do it for us, wouldn't you?" Rosalva asked, her accent thicker than normal. "Of course, we'll do it. Maybe it might take us a few days, but you're as good as in."

"But what if—" Maxine picked up her fork but didn't put it into her food. "What if he still doesn't come around?"

"Don't be silly," Bernice said. "You'll make him see things your way." There was something in her tone that worried Evie, and the zealous light in her eyes did little to alleviate her concern. This didn't seem like Bernice at all. What was up with her?

"You're right." Maxine took a deep breath and sat up straighter. "That's my goal, then. I want to talk to Harold and tell him what an idiot he's being. I feel better already." She looked at Evie. "You're next, dear. How is your goal coming along? I mean, we know you're doing well on the weight loss and exercises, but what's going on with the guy?"

Evie's eyes darted toward Jack's table. She'd had forgotten all about him! How could she have done that? With relief, she saw he was still there. "I haven't gotten far," she admitted. "We talked a few times, and I learned a lot about him from watching him at the gym. He's been divorced once, and he doesn't like carbonated drinks. Neither do I—isn't that cool?" She knew she was babbling, but she didn't know if she wanted to tell them he was in the restaurant. Would they think her foolish for falling for a man so much more fit than she was?

"What are you staring at?" Rosalva turned in her seat to look around the restaurant.

"No, turn around!" Evie hissed, waving her hand frantically a few inches above the table.

"He's over there."

"He's here? Right now?" Tina asked.

"Shhh." Evie needn't have worried. Jack was deep in conversation, pausing only to fork up something from his plate.

"Which one is he?" Maxine asked.

"The one nearest the wall. On the right."

Maxine squinted, and Bernice pulled out a pair of glasses which she used only when she drove her car. The others darted inconspicuous glances.

Tina arched a brow. "Looks strong."

"He lifts a lot of weights. You should see him. It's amazing."

"He's beautiful," Rosalava agreed.

Evie wasn't sure whether to be pleased or insulted. Women were usually beautiful, not men. There wasn't anything feminine about him, was there? Well, you could tell his bleached hair was styled, and he had dressed carefully. He always did, even at the gym. Not like Christopher, who wore baggy gray sweats that were a decade old and faded T-shirts with tiny holes in them.

"You have to speak to him," Rosalva whispered. "This is fate!"

Tina nodded vigorously. "Yes, fate."

"No way!" Evie's heart started pumping blood at a furious rate. "Besides, what would I say?"

Rosalva smiled, and Evie knew why—attracting men was easy for her. "You can introduce us," Rosalva began. "We'll walk by their table on the way out, and I'll drop my purse so they'll have to look up at us. Then you notice him and say, 'Oh, Jack. Hi. It's Evie. We go to the same gym.' Then he'll say something, and you introduce us. And so forth."

"She should ask him out," Tina said.

Evie put her foot down at that. "No, I would die! Simply die. He should ask me out. That's the way things work."

"Not anymore," Rosalva said. "Nowadays women have to be a little more outspoken. I could ask him if you two would like to double with me and Willard."

Evie glared. "No, I'm not ready. Not yet."

Rosalva shrugged. "Okay. I was just trying to help." Her voice sounded wounded, but Evie knew better than to apologize. If she did, Rosalva would ask him out for sure.

"I agree with Evie." Maxine readied a bite of her salad. "Men should do the asking and the paying."

Bernice nodded, but Tina was staring into the distance at nothing—oblivious to any of them. Evie envied her because at least she knew that the man she admired returned her affection.

During the rest of the meal Evie was so nervous she couldn't eat her salad. She kept darting glances at Jack to make sure he wasn't ready to leave. Hours seemed to tick by as she waited for the women to finish. At last they paid for their meals and pooled the tip on the table.

"I changed my mind," Evie whispered. "I'll talk to him later at the gym." She couldn't risk anything going wrong, and with her friends here, something was bound to happen. What if Maxine called him to task for not asking her out? If Rosalva invited him to double? Or if Tina chirped about how beautiful it was when people were in love? Worse, Bernice might start questioning him about his ex-wife.

"We're doing it," Rosalva said.

"No, please. Please." Evie wasn't above begging. "I can't."

"Evie, this isn't like you," Rosalva said, eliciting nods from some of the others.

"It's just too important."

Rosalva sighed. "Okay. It's your call." Evie could tell Rosalva was disgusted with her lack of courage, but that didn't matter because her relationship with Jack was safe.

"You could find out something he likes," Tina said in a low voice as they neared Jack's table. "You know, a play or maybe a singing group. Then you could get tickets and casually mention you have them."

That was the best idea yet. Evie smiled. "Thanks, Tina."

Unfortunately, she wasn't looking where she was going and ran into the edge of a chair someone had left pulled out from a table. Tripping, she lost her grip on her purse to save herself from falling on her face. She looked up in time to see her purse sailing through the air to land on Jack's table, upending his companion's soda.

In the men's flurry to stem the flood with napkins, Rosalva said dryly, "I wouldn't have thought of that, but it works. He will certainly notice you now."

Evie wanted to melt into the floor and vanish, but no such luck. Jack stared up at them, looking more puzzled than anything. Evie felt Rosalva's stare, but she was too busy praying Jack wouldn't recognize her to come up with a plan.

Rosalva, partially hidden behind Tina, shoved her purse at Maxine and stepped forward. "Oh, I'm so sorry," she said. "I tripped. Please forgive me." She held out her hand for Evie's purse, which Jack's companion passed to her. "Well, thank you. I hope you didn't get wet."

"No, no, it's fine," Jack said. A waitress had appeared and promised to replace the drink and the food that was spoiled.

"No need," Jack's companion said. "I was through."

"No, bring it," Jack ordered the waitress. "We'll still be a while."

Evie loved the way he took control. She hoped her mouth wasn't open. He was looking at Rosalva again, and Rosalva was staring at her. So were her other friends. Evie opened her mouth to say something about the gym, but nothing came out.

Rosalva's jaw tightened slightly. "Oh, I know you. You're Jack. Evie and I met you at the gym. Isn't that right, Evie?"

Jack's eyes went briefly to Evie and nodded. "Yeah, I

remember," he said. "You're new." He looked back at Rosalva, a question in his eyes. "Are you new, too?"

"Just a visitor," Rosalva said. "In fact, we may not have even officially met."

"Well, it's nice to meet you . . ."

"Rosalva." She smiled. "And you know Evie, of course."

Jack smiled back. "We've talked."

Determined to leave a better impression in his mind, Evie finally found her voice. "Well, it's really nice seeing you, Jack."

"Yeah, you too."

Bernice and Maxine nodded politely and started again for the door. "Bye," Evie called, having to push Tina along. Rosalva followed. When they were several tables away, Evie dared to glance back. Jack was still watching them.

When they were out of his sight, Evie found Rosalva's hand. "Thanks," she whispered.

Rosalva shrugged. "What are friends for? One thing's for sure—he won't forget you after this."

"Still, do me a favor. The next time I decide to throw my purse at a man, please stop me."

Rosalva laughed. "I'll try."

"I hope he's at the gym today," Evie added. Maybe today they would have a whole conversation that didn't involve directions to the treadmills or apologies over spilled drinks. Maybe he might even ask her out.

CHAPTER

14

Rosalva

We all sort of met Evie's Jack yesterday at Mimi's. He seems like a nice enough guy, though it's hard to get to know someone in a few seconds. Anyway, he doesn't seem to be the complete hunk Evie thinks he is. I think she's far prettier than he is good-looking. Yeah, there's the weight issue and that throws people off, but she's so loving and caring and beautiful that any man would be lucky to get to know her. I just think . . . well, I guess I sort of hate the fact that Evie's started focusing on changing herself for him instead of for herself. I tried to be everything for Enrique and look where that got me. Evie is special—inside and out. She's my best friend and always will be, though we haven't had as much time together lately.

We didn't make it to the hospital last night to find Harold because Evie and Bernice had other plans, but we're going tonight as soon as dinner is over. I'm sure I'll find Harold, and when I do, I'm going to give him a piece of my mind. I used to feel sorry for him that he was so in love with Maxine, but now I'm mad that he would treat her that way. If men would say what they feel, it would make life a lot less complicated. We wouldn't always have to guess what's wrong and scramble to make it all better. Really, men are much like children sometimes.

I saw Willard yesterday, and the funny thing is that he showed up with two men who were supposed to look at my lawn. I hadn't even mentioned it to him! The men were from Mexico, and both spoke Spanish to me, though they also spoke English as well as Willard. Better than me. They probably came here as small children. The older one was my age—named Spencer after President Kimball—and he had met Enrique once on a job he did for one of Enrique's friends. He was kind of cute, but as they were looking at my excuse for grass, Willard made a point of telling me both the men were married. I almost burst out laughing. Still, it was nice to chat for a minute in my native language, something other than "We need to fill the salad bar" or "How many orders of cheese bread did you say you need?" My boys hardly speak any Spanish at all, but I wanted it that way. I want so much for them to fit in here. After all, this is the only country they know. I still have memories of Mexico before my family immigrated, but to my sons Mexico is only a place we went to visit once when my grandmother died.

Willard met Spencer at Family Services, where he's been volunteering a few hours a week to help with legal matters. Apparently, Spencer's daughter was there because of an abusive marriage, and they struck up a conversation. Willard discovered they needed help on a custody issue, so he offered to trade services with them.

I thought before that people never truly change, but maybe if *they really want to, they can. Willard seems to have come a long way from the man whose wife had to divorce him.*

Anyway, Willard will be coming over to be here when Spencer returns to work on my lawn (he's doing it after his regular hours). I feel excited to see Willard, no matter how I want my heart to remain calm. It's not just my lawn and all the other things he's doing. It's that someone's trying to take care of me. Since my parents died, I haven't had that. I've always taken care of myself.

Rosalva shut her journal and ran her fingers under her right eye to catch the moisture there. *It's not a tear,* she assured herself.

The day had been a good one, though she was beginning to dread the fact that Lucas would be going to Enrique's tomorrow. She would worry the whole weekend. But unless Lucas himself refused to go, there was nothing she could do about it. Poor influence or no, Enrique was Lucas's father.

"I don't see why you want to even go there," Jaime said, his voice floating in from the boys' room where they were playing a video game.

"He's our dad, duh."

"Yeah, some dad. He's just a lazy bum. I bet he borrows money off you, doesn't he?"

"He pays me back."

Jaime snorted. "Mom hates it when you go."

Rosalva went to their doorway, knowing she had to put an end to that. She would not have Jaime force Lucas to choose between her and Enrique. "Hey, you two. Time's up. I know you played your half hour."

"Oh, Mom," Lucas groaned.

"It's not good for your brain to do more."

"Actually, Mom," Jaime began, "video games can help our, uh, reflexes and our reasoning skills. It's a proven fact."

"Yeah!" Lucas agreed, his face hopeful.

Rosalva laughed and gave them her sweetest smile. "Turn it off now, or I'll chop off the plug."

The doorbell ended further debate, and Rosalva hurried down the hall to open the door for Willard, the boys following close behind. "Hi," she said, a bit breathlessly—but only because of her quick dash, or so she told herself.

"Hi." His eyes were warm, and she felt his stare almost like a hug.

"Hey, Willard," Jaime said from behind her.

"Jaime, Lucas." Willard nodded to the boys. To all of them, he added, "They're going to start work on your lawn."

Piling onto the porch, they saw Spencer and his friend—Rosalva couldn't remember his name—unloading a machine from a truck.

"They're going to cut out all the grass," Willard said, "and then do the sprinklers and put down sod. It'll be the easiest way at this point."

"Cool." Lucas eyed the machine that wasn't much larger than a lawnmower. Rosalva was surprised because so far Lucas hadn't been pleased with anything Willard said or did.

"Well, come on in." Rosalva retraced her steps, leading them to the kitchen table. "I just kicked the boys off their video game, so maybe we can have some dinner. I have to go to the hospital tonight."

"I thought you said that guy was out of danger." Jaime sat in a chair by the table.

"He is, but he's kind of lost. It's a long story."

Willard took the seat next to Jaime. "Your mom's going on

a covert mission to find what room he's hiding out in. I was thinking I'd tag along. It might be fun looking into all those rooms."

"No," Rosalva said, shaking her head. "You won't blend in."

"Aw, come on."

"In that suit? Everyone will notice you."

"Maybe they'll think I work for the hospital."

"I doubt it, but come along if you want. That means fewer rooms for me to search."

Willard didn't look offended at her lack of welcome, nor did his confidence appear shaken. "I do have to drop something off at my brother's first," he said, "so I'll meet you at the hospital."

"That'll probably be better anyway, since I don't know how many of the ladies are going and how much room we'll have. Besides, then you won't have to come all the way back here to get your car."

"I wouldn't mind." Their eyes locked, and Rosalva felt her emotions spinning out of control. She tore her gaze away.

"Well, I think you should just ask where he is," Jaime said. "I bet I could charm it out of the nurse."

"You're staying here to make sure Lucas gets into bed on time."

Leaning against the counter, Lucas grimaced. "Aw, Mom, I'm not a baby."

"Okay, then, set the table. It's your day anyway. And make sure you set a plate for Willard." Rosalva walked to the stove where she was reheating food she'd brought from work. It was never quite the same reheated, but her boys rarely complained. When she had time, she liked to make food from scratch, and their favorite was homemade tortillas covered with a secret family recipe of beans and beef.

"You sure you have enough?" Willard asked.

"I planned on you," she said. "Besides, it's the least we can do with you arranging for the lawn."

"Well, Spencer's daughter doesn't have any money, and this way it works out well for everybody. She'll get custody of her son without a problem—I'm sure of it."

"That's a relief. The father doesn't sound like a responsible guy. It's good she has Spencer. Seems like a nice man."

"I think he is."

Lucas was laying down plates with more force than necessary, and Rosalva could barely hear Willard. She bit back a useless reprimand, having learned long ago that distraction was the best way to deal with her younger son's rebellious attitude. "So," Rosalva said to Lucas, "did you think of any lessons you'd like to take?"

He shrugged. "Naw. Maybe I don't wanna do anything else. I wish I was old enough to work."

"Your grades have to come first."

"Dad didn't graduate."

Rosalva set the serving plate on the table with a loud *thump,* willing herself to be calm. No wonder Lucas banged things when he was upset. She felt a strong desire to rant about where her ex-husband was in life now compared to where he could have been with an education, but that was another thing that always ended in disaster. "You are not your father," she said, in control once more. "You will finish high school and go to college."

"It's a different world out there now than when your father

was young," Willard added. "Now education is more important than ever. What do you think you'd like to study, anyway?"

"Nothin'." Lucas slumped into a chair.

"I used to want to be a pilot," Jaime offered, filling his plate with fries, salad, and steak. "Then I decided to design video games. But after taking biology this year, I've decided to go into some kind of science."

Rosalva blinked. "When did this happen?"

He shrugged. "I just decided, that's all. I was going to tell you but I forgot. I talked to the counselor at school. He said I might be able to get a scholarship if I get my ACT scores up."

"Let's get you on a mission first." She held her breath for the answer. Jaime was a good boy, but he had to fight a lot of negative peer pressure.

"Of course," he said. "But I'll have to take the ACT again in June. I don't want to wait until after my mission."

Rosalva barely had time to relax before Lucas said, "I want to be a pilot. That'd be cool."

"I took flying lessons once." Willard's face looked strangely vulnerable. "Hey, maybe that's what you should do. You could take flying lessons and see if you like it. You could even get a pilot's license."

"I could?" Lucas was grinning, his attention riveted on Willard. "Really?"

"Why not?"

Rosalva stared. How could Willard even suggest such a thing? She was barely scraping by now, and flying lessons could be hundreds of dollars a month. Besides, she wasn't sure if she was okay with the idea of having Lucas up in a plane every week. "No," she said firmly. "It's too expensive. Now who's going to say the prayer?"

Jaime stopped eating, looking guilty. "I will."

"Please, Mom." Lucas had actual tears in his eyes. "It's all I've ever wanted to do."

"Then how come this is the first time I've heard of it? Look, you begged for a dog you never cleaned up after. I had to take care of it for four years before it got run over. Do you remember that?"

Lucas nodded mutely.

"And what about the skis you begged for?"

"Well, I didn't know I was going to hate the cold."

Jaime tapped his fork and knife several times on the edge of his plate. "Well, he begged for the drums, and he still plays those."

Rosalva scowled at him, and he fell silent.

"If he doesn't like it, he can quit," Willard offered. "It's only to see if he's interested."

That was it. He'd gone too far. "Can I talk to you outside for a minute?" Rosalva asked through gritted teeth.

His face showed immediate concern. "Sure."

When they were outside on the back patio, she whirled on him. "Look, where am I going to get the money for something like that? He's my son, and I know what he needs. I know what I can afford to do for him." She knew her accent had become pronounced again, betraying her anger, but she was beyond caring.

He stepped back, eyes widening in hurt surprise. "I guess I thought—hoped—that we were beyond that point. That we were close enough for me to—surely you know I'd never recommend something I wasn't willing to finance."

"You should have consulted with me first! I'm his mother. What if I don't want my baby up in a plane? What if I had

156

already found another solution? In fact, I was going to talk to him about taking a computer class."

"You're right," he said, his shoulders crumpling. "I should have talked to you first. I keep telling myself I have to think of things from your point of view before I act." He gave a chuckle that lacked any trace of real mirth. "I didn't do a lot of that during my marriage, as you can imagine, but I thought I was doing better these days. I guess not."

He looked so dejected that Rosalva felt sorry for him. After all, she had accepted his help with the sink leak, changing the oil, and the yard. She'd let him believe it was okay to take care of her. "It is nice that you want to take care of us," she told him more gently, "but I'm never going to sit back and take a passive role in my children's lives or in a marriage."

"I believe that." His smile was back, though it was only tentative. "That's one of the things I admire about you. If I'm stepping out of line, I know you'll tell me."

They were silent for a minute, looking over her backyard that had fared only slightly better than her front because of the water that sprayed over from her neighbor's sprinklers.

"So now what?" he asked. "Did you see Lucas's eyes? I was a hero there for a little while."

Rosalva knew this wasn't about him being a hero, but maybe she didn't need to say that aloud. "I don't know. I don't want to . . ." She looked away.

"Use me?" His hand touched her chin softly, guiding it back toward him. "I'm not a poor man, Rosalva, and I like helping you. I haven't done a lot of good in my life, but I want to change all that. I want to help you. You make me feel real, and I like who I am with you."

He kissed her then, and Rosalva let him because she was

touched and because she believed he meant the words. "I think," he said between kisses, "that we're meant for each other."

She wanted to believe that part, too, but sometimes it seemed they came from different worlds. One thing she did know was that if they had any chance at all, she had to tell him everything.

"I'm forty-two years old," she began.

"I know that. I asked Jaime. Our age difference doesn't matter to me in the least." He started to reach for her again, but she shook her head.

"You have to know something first. You've talked about having a child someday. Don't get this wrong—I really like you, and I'm attracted to you, but I don't know if I'd want to start a new family." She shrugged, trying to make her voice light. "Diapers, strollers, no sleep at night. Maybe once upon a time I would have wanted more children, but now my boys are almost grown. I'm content with that, where we are right now. I'm sorry." She thought about adding that she might not even be able to get pregnant but decided that would only cloud the issue.

He was quiet for a long moment. "There I go again, assuming things. I didn't think you might not want to . . ." He let the words trail away. "Okay, I appreciate your honesty. I really don't know what to think—feel—right now. I guess I need a little time."

Part of her was disappointed that he didn't immediately claim his undying love regardless of the child issue, but her logical side knew that if he had, she would worry about him changing his mind. It was only fair to give him time to ponder how a relationship with her would affect his future as a father.

If their roles were reversed, she knew she wouldn't give up her potential motherhood without deep consideration and prayer. Even then, she doubted she would have been able to trade the opportunity to be a mother for a life with any man—how could she expect him to do so for her?

This will never work between us, she thought.

A few painful seconds of silence passed between them before Willard took a deep breath. "So what are you thinking about the flying lessons?"

A smile fluttered on her lips. "I thought you'd rather wait until you decide abou—"

"You thought wrong. I can afford it, and Lucas deserves a shot. Look, if you really don't want him to do it, he shouldn't, but if the only reason is money and my own stupidity for not bringing it up with you first, then please accept my offer."

"What if we, uh, decide not to date anymore?" She made herself ask this for Lucas's benefit. If he began lessons and loved them but had to stop because things didn't work out between her and Willard, it wouldn't be fair.

"He can have the lessons for as long as he wants," Willard said, which Rosalva didn't quite believe, but perhaps it was possible. She'd heard of rich people giving away more money than she earned in an entire year.

"I guess it might prove to be useful—if he decides he likes it. Pilots don't make bad money, I think." More than anything she wanted her boys to be contributing members of society, able to support themselves and forward the cause of the Church by their work, service, and example. "Okay, he can have the lessons, but let me tell him. I don't want him to think I gave in or anything."

He gave her an elegant bow. "You're the mom. And I

promise, I'll watch what I suggest in the future." He thought a moment and then added, "Maybe we shouldn't tell him I'm paying because I wouldn't want him to feel awkward if you decide to dump me."

She managed a smile at his gallantry, though her heart ached. With her confession, it was he who had to decide if he wanted to pursue a life with her, not the other way around.

When they entered the house, the boys were eating with uncharacteristic dedication and both avoided looking at her. Rosalva began eating, but as soon as she'd taken her second bite, the boys quit pretending.

"Well?" Lucas asked.

Rosalva swallowed. "Well, what?"

"Can I please take flying lessons?"

She smiled. "I didn't think we could afford it, but after talking to Willard, I think I know a way we can probably swing it. But—"

"Yes!" Lucas punched the air with his fist.

"Let me finish." Rosalva raised her voice. "The minute you complain about going to class or show a lack of interest, you're out of there."

"Okay, but I promise I won't!"

"I told you after he kissed her that you'd be able to go," Jaime said, leaning back in his chair with a satisfied smile.

"You were watching us?" Rosalva refused to blush, but she did feel rather awkward when she noticed Willard looking at her with amusement in his gray eyes.

Jaime's smile vanished. "Just through the window. We couldn't hear what you said."

"Well, not most of it anyway," Lucas added, "only right at first when you yelled."

"Hey, you're not helping," Willard protested.

Lucas's brow furrowed. "I can still go, right? When can I start?" The change in Lucas's attitude toward Willard was amazing, and since he didn't know Willard was paying for the lessons, Rosalva could only hope the change was because someone was taking an interest in him.

"Tomorrow?" Willard suggested. "I mean, we'll have to call and see when they start, but it's possible we could at least sign up tomorrow."

"Cool." Lucas pushed back his plate. "I gotta go call the guys." Abruptly, he hesitated, his smile vanishing. "Oh, no. I forgot tomorrow's Friday, and I'm going to Dad's. Mom, do I have to go?"

"Well, you'll have to take that up with your father," Rosalva said, keeping her face expressionless, which was hard to do when her heart was singing. "He probably won't mind, though, unless he had something special planned."

"Naw, he never does."

Jaime opened his mouth to speak, but Rosalva shook her head. The last thing Lucas needed was to have to defend his father to Jaime.

"Well, you let me know," Willard said. "In the morning I'll make a few calls and see where we can take you. Might have to wait until next week anyway, depending on when they're open."

"I want to go tomorrow if I can," Lucas said.

Willard pulled a card from his wallet. "Call me when you get home from school, and I'll let you know what I've found out."

"Thanks." Lucas pocketed the card before going for the phone.

Rosalva ate a few more bites of dinner, but her appetite was gone. Jaime still resembled a cat that had eaten a jar of caviar, glancing back and forth between her and Willard. Rosalva wondered if her son was relieved that she might have found someone to depend on, freeing him from responsibility. She'd have to be certain she didn't put too much burden on him when Willard decided to find a woman who was willing to have another child. A younger woman.

It'll be for the best, she told herself.

Willard looked at his watch. "Don't you think we'd better get moving if we're going to scope out the hospital?"

She laughed. "You're not really coming, are you?"

"Sure am. In case you get caught, I'll be your lawyer."

"Well, Evie's picking me up in ten minutes. She's probably just leaving her house. If you have to stop at your brother's, you might want to leave before she gets here." She arose and took a load of dishes to the sink. Willard brought his own plate and Lucas's, who had forgotten in the excitement.

"Okay, then. See you in a little while." He made a move toward her but then stopped, as though becoming aware that Jaime was still watching them. Or was it because he'd remembered that she wasn't willing to have another child? For a fleeting moment she wished she were seven years younger. That would make her thirty-five, still young enough to have several children.

She walked Willard to the door and watched him drive away. Spencer stopped his work in the yard and came over to her. "I wanted to talk to you about what you'd like to do here," he said in Spanish, laying his shovel against the stair railing. He had to talk loudly because his companion was using a machine to tear out the old grass.

"Oh, whatever you feel is best. Didn't Willard say?"

"No, he just said to make it nice." Spencer smiled at her, his brown eyes looking even darker because they were framed by deeply tanned skin. He was shorter than Willard by a full head, but every inch of him looked strong and wiry, a consequence of his daily work.

"What do you suggest?" Rosalva asked.

He grinned a wide, white smile. "Well, once we get the sprinklers in, I was thinking of putting a flower bed over there, and in front of there where it curves down, maybe a little waterfall. Nothing too big or that requires a lot of maintenance but something that really catches the eye. Then along the property line, we could do a row of hedges about this high." He put his hand out at thigh height. "I'll use cement curbing around them and the flowerbed."

Rosalva was impressed. "It sounds beautiful. But isn't all that a little expensive? I thought we were just doing grass." She had a sudden sinking feeling that he was trying to get her to pay extra.

He gave her another smile that made her feel warm inside despite her growing suspicion. "I'm an artist. I like to try to match the yard with the owner. Though there isn't much space here, I want it to be different from your neighbors'—special. Something that is more like you." The compliment wasn't subtle, but she didn't feel he was hitting on her, only speaking from his heart.

"I can't pay you anything," she said.

His only reaction was the creasing of the skin between his dark eyebrows. "I don't expect payment, except Willard's help with my daughter's case. Yes, I could give you only grass and that would probably satisfy you both, but I want to do as good

163

a job as I believe Willard will do for my daughter. I wouldn't want him cutting corners, so I won't be cutting any, either."

Rosalva felt chastened. "Thank you. Anything you decide is fine."

"Well"—again the smile, and she was relieved it was back—"I wouldn't object if you would let me put a small sign in your yard while we work and for a few weeks after we're finished. We'll probably get some calls for additional work."

"Sure, go right ahead. I guess I didn't realize you worked for a landscaping company. I thought it was something you did on the side."

"It's a company," Spencer replied. "My company, actually."

Their conversation moved on, and Rosalva learned that Spencer usually did all the designs himself but hired men to do most of the labor. When Spencer wasn't designing or out giving bids, he was ordering supplies and driving around to check on the different job sites. He planned to work on her lawn himself after his regular day was finished in order to keep regular proceeds coming in.

"I'm sorry you're having to work so late." She knew his family meant everything to him, as it did to her—that was a part of their cultural heritage, ingrained in them from childhood. "I bet your wife isn't very happy about it."

He laid a hand on his shovel. "I'm not married."

"What?" It came out in English instead of Spanish, but neither really paid attention to the shift in languages.

"I was married—twice. My first wife came over from Mexico to study, and we met and married. But she went home to visit one day and never came back. After some months I went to Mexico to get her and my daughter, but she was with another husband—a very wealthy landowner—and my daughter was staying with her grandparents. I took my daughter and came home. My second wife helped me raise her, but she died five years ago from a tumor." He spoke matter-of-factly, but Rosalva could see the emotion in his eyes, could feel the pain he tried to hide. She was glad he'd spoken in English. In Spanish his double loss would have felt like an impossible load.

"I'm sorry," she said.

He shrugged. "I have my daughter and, thanks to Willard, my grandson. And I have my work. We are not a big company, but we have satisfied customers." He hefted the shovel, gave her another warm smile, and went back to work.

Rosalva watched him for a full minute before going inside to give her boys last instructions.

15

Tina

This is such a fabulous idea, us going to the hospital to help Maxine. I'm sure we'll find Harold, and when we do he'll change his mind about everything. No one could refuse Maxine. She's one of the best people alive.

Scott and I are still dating. I love him, and I think he feels the same way. Strange how in less than two weeks I can feel so strongly about a man. It almost seems too good to be true.

Maybe it is.

I am a little worried because Scott has been arguing with his daughter. Apparently, her mother left when she was about eleven or so and then came back into their lives three years later. When things didn't work out, she got custody of Callie, only to dump her off on Scott after six months. Scott, of course, was really glad to have Callie live with him, and Callie was happy too. But now it's two years later (Callie's nearly seventeen), and Callie has these moments when she really wants her mom and blames it on Scott that her mother didn't want her.

I suggested letting Callie visit her mother for part of spring break next week (he knows where she is now), but Scott doesn't think that's a good idea. He feels his ex-wife had her chance—twice—and blew it. He got a little upset, as he has every right to do given the situation, and his reaction made me feel like dying inside. Like curling up in a ball and hiding. But I had to speak for Callie's sake. I think she needs to see her mom, to know that her mom loves her even though she's chosen a life that doesn't include Callie. (Scott has told me his ex-wife does love her.)

I don't understand how a mother could ever leave her child, but I know it happens. I can tell Callie's hurting inside because of it, though she denies any feeling. I know the kind of hurt that you have to hide. Abuse and neglect are very similar. Poor Callie. She's happiest when she's at my house, and I'm hoping if Scott and I get together for good that I can give her what she needs in a mother figure.

Now for the real worry—for me, anyway—why did Scott's wife really leave? I love him so much, and I don't want to suspect anything, but I can't help myself.

Tina slid into the backseat of Evie's car next to Rosalva, smiling at Bernice who was in the front with Evie. "This is so cool," Tina said. "I'm glad we can all do something for Maxine. Where is she, the poor thing?"

"She's at home," Bernice said. "She wanted to come, but I made her stay home. Tomorrow is soon enough to face Harold. We have no idea how long it's going to take or if we'll get caught. We don't want them to recognize Maxine when she comes tomorrow."

"Good thinking," Evie said.

"I don't know." Rosalva took her compact from her purse and renewed her lipstick. "I'm having second thoughts. What if Harold's right? What if we're helping Maxine dig herself into a hole of slavery? I mean, Harold's a nice guy, but life as a nurse to an invalid certainly isn't the kind of marriage I'd want for myself."

Evie glanced over her shoulder as she stopped at a traffic light. "Don't be so dramatic. We'll just tell him to play along until we see where things are, that's all."

"He loves her," Tina added. "I think he'll do what's best."

Rosalva gave them a flat stare. "Well, he tried that already, and here we are."

"If he's really going to be an invalid, he won't marry her," Tina said. "The problem is he's giving up way too early."

"Maybe he knows something we don't." Rosalva's voice was ominous.

"That's what we'll find out," Bernice said.

"Yes, now talk about something else," Tina ordered. She didn't like the picture she saw in her mind of Maxine growing old and dull as she slaved over Harold's bedside. What if he really never walked again? What if things were even worse than they knew? And what was with Rosalva tonight anyway? Finding Harold had been her idea in the first place, and she had no right to put a damper on things now.

"I told Willard I didn't want to have more children," Rosalva blurted into the silence.

"And?" Evie prompted, not taking her eyes from the road.

"He said he'd have to think about that."

"I'm sorry, Rosalva." Tina put her hand on Rosalva's leg.

"I can't blame him," Rosalva said. "I wouldn't give up the chance of children for a man."

"Amen!" said Evie, and Tina nodded in hearty agreement.

Bernice shrugged. "Well, that's a dumb thing to say, seeing as we need men to have children. Besides, I wouldn't have traded my husband for anything."

Rosalva smiled sadly. "You were really lucky, Bernice. Really lucky."

"I know." Bernice's gray head dipped as though looking at something in her lap, but when Tina craned her neck she could see nothing but Bernice's folded hands. For a moment Tina thought the older woman was going to say something more, but instead she clamped her mouth shut and stared out the window.

Something's up with her, Tina thought. She wished Bernice would share with them her problem—whatever it was. Maybe they could help. But Bernice had always been more reserved than the others in the Independence Club.

Independence Club. Tina smiled. After years of an abusive marriage, that was what the women had been for her—an independence. They had given her balance as she struggled to regain normalcy after Glen's death. But now there was Scott. Tina wished the hospital visit were over so she could see him. He'd said he'd wait for her call no matter how late she returned.

When they arrived at the hospital, no one paid them any attention. Most of the doors were open, so all they had to do was to stroll by and glance inside—all the while pretending they weren't seeing anything. At the doors that were half shut, they waited briefly to see if someone emerged, and if that didn't happen soon, they would walk in a line, one behind the other, the first person sticking out her hand and giving the door a slight shove. The women behind her would then glance inside as they strolled by. Some of the people didn't notice them, but others were obviously upset.

"Can't a guy have a little privacy?" one old man shouted at them. "Sheesh!"

"Sorry," Tina called.

"This isn't working," Evie said, coming to a stop at the beginning of a hallway where most of the doors were barely ajar.

"We'll try something else." Tina lifted her chin in determination. Maxine was always there for her, and she was not going to leave this hospital without a room number to give her.

"But what?" Bernice asked.

"Come on, I'll think of something." Tina led the way. At the next half-closed door, she knocked. "Come in," said a gruff voice. Inside, a huge man lay in a bed that looked way too small for his frame. "Oh, sorry," Tina said. "I thought this was my friend Harold's room. Please forgive me."

The man smiled. "That's okay. Haven't had any visitors today." He pointed to the television. "You like this show?"

Tina took a few more steps into the room so she could see the screen. "I've never seen it before."

"You can stay if you want."

He was lonely. Even if he hadn't invited her to stay, she'd felt that way often enough to recognize the expression in his eyes. "Thanks," she said. "Maybe another time. I'd better go find Harold. You don't know where he is, do you?"

"No, sorry. Ask the nurse. She can tell you."

"Thanks."

Out in the hallway the others congratulated her for getting inside the room. "This would be a lot easier if we could look like nurses," grumbled Rosalva. "And where is Willard, anyway? He should have been here by now."

"I'm sure he's okay," Tina said. "He probably got caught up with his nieces and nephews. That's all. Those kids are adorable."

"Well, back to it." Bernice knocked at the next door and went inside when someone called out. She was back within two minutes, her face drained of all color. "A man but not Harold," she said. "Harold would have the good sense to be wearing clothes. No wonder that guy's door is closed."

Rosalva and Evie burst into laughter. Bernice looked so shaken that Tina couldn't help giggling herself. Giving them a disdainful glance, Bernice stalked down the hall.

"We really should split up," Tina said.

"Yeah, maybe we'll find him faster." Rosalva turned and went another way, followed closely by Evie.

Tina sighed and returned to one of the hallways they'd already canvassed. There had been two doors shut here, but they hadn't dared open them. Now they had no choice. She came up short in the hallway, as a doctor emerged from the first room, nearly barreling into her. He had very blond hair and blue eyes as deep as the ocean.

"Oh, excuse me," he said.

Tina saw her chance. "Is Harold okay?" She glanced at the door with apparent concern.

"Harold?" His handsome face wrinkled a moment.

"Not Harold, huh." She sighed. Great. Now she'd have to find a way to get inside that last door—and then inside of who knew how many other closed doors down other corridors.

"Uh, let me guess. You're looking for Harold." He had a nice smile.

"Yeah. He's a friend of a friend of mine—well, he's sort of my friend, too—but they're more than friends. Only he's acting really weird, and now we don't even know what room he's in."

"Wait a minute. I think I heard something about that." His stare became grave. "Should I call security?"

"No, really, it's fine." She started backing away. "I'm sure Harold will give us a call as soon as he feels better—unless of course he's never going to feel better and then he's basically consigning himself to a life of utter misery without Maxine. But you don't need to concern yourself with that."

"I'm kidding," the doctor said, smiling at her. "I'm not calling anyone. Honest."

"I thought doctors only visited patients during the day—or in an emergency." During her years of marriage to Glen, she knew one sure way to take blame off oneself was to go on the attack. Glen had been a master. "So what are you doing here, anyway?"

The doctor chuckled at her audacity. "I'm here making sure there won't be an emergency. I like to sleep nights."

He was nice *and* conscientious, and Tina knew if she hadn't been so in love with Scott, she might care more that he wasn't wearing a wedding ring. Or did doctors even wear wedding rings? She seemed to remember reading once that they didn't, but her family practitioner always had.

"I'm not married," he said, seeing her attention to his hands.

She flushed. Was she that obvious? "Oh. I'm not either.

I'm—I'm seeing someone, though." Even thinking about Scott made her heart feel like flying.

"Just my luck." He actually looked disappointed. "Well, here's my card," he said, handing it to her. "In case you . . . well, need a doctor, I guess." Giving her another smile, he strode down the hall, his thin white coat flowing behind him.

Tina blinked. Things like that never happened to her. Two weeks ago, she would have jumped at a chance to meet such a kind man, but now she had a future with Scott—she was sure of it. She didn't need this doctor. Except for one thing.

"Hey," she called out. "So do you know where Harold is?"

He turned around slowly, hands in his pockets. "You're getting warm." With a wink, he went on his way.

Tina eyed the last door. Could Harold be in that room? She hurried over and tapped on the door.

"Come in."

Sure enough, Harold was sitting in the bed. The room was darkened, but she could see him in the dim light coming from the TV.

"You found me," he said, a half-smile fluttering on the right side of his face.

"I found you." She turned on one of the lights and walked over to the bed. "You've not been very nice, Harold. Maxine's going out of her head with worry."

He lifted his right hand, indicating the inert half of his body. "I can't consign her to this."

"And what if it had happened next year, or the next? After you were married?"

"Then it would have. Besides, Maxine might never have married me. I don't want her doing so only because she feels sorry for me."

"If you believe that, you really are crazy," she said. "We all knew it was only a matter of time before she married you." Still, she had to admit to herself that seeing him like this unnerved her more than she expected.

He shrugged, apparently not willing to risk answering.

Tina felt a rush of anger. "Darn it, Harold, you can't treat her this way! The least you could do is go along with her. Then if you find out that you won't get better, you can decide what to do later. This way is just plain mean."

He was silent a moment, his eyes reflecting the figures on the muted TV screen. "I love her so much. If I agreed now, how could I ever give her up?"

"Same as now," Tina said simply. "Besides, having her help could make all the difference in your recovery."

He opened his mouth to reply when a knock sounded on the door. "Grand Central Station," he muttered as the door opened, spilling Evie, Bernice, Rosalva, and Willard into the room.

"There you go," Willard said with satisfaction. "Just like they told me at the front desk."

"What?" Tina asked.

Bernice pursed her lips sourly. "He told them he's Harold's lawyer. We look for an hour, and he gets the room number in two minutes." She shifted her sharp gaze to Willard. "Next time come on time. My back is aching from all this skulking around."

"Skulking?" Willard grinned.

"There's not going to be a next time." Rosalva sauntered over to the bed. "So, should we kidnap him? Tie him to a bed in the basement of Maxine's house?" Her voice was completely serious.

"She's joking," Tina assured Harold.

"Maybe not." Willard smiled at Rosalva, and Tina could feel the pull between them. Agreement about a baby or not, these two meant something to each other, Tina was sure of it.

Harold laughed. "I should have known." His smile was lop-sided, but Tina thought it rather endearing.

"So what's it going to be, Mister?" Bernice demanded.

"We know you think it's best for her," Evie added, "but Maxine's hurting—badly. You can't want that."

Harold sighed and muttered something no one understood. With evident frustration, he repeated, "I need to think."

"Haven't you had enough time?" Bernice put her hands on her hips, and Harold's eyes slowly followed the movement.

"Seems to me we all need to think." Harold rested his gaze on Bernice, then Evie, and Rosalva. He even studied Willard before shifting his eyes to Tina. There was something odd about his gaze, though Tina couldn't place the difference. He seemed to see into her soul. Did he wonder why she hadn't spoken to Scott about her life with Glen? But how could he even know that she hadn't? And did it really matter if she ever told Scott? Glen was dead and couldn't hurt her or the children anymore. No, Scott never had to know. She didn't want the past coming between them. She didn't want him to know that she had been a woman someone had hurt. Hit, beaten, abused. Surely that would change her in his eyes.

The others were quiet, and Tina hoped they didn't guess at her consternation.

"Well," Tina said, breaking the silence. "We're all here for you, Harold. We want to help, but you have to let us before we can. Promise you'll give us a shot?"

Harold nodded, and Bernice looked satisfied. She rubbed

her hands together. "Let's go, then." She twisted the ring on her finger in a nervous motion. Something glinted briefly, but Tina decided it was the light reflecting off the plain gold band she always wore.

With a few more words of encouragement, they left Harold. "It's going to be all right," Tina said brightly as they made their way to the cars. She wasn't sure about that, though. In fact, she had a terrible black feeling inside that threatened her peace of mind.

"Sure it is," Evie agreed. "You did write down the number, didn't you?"

Bernice nodded, but she seemed far away.

"Hey, I'm driving home with Willard," Rosalva called to them.

"Fine." Evie took out her keys and pressed the button to unlock her car doors.

The last glimpse Tina had of Rosalva and Willard was of his taking her hand.

I do have to tell Scott, she thought. Harold was right. But how should she broach the subject? And what would he say when he knew?

Tina wouldn't have worried except the anger in his voice when Callie had gone to the mall without permission had reminded her exactly of Glen's.

CHAPTER

16

Bernice

*Harold's right. I have to tell them. I could tell that he saw my
ring last night. I tried to keep it turned inside, but it was chafing me.
For having something wrong with his eyes, he is sure perceptive. I
guess I was standing too close to the bed. At least none of the others
noticed. I promise I will announce my engagement at the next
Independence Club brunch. I've thought about telling just Maxine,
but I think she'll keep her comments to a minimum if the others are
there—especially Tina. She's usually too sweet to be real, but I know
she'll be truly happy for me. Clay keeps asking about meeting my
friends, and I keep putting him off. I am such a hypocrite. Well, I'll
make up for it later.*

I'm going over to Maxine's later. I know she went to see Harold this morning, so I'm positive things will be all right now, but I need to make sure. I really do want her to be happy.

Bernice had been waiting on the front porch for a full two minutes. "Maxine!" she called, pounding on the door and leaning closer. "I know you're there. I saw you come home."

At last there was a clicking sound as the door unlocked and opened. Maxine stood there in a summery pink suit dress, her eyes red but dry. The fine lines of her face were more pronounced.

Bernice took one look at her and stepped inside, folding Maxine into her arms. *I'll kill him,* she thought. Harold had seemed so reasonable last night, and she could tell he missed Maxine, but somehow he'd gone and blown it.

Maxine wasn't stiff in her embrace, but she wasn't exactly malleable either. She returned the hug without effort.

"What happened?"

Maxine walked to the couch and sat down gingerly as though she were in someone else's house. "He's not there."

"What?" Bernice sat beside her. "We all saw him—did he change rooms again?"

"He checked out, but he's not home. I already went over there."

"I don't understand. He's got weeks of therapy to go through—he couldn't have just left."

"Well, he's either doing outpatient therapy or he's moved to another hospital." Tears welled up but didn't spill from her eyes. "Oh, Bernice, I've been such a fool, and now I've lost him." Maxine looked delicate and beautiful, quite the opposite of how Bernice knew she looked when she was upset.

"Don't talk that way," Bernice chided. "Maybe he needs a little time, that's all."

"No. It's over."

"Maxine! Stop that. You can't give up!" Guilt fell over Bernice like a heavy cloud that covered every inch of her, choking her and dousing her spirit. This was partly her fault, she knew. Why had she gone to talk to Harold that first time? If not for her big mouth and her selfish attempt to use Maxine's relationship to downplay her own, maybe things would have been different. Harold might never have come up with the idea of sparing Maxine the trouble of taking care of him.

Maxine's chin lifted. "I'm not giving up. I'm being realistic." She stood, running her hands lightly down the front of her skirt. "And one thing's for sure, I'm not going to shrivel and die. No, I'm going to figure out how to use that stupid website. You got any idea how it works?"

Bernice didn't. She didn't even have the Internet, though Clay was quite proficient. He'd promised to show her how to look up references on the official Church website. Of course, she couldn't bring up Clay now. Though it might distract Maxine, doing so would also highlight her loss. "Tina will know," she said. "Or Evie. Let's go call them."

In less than five minutes both women were there, bringing not only their expertise but also their sympathy and their love.

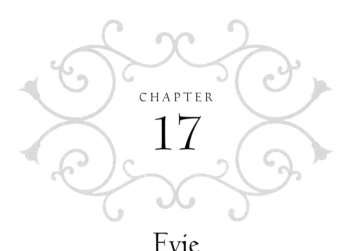

CHAPTER

17

Evie

I haven't told Maxine, but I've found Harold. He's at his daugh-ter's, though, which she probably guesses. I wrote him and told him that we were planning a French honeymoon for them. Hey, Maxine might be giving up, but we're not. Tina's going to send him something next. We'll get through to him one way or another. Somehow we'll make him understand that it doesn't really matter if he's in a wheel-chair or can't drive. What really matters is that they spend the rest of their years together.

I've lost five more pounds, and I'm feeling really great. I think I look good, too, though I know I have a ways to go. It's okay—I'm becoming a patient woman. I'm so excited to see Jack today. Last Friday he stopped and talked to me. He'd remembered me from the restaurant. I hoped he'd ask me out, but he didn't. Oh well, it'll happen. Maybe tomorrow I'll have something really neat to share with the ladies at our brunch!

Evie held her stomach as she walked on the treadmill. She had never laughed so hard in her life, but that didn't stop Christopher from recounting yet another story of a not-so-intelligent thief who had been caught by his own stupidity.

"You see," he said, "the boy had his hands full of stolen goods, and he was well out ahead of us. There was no way we'd ever catch up on foot. But he'd forgotten his pants."

"His pants?"

"Yeah. They were about four sizes too big, held up with a belt around his hips. Not tight enough, though."

"They didn't!"

"Yes, they did. Pretty soon those pants were around his ankles, and we got him."

Evie giggled. "Serves him right. I can just see it. Pants down around his ankles, cops—uh, officers—trying to read him his rights—"

"And laughing so hard it was almost impossible to get the cuffs on him." Christopher chuckled. "Exactly right." He sobered a little. "I saw him again, though, a few months later. Looks like he's doing better. I go see him sometimes at his high school."

Evie bet he did. Christopher was a nice man. "How come you never married?" She asked the question before she thought it through. They'd become quite good friends, these past weeks, but she wasn't sure they were close enough for a question like that.

"I was engaged once," he said with a shrug. He looked

around as though checking to see if anyone else was listening, but the only person nearby was Cecilia, and she was wearing her headphones. "It didn't work out. She went off and married someone else. Said she didn't want to be a cop's widow. But look at me, I'm still here." He raised his arms, and Evie noticed that his belly wasn't as large as it used to be. She sort of missed the comfortable bulk.

"I'm sorry," she offered.

He grinned. "Don't be. What kind of marriage could it have been? She didn't even like Billy Joel."

"She didn't?" Evie gaped. "How could anyone not like Billy Joel? You are so lucky to have escaped!"

He laughed.

"Seriously, though," she went on, "at least she didn't marry you and then cheat, like my husband did."

Christopher studied her, his brown eyes a safe haven for her confessions. "He blew it," he said simply. Glancing past her toward Cecilia, he added, "He blew it twice."

Evie's treadmill slowed to a stop, and she rubbed her towel across her face. "You got that right. And he even liked Billy Joel."

"Did someone say Billy Joel?" Cecilia had taken notice of them and punched the off button on her MP3 player. "I've got something here by him." She clicked a button a few times, and soon they heard the strains of "Piano Man" coming through her headphones. Evie began humming along as Christopher mimicked a guitar solo.

The next minute Cecilia was digging her elbow into Evie. "Don't look now," she muttered.

Of course Evie looked and saw Jack coming her way. Her heart leapt. Was he actually coming over or just passing by? *Oh, please notice me,* she thought. *Please, oh, please.* He stopped, and Evie's legs felt weak. He was so handsome and young-looking for his forty-eight years—she'd just learned his age by talking with the lady at the registration desk.

"Hi," he said. "From the restaurant, right? You and your friend, Rosalva, wasn't it? Nice girl."

"She's the best."

He glanced at Cecilia's headphones, which still gave out barely audible strains of music. "Ah, Billy Joel. Nobody does it like he does."

"You can say that again." Christopher strummed his pretend guitar again. Evie was a little embarrassed to have him do that in front of Jack, but Jack didn't seem to care.

"Saw him once a long time back," Jack said. "Worth every penny."

Evie wondered how she could somehow talk to him alone, sure that he wouldn't ask her out in front of the others. She tried signaling Cecilia with her eyes, but it was Christopher who understood. "Come over here for a minute, would you, Cecilia? There's something I want to show you." He and Cecilia moved away, and Evie sent a silent thank-you toward Christopher. He was really a good friend.

Ask me out, she thought at Jack. Was she still too overweight for him? She felt good, but she knew that was deceptive because she'd been so heavy. She certainly would never be as skinny as Tina or as shapely slender as Rosalva.

"Well," Jack said, "nice seeing you. Tell your friend 'hi.' "

For a brief moment Evie was jealous of Rosalva. Was it Rosalva that Jack wanted to meet or was that simply his way of talking? Then he smiled, and Evie forgot all that. "Bye, Jack," she breathed.

Christopher and Cecilia hurried up to her. "Well?" Cecilia asked. "Did he ask you out?"

Evie shook her head, trying not to show her disappointment. "No, but it's okay." She smiled at them. "There's always Billy Joel." She reached for Cecilia's headphones.

"Uh, there really *is* Billy Joel," Christopher said. When they looked at him blankly, he continued. "He's coming in concert. Not here—Las Vegas. First week in June. And of course the tickets are priced out of this world, and all the good seats are sold out. But my sister's friend's cousin works at a ticket office, and she snatched up a couple of great tickets. Turns out she can't go. My sister said I could have them, and if you want you could—"

"You could take Jack!" Cecilia squealed. "Christopher, that's a great idea!"

Evie gasped. "Oh, Christopher, would you really let me buy them?"

"Uh—uh." An unreadable thought was in his eyes, but when he blinked it was gone. "Sure, if that's what you want."

"You could rent two hotel rooms, of course," Cecilia said. "And I'll go with you, so it's on the up and up."

"You really think he'd go?" Evie asked.

Cecilia nodded. "Of course. You heard what he said about Billy Joel. Why wouldn't he?"

Evie's heart was beating hard as she considered the possibility. She was a modern woman. She could ask a man out to a concert. And if they happened to get to know each other a bit better on the long ride to Las Vegas, well, that was great. In the six weeks before the concert, she would have lost most of the weight the doctor recommended—maybe more. If only she could keep up her pace.

"I'll do it!" She hugged Christopher. "Thanks so much."

"No problem." He hugged her back, not seeming to mind that they were still sweaty from the treadmills.

"It's settled, then," Cecilia said, grinning. "When do you get the tickets?"

"They're coming in the mail." Christopher drew away.

"You should wait another few weeks to ask him," Cecilia said. "And buy a new outfit."

"A date-asking outfit." Christopher looked amused. "I use them all the time. Unfortunately, I haven't yet found the right outfit."

Evie laughed. "Well, we can only try."

"Hey, what do you say we all go out to a movie to celebrate?" Christopher asked. They had been to a movie last week and enjoyed themselves.

"I'm game!" Evie said.

Cecilia's brow furrowed. "What about your grandchildren? Isn't your daughter bringing them over tonight?"

"Oh, that's right. I forgot."

"That's because you're too young to be a grandmother," Cecilia said.

"Forty-five is plenty old to be a grandmother."

"We're not turning them away, are we?" Cecilia's tone was pleading. In the past weeks she had become more involved in their lives than she had been before she filed for divorce from Jason. At first this had disconcerted Evie, until she realized that while she would have many more grandchildren, Cecilia would never have any children or grandchildren of her own. Evie decided she was glad to share—her grandchildren could never have too much love.

"Of course not," Evie said. "But there's no reason we can't do both. Prepare yourselves for cartoons, folks. I think there's a new feature down at the local theater."

CHAPTER

18

Rosalva

I've never been so disgusted in my life. Willard took me over to his brother's house for a Mother's Day barbecue on Saturday. At first everything was perfect. Willard's brother, Ryan, has only been married to Kerrianne a month, but with their combined five children, there's the feeling they've been married a lot longer. They're both nice people. The children are, as Tina would say, adorable.

My boys were also invited, and they were having a good time. Lucas has started his flying lessons, and he was describing them for the younger boys, who begged for every detail. Jaime talked about his mission plans, and the two girls hung on his every word (they both seemed to have a little crush on him, though they're only nine or so). Willard was attentive and polite to me, but I could sense he was being careful with his feelings. It's been more than two weeks since we talked about my not wanting a child, and he hasn't made any decision. Even so, things were comfortable between us. I could imagine us having a good life together.

Then Willard's parents arrived. I could tell right away they weren't pleased with me. I remembered they hadn't liked Willard's sister-in-law when she was alive because her grandmother was Mexican. Sure enough, they acted like I wasn't even there, like I wasn't good enough to acknowledge. I felt so hurt, even though I know that people who act like that aren't worth crying over. I kept wanting to tell them that I worship the same God they do.

Kerrianne could see I was upset. She took me aside and told me they had treated her nearly the same way because they thought she was from a poor, uneducated family. According to her, they'd changed a great deal. She said they were actually warm to me compared to how she'd been treated. Well, it sure didn't feel that way. And the strange thing is they practically worship Kerrianne now.

Willard seemed to stay away from me while they were around, though that might only be my imagination because he did hold my hand at one point. I didn't notice him slighting my boys at all. He told everyone all about Lucas's lessons like they were his own. Lucas is a changed boy around Willard these days.

I'm so confused. I really like Willard—more than a lot. He's far from perfect, but he's come a long way, and he's worked hard to correct his past mistakes. But I don't know if I could be involved in a life where my in-laws hate me because of the color of my skin. I guess it's just as well that Willard is undecided about me. I am undecided about him, too.

Fortunately, I had a much more enjoyable time at Mimi's yesterday. I'm so glad I have those women for friends. When I told them what happened on Saturday, they were unconditionally in my corner. They'll help me hang on until I know what it is that I want. Both

Tina and Evie are so happy right now that the rest of us really don't have to say anything during our meetings, though we do try to keep working on our goals. I'm sure any day now Tina will tell us she's getting married. I hope so. Scott seems great.

Evie still hasn't asked Jack out, and she's had the actual tickets for more than a week. I think she's afraid. Something's up with Bernice, too. She only talked for a minute about her Bible studies. I wonder if she's dating again. Maybe someday I'll ask. If only Maxine were her regular self, she'd get to the bottom of it.

I hate seeing Maxine so lost. It's just not like her. It's my turn to send Harold something to remind him of her. Evie wrote a letter and told him about France, Tina put together a bunch of scrapbook pages of all the pictures we had of Maxine, and I kept the best picture to print on a shirt for him. Irresistible!

That reminds me. I found out Harold ended up asking Willard to be his lawyer to draw up his will. I guess they really hit it off that night at the hospital. I haven't told Maxine. I doubt I will.

"How's it coming?" Rosalva asked, standing on the porch and gazing out over her front yard. The old grass was gone, the sprinklers were in place, and the new cement curbing arced gracefully around the flowerbeds, waterfall, and decorative bushes. Everything was perfect, except for the grass that would make the yard look finished.

"We'll sod tomorrow," Spencer said. "Only takes us a few hours to get it done."

"It's beautiful." Rosalva sank down on the top step, letting her eyes wander again over the yard.

"I'm only sorry we didn't finish sooner for you." There had been a delay with the concrete and another with parts for the waterfall.

"Pretty fast, if you ask me," she said. "I once waited two months for a guy to finish my roof. Maybe that's because we were dating."

Spencer smiled, and Rosalva grinned back. She felt so comfortable with him. Not like with Willard's family.

"What's wrong?" Spencer asked. "You seem a little sad." They had talked every day he'd come to the house and become friends of a sort.

"It's nothing. I just met some people who weren't very nice because of the color of my skin."

"The world is full of people like that." He was leaning on the railing, looking down at her. Rosalva knew he liked her. She could always tell when a man was interested. Being with him might not be as financially secure as with Willard, but there would be no racial dilemma, and he was a good, hardworking, honest man. Maybe she could even grow to love him.

Love? Was that what she felt for Willard? *It can't be*, she thought. If so, Willard would hurt her—she knew it. And why was her ethnic heritage even an issue? She was an American, a hardworking American, and a member of the Church as well. There shouldn't be a problem—but there was.

"The only thing we can do is keep being nice to them," Spencer was saying. "I tell myself every day that they get up every morning and eat breakfast just like me. They put their pants on one leg at a time. They are children of God." He grinned. "It helps—sometimes."

Rosalva didn't want to think about it anymore. "How's your daughter's case?"

"One more time we have to go before the judge," he said. "Then it'll be over. My grandson will be safe."

She envied him that grandbaby. "I'm glad."

"I'll miss talking to you when it's all done." He motioned to the yard with a gesture that was oddly graceful.

"Me, too."

But maybe she wouldn't miss him. Willard was coming over to talk tonight, and there had been a seriousness in his voice that made her heart feel like lead.

"If you decide your back lawn needs doing, you could call."

"Thanks. I have your number."

She watched Spencer stride toward his truck, every motion of his lean body fluid and powerful. For a moment he reminded her of Enrique when they first met and later as well when she'd given birth to Jaime. Those had been happy times. Melancholy flowed through her. Life was passing so fast now, almost slipping between her fingers. Before she knew it she would be Bernice's age and then Maxine's. She would have her own grandbabies to hold and love and cuddle.

What was Willard coming to say?

Spencer stopped at the truck and turned toward her. "Your younger son," he called. "He helped me here yesterday. He's a good boy. I could use help sometimes after school, if he's willing. I pay well, and I hire only good men so he'd be in good company."

She knew the offer was his way of leaving things open between them, and the fact that he understood her concern for her son made her like him even more. He cared, and regardless of what happened with Willard, Lucas could use the work experience and another good role model. "Thank you," she said. "I'll talk to him and have him call you tonight."

He nodded and lifted a hand in farewell.

Willard didn't arrive until after dinner. Jaime was still at work, and Lucas was doing homework and dreaming about his new job. He'd already talked about a schedule with Spencer and planned to work three hours a day after school, except for the day he had flying lessons. He'd also work Saturday morning. Rosalva was content that he'd be out of trouble and well on his way to becoming a contributing member of society. "But I'm keeping an eye on your grades," she'd warned him. "One little slip, and good-bye job. Your real job is to get through school." He'd agreed, and his doing homework without prompting was a sign of good things to come.

When she opened the door to Willard, the smooth dirt in her yard reminded her of Spencer. Both good men but so different. She felt numb inside.

Willard wore a suit, as if he'd come directly from work, though she knew he'd likely gone home first, given the hour. She thought back to her telling the ladies at Mimi's yesterday about his parents and how their reactions had varied. Evie had wanted to confront them, Tina had suggested they'd soften up after getting to know her, and Bernice had said to ignore them altogether. Only Maxine hadn't commented. She'd asked how Willard felt about their treatment of her and how she felt about him. Rosalva didn't know either of those things. There hadn't been any time since his parents' visit to explore those feelings.

"You look great," Willard said with appreciation.

She had dressed carefully, wearing a colorful gypsy skirt and blouse that was dressy enough for anything but still casual. "Where are we going?" she asked. Since it was Thursday night and she'd have to make sure Lucas was in bed so he could get up for school, she couldn't be out late, but he should know that by now. They'd been seeing each other almost every day for more than a month.

Of course, after tonight it wouldn't matter. She knew the

choice he had to make—it was the choice she would make. So why couldn't she be happy envisioning him with a family?

"Do you feel like walking?" He looked doubtfully at her high-heeled sandals.

"Sure." The sandals were comfortable to walk in, as long as the ground wasn't uneven.

After telling Lucas she was leaving for a few minutes but would have her cell phone on, they walked together along the sidewalk, not touching, though their hands brushed occasionally, sending a longing through her that she could not describe. A need for belonging, for a future, for an eternal relationship. The feeling made her want to cry.

Why didn't he get it over with? She wouldn't try to convince him otherwise. She wouldn't even flirt. She would let him go with dignity.

The May evening was beautiful and warm. It was light enough that people were still working in their yards, and children passed them on bicycles. The neighborhood was an older one in the middle of Pleasant Grove. Rosalva liked most of her neighbors, though there were a few new ones she didn't yet know. She worried only about two of the families. The parents were gone a lot, and their children often roamed the neighborhood unattended. She'd taken one toddler back to her parents' house several times, and she was sure their teens were responsible for toilet-papering the house of the widow across the street. She knew the people next door to one of the families, and they were constantly tossing back the beer cans the teens threw over their fence.

They had reached 100 East when Willard took her hand to cross the street. Soon they arrived at Discovery Park with its large wooden structures and numerous play areas. The laughter of children filled the air.

"There's a path. It's even paved." Willard pointed, and they walked toward the path that led to the adjoining Manila Park. They passed a huge baseball field, soon reaching the other side of the park and a smaller set of play equipment. Her feet were beginning to ache after all, so she kicked off her shoes and headed over the grass to a bench facing the play equipment. A mother and her two children, the only occupants, were leaving. A perfect place for a good-bye.

Willard had kept hold of her hand. He rubbed it now as they sat in the fading light. "Rosalva," he began. She liked the way he said it, with the hint of a Spanish accent as though he cared about trying to make it sound as it was supposed to. Not like his parents, who had called her Rose the one time they had addressed her.

"It's okay," she said. "You don't need to say it. I already know."

He looked at her, tilting his head, those steel gray eyes taking her in. "But I want to, anyway. I want there to be no mistake." He paused for several heartbeats. She almost lost it then, but she blinked her eyes and willed herself not to break down. *Later,* she told herself. *Not in front of him.*

"During these past weeks," he said at last, "I've thought a lot about what I want out of life—from you, from myself. There was a time when I would have gone after what was best for me, regardless of the consequences. I would have forced the woman in my life to conform to what I expected."

Well, he had learned something at least. That should help him in his next relationship. The thought wasn't as consoling as she'd hoped.

His hand tightened. "What I'm trying to say, Rosalva, is that I've come to an understanding that is as clear as any I've ever had. I want to be with you. On your terms—however you'll have me."

With those few words, the future she expected shifted like a ripple through the fabric of time. With one shake, all the valleys and hills were different. New. Promising.

"What about a family?" she choked out.

He shrugged. "I can't imagine my life without you and the boys. I'd like you to be my family."

"But your parents . . ." She almost regretted bringing them up. Would he take it all back? She waited, scarcely breathing.

He frowned and looked over the empty playground. "My parents certainly have their problems, and I admit that I used to be a lot like them. It took losing everything before I realized what was really important."

"You don't know what it can be like," she countered. "Race is very important to a lot of people. There are too many like my ex-husband who make it bad for all of us."

His gaze shifted back to her. "Oh, honey, people like that come in all colors. Believe me, I see it every day at work. But the thing is, none of that matters if we're willing to do what it takes to make *us* work. I believe we can do it—regardless of how my parents choose to act. We won't be alone. We have each other, we have my brother and his wife, and we have the—"

"Independence Club," she finished with him.

He was right. They had a lot of friends, more support, in fact, than she'd ever had at any other time in her life. If his parents hated her, if they were angry because of the lack of grandchildren from their firstborn, well, that was something they would have to deal with, not something that would prevent her and Willard from finding happiness. As long as her friends were there and as long as Willard was the man she believed he'd become, she could face anything.

"I love you, Rosalva," he said softly. "I want to spend the rest of eternity with you."

She took her hand from his and placed both of her palms on his cheeks. Every line in his face was dear to her, every inch spoke to a place within her heart. "Yes, Willard," she whispered. "I'll marry you."

CHAPTER

19

Tina

I can't believe another week has passed by, and it's already the middle of May. I'm going to Mimi's later to meet the girls, but the only thing I really have to tell them is that things are going well with Scott. Too bad it's not exactly true. I really care for him—so much, in fact, that I'm scared. Is he simply too good to be true?

Why did his wife leave him? I can't stop wondering. Was she really chasing rainbows as he implied? That's her name, by the way. Well, not her real name, but the name she goes by now. Strange.

Scott's been tense because of Callie's grades, but she's gotten them up again, thank heaven. I forgot to mention that she talked to her mother last week for Mother's Day. I think Scott let her do that to sort of make up for not letting her visit during spring break.

Things have been quiet since, but I can't help feeling a storm is brewing. It's frightening because the last thing I need is more rain.

Scott has been asking me about Glen, about our life together. It bothers him that I don't want to talk about my life before. I wish I could tell him everything, and I do think I should tell him, as I'm sure Harold was hinting that night at the hospital. But if I did, Scott would know I'm not the capable woman I pretend to be, and I don't want his pity. (Maybe I understand a little how Harold feels in regard to Maxine.)

Sometimes I want to be alone. Sometimes I think it would be easier. Mostly, I'm afraid of trusting him too much.

Why did his wife leave?

S o you still haven't asked him?" Tina lifted her sandwich with both hands. "Evie, the concert isn't that far away. It's on a Friday, right? You have to give him time to get off work. You'll need time to drive to Vegas." She bit down on her sandwich, setting the rest back on her plate.

"I know." Evie sighed and nibbled halfheartedly on a piece of lettuce at the end of her fork. "And that's what makes me want to take all the pieces of that sweet bread and eat every last crumb."

Rosalva reached hurriedly for a slice of bread, as did Bernice and Tina. "Sorry," Tina said sweetly. "Only one left." She was still speaking when Maxine put the last piece on her plate.

"You guys are the best." But Evie watched them a little enviously as they ate.

"Did I hear you say you're still on the no-sugar diet?" Bernice asked.

"Well, I did it for two weeks and then stopped for a while,

but I started again this week. I lose more when I cut out the sugar—especially raspberry-filled donuts."

Tina hated the worry in her friend's voice. "But you still lose when you eat some sugar," she pointed out. "You don't have to do it so fast."

Rosalva swallowed her mouthful of bread. "Slow or fast, Evie, you're looking too great to stop now."

Evie smiled, and Tina realized how much her face had changed with the weight loss. She was still beautiful, her skin like porcelain, but the shape was oval now instead of round.

"I did lose another three pounds this week," Evie told them. "That makes twenty since I saw the doctor, thirty-five if you count the fifteen I lost before. So that means only twenty-five more pounds until the doctor says I'm healthy. Of course, after that's gone, I'd like to lose another fifteen pounds."

"Who wouldn't?" Bernice looked down at her hand on the table, and Tina thought she saw something shining. She peered closer, but Bernice quickly cupped her hand, laying the other one over it. Tina couldn't think what she might possibly be holding. Or had her wedding band simply reflected the light again as it had in Harold's hospital room?

"So when are you going to ask Jack?" Tina prompted Evie.

"What if he says no?"

Tina let out a laugh. "It's Billy Joel. He wouldn't. Those tickets cost hundreds."

"So basically I'm buying a date." Evie looked glum.

"Yep," said Rosalva. "And why not? That's what men do."

"And if he doesn't ask me out afterward?"

"Then he's a jerk." Rosalva stuffed the last part of her bread into her mouth. "But I agree with Tina. You really need to ask right away. Executives have to plan if they're going to be away."

"That's right. You're engaged to one," Bernice said. "You would know." She glanced down at her hand, but she didn't open her fist.

Rosalva shook her head. "Willard's not an executive. He's a lawyer. A very good one."

"Have you decided on a date yet?" Tina asked Rosalva.

"He wants to have the wedding in July, but . . ." Rosalva's smile vanished.

Evie wrinkled her nose. "Oh, don't tell me you're having second thoughts. It's like a disease around here."

Tina understood her meaning immediately. First Maxine had changed her mind about Harold, and then Harold had changed his mind about Maxine. Evie, who had been so sure of her passion for Jack, was now teeming with indecision. Bernice had gone from never dating to dating and back again without so much as admitting anything. *And I can't seem to take my relationship with Scott to the next level,* Tina thought. She knew this was her fault, that she needed to open up and communicate more, but the idea absolutely terrified her. Maybe she was also on the verge of changing her mind about relationships. Having no relationship at all did seem safer.

"It's not me," Rosalva said. "I feel sure about him, more sure than I've felt about anything. I am worried, though. What happens if in ten years he looks back and regrets that he never had a son or daughter? What if he blames me?"

Tina put a hand over hers. "In ten years he'll be only that much more in love with you. It won't matter one bit. And by then you'll have grandchildren—"

"*My* grandchildren."

"Both of yours," Tina said firmly. She'd seen how taken Scott had become with her own boys, and though she thought it would be wonderful to have a baby with him if they decided to marry, she knew he would still be content if that didn't happen. Of course, he had a daughter already—Willard didn't.

Rosalva made a face. "It doesn't seem fair. I wouldn't give up my chance to be a mother for him."

"It's different for women," Evie said. "We crave babies. I would have had eight or more if Jason had been willing."

"That's exactly it." Rosalva snapped her fingers. "You resent Jason for it, don't you? I made sure that Willard came to me on my terms, and now I feel as if . . . Well, if I really cared about him, wouldn't I want him to have a chance to be a father? I mean, you should see him with his nieces and nephews. Kerrianne says they used to dislike him in the old days, but now he's become a favorite with them. I just think he would make an awesome father, and I care enough about him to want him to have that opportunity."

Everyone was silent a moment, stunned. Tina didn't know what to say. This was so unlike Rosalva—she'd made no secret that she was sure her childbearing years were over.

"Well, it's something only you can decide," Evie said, "but I'd baby-sit whenever you needed me."

"Me, too," Tina said brightly.

Bernice gave them her sour smile. "Don't look at me—I've got grandbabies up to my ears. I would throw you a baby shower, though. After fifteen years, you'll need a lot of things."

"You can say that again," Tina agreed. "And I doubt you'd regret having another child. Think of how precious your babies were—a sweet slice of heaven. I'd like to have at least one more myself."

"Wait, wait, wait! I didn't mean that," Rosalva said forcefully. "I meant that maybe if I truly loved Willard, I wouldn't marry him, and then he'd be free to find a younger wife—one who is willing to give him a child."

Tina thought that was a ridiculous idea, but she wasn't about to say it to Rosalva. What did she know, anyway? It wasn't as though she had a great track record with men.

"I'm sorry, Rosalva," Evie said a little too loudly, "but that's just plain stupid. You love Willard. You can't give him to some-one else."

Rosalva dropped her gaze and didn't reply.

Maxine cleared her throat, causing Tina to start with surprise. She'd become accustomed to Maxine's silences these past weeks and hadn't expected her to weigh in on the baby issue. "I think," Maxine said, "that you should pray about it."

Bernice nodded emphatically. "Good idea."

Again Tina caught sight of a shining thing in Bernice's hand, but she didn't appear to be holding anything. Then Tina understood. Her ring was flashing, not from the gold but from one or more diamonds. Yet Bernice's wedding band never had a diamond. Tina knew because Bernice was the only one who'd kept wearing hers. Tina had sold hers in the newspaper the day after Glen's funeral. She'd used the money to buy the boys clothes.

Bernice is seeing someone—and seriously, Tina decided. But why hadn't she told them?

"You know, it would be different with Willard," Maxine continued. "You wouldn't have to worry about supporting another child. I bet you could even quit your job—I mean, if you want." This last was given so offhandedly that Tina knew Maxine had made it up on the spot. But she was right. Rosalva's relationship with Willard was nothing like her relationship with Enrique. It required a different way of thinking.

Rosalva lifted her eyes and stared at Maxine. "Stay home? It's a little late for that—I think."

"But you hate being away from the boys," Evie said.

Rosalva wet her lips with her tongue. "That makes it just that much more wrong. Me staying home with my children, while he works."

"Oh, but he'll have what he wants most," Tina said. "You."

"And what if he . . . what if I end up needing to support myself?"

"Either you trust him or you don't," Maxine said firmly. "That's another thing you have to decide. You can always keep on working."

Silence. Not even Tina could think of something to say. If only she could peek into the future and see what was best for her friend. Maybe for herself, too.

"By the way," Maxine said, in a tone that clearly changed the subject. "I want you all to know that I signed up for a summer French class." Her chin lifted slightly, as though in challenge.

Tina grinned. "That's fabulous, Maxine!" Maybe now her friend would find the part of herself she'd left with Harold. "I've mapped out a few possible vacations for you if you want to look at them."

"Maybe I'll do that." Maxine didn't act as happy as she once had, but Tina could tell she was working on it. Eventually, she'd be all right again.

The best thing we can do is be supportive, Tina thought. *And maybe try not to worry her too much.*

"Are we done?" Rosalva asked. "I've got to get to work." She put down money for her meal. "Pay for me, would you? You guys are the best—I really love you." With that she was gone, walking briskly through the restaurant as heads turned in her direction.

Tina said good-bye to the rest of the women and slowly drove home. Maybe it was time to get things out in the open with Scott—Maxine would surely tell her that if she asked. Of course, she couldn't tell Maxine anything right now. Maxine had her own concerns.

Besides, how could she begin such a conversation with Scott? "You wanted to know about my husband?" she might say. "Well, his favorite pastime was to yell at me if his food wasn't ready when he came home from work, or if it wasn't the right temperature." Or maybe, "He brushed up on his high school wrestling skills by slamming me into the wall."

No, she wouldn't tell him any of it. They could build from what they had—why dredge up the past? Tina began humming softly to herself. It might take more time, but Scott would have to get to know her without the secrets she had buried.

Tina's cell phone rang as she entered Pleasant Grove. Fumbling for the phone in her purse, she pulled over, glancing at the number. Not the boys or the school—Scott. Her heart jumped. Only as she answered did she wonder why he was calling her from home when he should be at work.

"Callie's missing," he said without preamble. "The school sent an e-mail to tell me she was absent. I came right home, but she's not here. Is she at your place?"

"I'm almost home. I'll check and call you back. I'm sure it's okay. We'll find her."

"I know, but with how she's been acting lately, I keep thinking about all those other girls, the ones they don't find." His voice sounded odd, and she suspected he was crying.

"If she's not at my house, I'll go to the school and talk to Ashley."

"Call me first, okay? I'll go with you. Then I'm calling the police."

Tina had an idea. "Are any of her clothes missing?"

"I don't think so, but I can't be sure. Her room's a mess, and I can't tell one outfit from another."

"I see what you mean." After a certain age, she hadn't been able to keep track of Ashley's clothing, either. "I'll call you," she promised.

Minutes later, Tina pulled up in her driveway and jumped from the car. She had a secret place by the drainpipe from the rain gutter where she kept an extra key when she was out of the house, in case Ashley or one of the boys walked home early from school. Callie knew where it was. *Please be there. Please be there,* Tina thought, her words becoming a silent litany.

Callie was nowhere in the house. By the time Tina reached for the phone, Scott was already knocking on her door. "I'm sorry," she said. His face was gray, and his usual happy smile was absent.

"What if she . . ."

"No." She put one hand on his chest, feeling the thudding of his heart. "Let's go to the school. Don't worry. We'll find her." Even as she said it, she wanted to fall into his arms and weep. *Where are you, Callie?*

Ashley was surprised when they pulled her out of class. "Callie's gone? Oh, I can't believe it!"

"Do you know where she is?" Tina demanded. "Do you have any idea at all?"

"No, I don't! Promise." Ashley tucked a strand of her strawberry blonde hair behind her ear. "But she is so dead when I catch up with her—we're best friends. She should have clued me in."

Scott looked physically ill, and Tina knew he was thinking the same thing she was. If Callie hadn't given her best friend an indication of her departure, maybe it hadn't been planned. "Okay," Tina said. "You go back to class, and I'll see you at home. If you hear anything—call me."

"Wait! Have you called Callie's phone?"

Tina looked at Scott, and he nodded. "No answer," he said.

"Oh." Ashley's brow furrowed. "I'm sure she'll be back soon." She gave Scott a sympathetic smile, and he put his arm around her shoulder in a half hug.

"Thanks, Ashley." After Ashley was gone, he said, "Let's go talk to the police."

He didn't speak all the way to the police station. "What about her mother?" Tina asked as he pulled up at the city building. "Could she have gone there?"

Scott froze, his face solid granite. "I told her she couldn't go see her until school was out—if then." There was anger in his voice, no matter how obviously he tried to control it. She felt the emotion in every pore of her body. Her stomach tightened, and her heartbeat quickened. He dropped his head to the steering wheel. "Oh, if she hurts her again . . ."

Tina said nothing. She was too afraid of his anger. There was nowhere to run inside his truck.

He lifted his head, and she could see the tears. Glen had cried too, after he'd hurt her. He'd begged her to forgive him, and for a while everything had been okay. Until the next time.

"I did call Rainbow," Scott said brokenly. "I left a message. She didn't answer, and she hasn't called me back."

Her heart went out to him. "Come on. Let's go inside. They'll know what to do."

They spent the better part of two hours at the police station, finding the short, bulky man who assisted them efficient and helpful. He gave Scott a list of things to do—including finding recent pictures, making a list of relatives and friends, and keeping everyone out of his house until the police could examine it thoroughly. The officer also recommended registering Callie with several national missing child sites on the Internet.

"We'll send officers to the school and to your neighborhood," the officer promised. "And we'll contact your ex-wife. Meanwhile, let us know if you hear anything at all."

"What about the media?"

The officer nodded. "The sooner they get involved, the better. But it's difficult because a lot of teens these days get mad and run away for a while. The media likes to make sure they're really missing—or have proof of something suspicious. That's what we'll try to give them. Those sites I gave you will also help. The more active you are, the better."

Scott ran his hands through his hair, his expression close to despair. The officer reached up and laid a hand on his shoulder. "Keep your head," he said. "Given your daughter's age, the time of year, and the conflicts you've been having recently, I'll bet you this is something she's planned and that she'll be back once she feels she's proven her point."

"Thanks," Scott managed.

As Scott drove toward home, Tina read aloud the lists they were given. One mentioned getting others involved in the hunt. "Hey, I just thought of something. Evie knows this police officer. He doesn't work in Pleasant Grove, but I'll bet he'll have some suggestions or maybe could do some checking on his own." At Scott's nod she took out her cell phone and dialed Evie. She was relieved when Evie answered almost immediately.

"I'm ready to head to the gym now," Evie said after Tina had explained the situation. "I'll get right on it. I'm sure Christopher will help. He's a great guy. Let me get a paper, and I'll write down the particulars. Have you called the others?"

"No, we've been at the police station. But Rosalva's at work, and I remember Bernice saying something about going to her son's in Fillmore. And Maxine . . . well, she's been so down lately that I didn't want to add to her problems."

"I know what you mean, but she'd want to know. Tell you what. I'll call Bernice again after I talk to Christopher. I'll keep calling until I get her, and after Rosalva gets off work, I'll talk to both her and Maxine—maybe then we'll know more. I just hope Rosalva's going home and not out with Willard. Meanwhile, Christopher will probably have something I can do to help him on this end. We'll check back in with you later."

"Thanks, Evie. You're a real friend."

"Be strong," Evie replied. "We'll find her."

Back at her house, Tina convinced Scott to stay for a late lunch. "Just a quick sandwich," she said. "Taking care of yourself is on that list, too. Look, I've got everything cut and ready. It'll just take a second to put it together."

Moments later, he picked at his sandwich, barely able to sit still. "I need to get the pictures to the police," he said after taking only a few bites. "And start on the rest of the list. I should be out there looking." His chair scraped backward as he stood.

"Take your sandwich, then." She walked with him to the door. "While I wait for the kids to come home, I'll call everyone in the ward to see if they've seen her. I'll let you know if I hear anything. You do the same, okay?" He nodded and left, looking heartsick and close to breaking down. Blinking back her own tears, Tina walked woodenly to the kitchen and picked up the phone.

Ashley arrived home from school first, followed by Skip from the junior high, both on foot as usual. Tina sent Ashley in the car to the grade school to pick up the younger boys. Scott still hadn't returned or called.

Tina's heart felt tight as her worry grew. Where could Callie be? She was a smart young woman and should know better than to get into trouble, but she was also very innocent. *Anything could have happened,* Tina thought. *Anything.*

Evie's friend Christopher called shortly, wanting to talk to Scott, so she gave him Scott's cell number. Then Evie got on the line. "Rosalva's at an event with her son," she said. "I'd forgotten that he was performing on the drums tonight. She'll call me as soon as his part is finished. Maxine's phone is busy—I think she must be trying to do her orders on the Internet again. But I called every Stubbs in Fillmore and found Bernice at her son's. She's driving straight from there to my place, and we'll make a flyer to distribute in the neighborhood. We need Scott to e-mail us a recent picture."

"Tell him about the picture when Christopher talks to him. I know he took one down to the police station."

"Will do."

Tina hung up, shutting her eyes for a minute to pray for Callie's return.

"Mom, I'm hungry," Ronnie complained, appearing from the hall.

"Me, too." Dallin was behind him. "Are we going to have dinner today?"

Skip looked up from the table where he was doing home-work. "Let's have something good."

Tina looked helplessly at Ashley, who was calling all of Callie's friends. The last thing she wanted to do was to think about making dinner, but she had to take care of the boys.

"We can make taco salad," Ashley offered. "That's easy, and everyone likes it." Her suggestion was met by a general mur-mur of approval.

"Good idea," Tina said. "I'll fry the meat and beans, and you do the salad. Boys, set the table."

"Then can we play Uno until dinner's ready?" Ronnie asked.

"Sure, sweetie."

"Wanna play with me, Dallin?"

"All right." Dallin headed for the dish cupboard while Ronnie went to the drawer where they kept the game.

"You know," Ashley said as she began washing the lettuce she had taken from the refrigerator, "I really think Callie must have gone to see her mom. She's been talking to her."

"You mean for Mother's Day."

"No, on her cell phone. It wasn't on Mother's Day. They talked at least twice that I know about besides then."

This was one of the unusual things the officer had warned them to be alert for. Tina immediately left the meat in the pan and called Scott on his cell phone. "I think you should come over," she said.

"What's up?"

She didn't want to tell him what Ashley had said over the phone because she wanted to make sure he ate something for dinner. "Well, it might be nothing, but could you please stop by?"

"Okay. I'm not too far away."

Scott arrived in minutes. "I've driven every street in Pleasant Grove," he told her as they walked into the kitchen, "and checked inside every store. What did you hear?"

Tina took a deep breath. "Ashley says Callie's been talking to your ex-wife on her cell phone."

"So you think she's there?" Hope vied with anger in his face.

"It's the only thing that makes sense. I know you said you called Rainbow earlier, but maybe she's home now."

"She could have been home before. She never answers the phone when she hears my voice on the answering machine." The admission made Tina feel sad because even after all the time he'd been divorced, it still hurt him that Rainbow wouldn't pick up the phone when he called.

Scott pulled out his phone and began to dial. "Look," he said after a few seconds, his voice harsh, "I know you're there, Rainbow. Pick up the phone. It's about our daughter. I've already reported her missing to the police. I gave them your address and phone number. I know you've been talking to her. Pick up the phone! Please?" He sighed in frustration, an angry sound that made Tina's heart numb. "Answering machine," he said unnecessarily, slumping into one of the stools near the counter.

"Try again," Ashley suggested, looking up from the tomatoes she was washing at the sink. "Maybe she's sitting there listening. I do that sometimes when it's someone I don't—well, when I don't feel like talking." She flushed and added quickly, "Not that I don't like them or anything."

Scott gave her a wry smile. "It's okay, Ashley. I don't care that she doesn't like to talk to me. To tell you the truth, talking to her isn't a picnic for me, either."

"Maybe she's in the bath and couldn't get to the phone in time," Skip said from the table.

"I'd like to take a bath," Ronnie said, making Skip and Dallin laugh. At the sound, the numbness in Tina's heart eased.

Scott called again, with the same results. Disappointed, he stood and began pacing the floor, jabbing the redial button. After the fourth call someone finally picked up.

"Where is she?" he demanded, turning on his heel as he reached the glass doors leading to the patio. "What do you mean you said it was okay? I'm the one with custody. You're the one who walked away." There was a long pause, and Tina could see his frustration building. His entire body was taut, his face flushed with anger. "I don't even know those people, and you told her to catch a ride with them? Look, that's it! I'm calling the police right now. Either you get my daughter back here tonight, or you'll be spending time in jail." Scott paused for a few seconds, listening, and then he took several irritated steps toward the counter. "No, you listen. You had no right to invite her without my permission—no right at all!"

As the argument continued, Tina backed up against the opposite wall where she had removed the wallpaper. She still needed to paint, but at least the ugly paper was gone. Maybe she should think about doing it soon. *That's it,* she told herself, *focus on the painting.* Anything so she wouldn't have to dwell on Scott's fury and what it might mean to her children.

"Don't you dare hang up on me," Scott was saying into his phone. "We have to deal with this now!"

Tina's body began trembling. She needed to get away—to run, yet she couldn't leave the kids. Neither could she abandon

Callie to her father's rage. She had to smooth things over between them.

"She wanted to see her mother," she managed to say. "You weren't listening."

Scott didn't hear her. "She hung up!" He slammed his phone shut and the impetus caused him to lose his grip, sending the phone crashing to the floor. The back popped open and the battery slid across the floor near Tina's feet. Frustrated, Scott slapped the counter with his open hand.

Tina felt the scream tear from her throat, though she didn't hear the sound. Suddenly she felt as though she were under water. Everything was muted—movements, the voices around her, her own heartbeat. Scott was speaking, but she couldn't hear the words. She had the overwhelming urge to scurry under the table for protection.

"Mom!" Skip and Dallin were at her side in seconds, Dallin's cards falling to the linoleum.

"Go get Maxine!" Was that frantic voice hers? It sounded far away, separate somehow from her. She pushed Skip toward the door leading to the living room. Maxine would help. Maxine always knew what to do. Funny how she'd not wanted to burden Maxine with Callie's disappearance, but of all her friends only Maxine could help her now.

"Take your brothers." She tried to make her voice calm, yet panic laced every word. No matter. She had to get them out of here. She had to make sure they were safe. Ronnie ran toward Skip, scooping up a few cards on his way, but Dallin clung to Tina. At the kitchen sink Ashley's eyes were wide with fright. Skip stopped at the door.

Scott was talking again. His arm came up. Tina crossed her

213

hands in front of her face, cowering despite her determination to be strong. "Don't!" she cried, her heart pounding in fear.

Skip left at a run, taking Ronnie with him. Two of her children were safe—now she had to protect the others.

Scott was still talking, but Tina didn't understand his words. He took a few steps, reached out to touch her arm. Breathing heavily, Tina sidestepped him, a difficult feat with Dallin plastered to her body.

"Mom?" Ashley was coming toward her.

Scott's hand reached out to her again. "Tina?"

Swallowing a scream, Tina grabbed Ashley's hand and pulled her down the hall toward her bedroom. Dallin came along with them, still gripping Tina's waist.

"What are you doing?" Ashley said, her voice high and anxious.

Hysteria, Tina thought. *She sounds funny because she's so afraid.* She gripped Ashley's arm tighter. Scott was following them. No, it was Glen. She had to hurry.

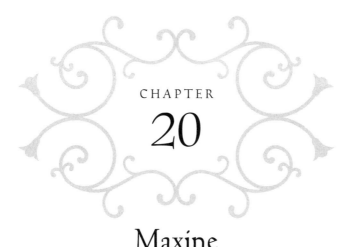

CHAPTER

20

Maxine

The color has gone out of my life. I miss Harold.

I have plenty to keep me busy—my cosmetics sales, worrying about Tina, and wondering what Bernice is hiding—but it's not the same. My heart's not in it. I never thought I would be one of those ladies who was so hung up on a man that she couldn't function. And you know what? I refuse to be that way. I am a person in my own right. I have a lot of fun. I loved life before Harold came along, and I will love life again. Giving someone else the power over my happiness is ridiculous. I am the author of my life.

axine felt a sinking sensation in her chest when she saw Tina's son Skip at her doorstep, his little brother Ronnie climbing down from his back. Skip's eyes were huge, and as he tried to speak, he sounded close to tears. "My mom—she needs you."

"Come on, I'll get my keys." Maxine motioned them to come inside. "What happened?"

Skip shook his head. "I don't know. Nobody was fighting or anything. Scott was mad, though, because Callie was missing. She went to see her mom—she lives in Idaho."

"She shouldn't go without asking," Ronnie put in. "That's bad."

Maxine led them through the kitchen to the garage, trying to piece the information together. "Scott was mad?" she prompted.

"He was yelling on the phone," Ronnie said helpfully. "He was talking to a rainbow."

"*To* Rainbow," Skip corrected, "not *to a* rainbow. Rainbow is Callie's mom's name, but not her real one. She changed it when Callie was little. Still, Scott shouldn't be so mad. Callie just wanted to see her mom." His voice was defensive, and Maxine guessed the thirteen-year-old had a crush on Callie.

They clambered into the car, and she reminded them to buckle up. Maxine checked for traffic before backing out of her drive. "That's all he did? Yell into the phone?"

"Well, more like he was just mad-sounding," Skip said, confusion lacing the words. "And it wasn't at us, but my mom . . ."

"She was scared."

He nodded.

"Was Mommy scared of the rainbow lady?" Ronnie asked.

"Because I know Scott wouldn't let her hurt us or anything. He's probably way bigger than her. And strong. He's stronger than anyone."

"What did your mother say?" Maxine wavered between thinking Tina might have understood something the boys hadn't and the possibility that she had let her past influence her perception about what had actually happened.

"Mom was acting funny," Skip said in a whisper, presumably so his little brother in the backseat couldn't hear. "She was, well, kind of scrunching up a bit." He showed her, raising his arms over his head.

"Cowering?"

When he nodded, Maxine decided to step on the gas. They covered the space in record time and hurried up the walk. Scott was pacing in the hallway and looked up with relief as they entered the house. "She won't open the door," he said, glancing down the hall toward the bedroom. "I don't know what to do."

"Tell me what happened." Maxine let a touch of asperity color her voice in case he wasn't as innocent as he appeared.

"I'm not sure." Scott ran his hand through his hair. Maxine could see the expanse of his arm and the muscle underneath the skin. Ronnie was right, Scott was strong—much stronger than the too-thin Tina. "I found out my daughter is on her way to my ex-wife's apartment in Nampa," he began, "and I guess I was a little upset. I mean, we've been so worried—we went to the police and everything. That reminds me, I'd better call them and let them know she's been found. And I should call Tina's friend Evie, if I can find the number. She knows a police officer who was helping look into things. Nice people, both of them. They've really gone the extra mile. Callie's picture is all over the Internet already, and they're putting out flyers. Christopher was trying to get the media to run something on the late news."

Maxine could tell he felt bad about wasting everyone's time, but she was glad so many had responded to help find Callie. If someone had bothered to inform her, she would have helped, too. Not that she was surprised no one had called; since Harold had refused her, the ladies in the Independence Club seemed to go out of their way to avoid causing her worry. "Evie's number should be programmed into Tina's phone," she told Scott. "Or if she called you on your cell, you should have the number."

"Oh, that's right." He shook his head at his oversight. "Anyway, I was talking to my ex-wife on the phone when Tina started looking at me funny. I thought she was just worried about Callie like I was. Then I dropped my phone and it broke apart, and I hit the counter—it was the last straw, you know—and suddenly Tina's telling Skip to go get you. She's sort of yelling, not really loud but sounding really worried—tight, if you know what I mean. By that time Dallin's clinging to her waist, and Ashley is completely pale. I tried to ask her what was wrong, but she starts raising her hands over her head like I was going to hit her." Scott grimaced, his brown eyes revealing his hurt. "Why would she think that? I've never hit anyone in my life—well, maybe my brother a couple of times growing up—but I would certainly never, ever hit a woman, and especially not Tina." Scott's hand went out to tousle Ronnie's hair absent-mindedly.

"My dad used to hit her," Skip said. The words cut through the silence, sharp enough to deafen their ears and wound their hearts. Scott's hand froze on Ronnie's head, and Maxine was glad the child couldn't see the horror that came to Scott's face.

"He yelled a lot," Ronnie offered. Now he looked up at Scott, but the horror had faded to shock. "I didn't like it."

"It was worse when he didn't yell," Skip countered. "Kind of like . . . like riding in an airplane and the pressure is building in your head and then it sort of . . . well, explodes."

Now Scott seemed to be using Ronnie's head to support himself. His face was pallid. "This is what you meant, wasn't it?" he said to Maxine. "When you told me to ask her about her husband."

Maxine nodded and then clapped her hands briskly. "Okay, kids, everything's all right now. I'm going in to see your mother, and you boys are going to stay here with Scott while he calls the police to tell them Callie has been found."

"We should call the neighbors, too." Skip started for the kitchen. "I can do that, if you'll use your cell phone, Scott. If it's not broken."

"Good idea." Scott took a step before looking back at Maxine, his face questioning. Instinctively Maxine knew what he wanted. "She'll be fine," she said. "I'll be with her. Go on, now."

With a longing glance toward the bedroom door, Scott scooped up Ronnie and carried him into the kitchen. Their voices followed Maxine down the hall.

She knocked softly on the door as she called out, "Tina, it's me, Maxine. Skip came over to my house. I'm here. Will you let me in?" She heard Ashley's voice on the other side of the door, but someone hushed her. "Hello, Tina?" she called louder. "I have the boys. Everything's all right, but you have to let me in."

The door unlocked and the knob slowly turned. Tears ran in mascara-laden rivulets down Tina's face. "Is he gone?"

"We'll get to that in a minute." Maxine pushed into the room and put her arms around Tina. Ashley and Dallin were seated on the bed, looking somber. "What happened, honey?"

"It was horrible, Maxine! I didn't know him. He was . . ." Tina paused, confused. She tucked a strand of strawberry-blonde hair behind her left ear. "He was so angry. I won't live like that again, Maxine—no matter how much I love him. I can't!"

"Nobody's asking you to. But that's not really the problem, is it?"

Tina drew away slightly. "What do you mean?"

"I mean that you need to see someone."

"It's not me. It was Scott." Tina's voice was tiny like a young child's. "He was furious. He was screaming. He was out of control." A longer pause. "I was so afraid."

Maxine's eyes went to Ashley, who was shaking her head. "No, Mom. It wasn't like that." She came to her feet, hands clenched at her sides. "Yeah, he was angry, but not at us. And he wasn't screaming. He was in control. That's what I've been trying to tell you. You've got it all wrong. Scott's not like Dad. He's not! He would never hurt anyone. Even when Callie does the most stupid things, he's never been mean to her. A little upset and, well, strict about punishment, but he's never hurt her. Honest. She would have told me. We tell each other everything."

Tina turned toward her, stumbling almost like a blind woman. "What are you saying? You were there, Ashley. You heard him!"

220

Ashley shook her head, a tear rolling down her cheek. "It wasn't like that."

Tina turned to Dallin. "What about you?" He was silent, his face troubled. "Dallin, please."

"I don't know what happened, Mom, but I wasn't scared . . . of Scott." His words hung in the air, telling and painful. Maxine watched as Tina stared into her children's eyes, seeing the truth. They hadn't been afraid of Scott, but of her—or at least for her.

Tina's hands clutched Maxine's arm. "Oh," she said. Just that, no more. A sigh of surrender.

Maxine walked with Tina to the bed. "Okay, kids, why don't you all go out and help Skip call the neighbors and tell them Callie's been found?" She purposely left out Scott's name and the fact that he was still in the house. "Ashley, maybe you can call for a pizza—my treat. You guys have a picnic in the backyard, okay?" She pulled out a few bills from her purse. "Save your mom and me a piece. We'll be out in a minute. Go ahead. Everything's okay."

When the children were gone, they sat on the bed together. Tina shook her head, gazing at Maxine with eyes full of tears. "Could I have really been so wrong?"

"Remember the spilled juice?" Maxine spoke gently but firmly. Tina had to face the truth. "None of you were in danger then, either. It's time to talk to someone about it. You need to get a handle on it, like your children have."

"I'm fine."

Maxine didn't respond. Tina was obviously not fine.

"I feel fine most of the time," Tina qualified, her voice defensive.

"You can't flip out every time someone gets angry, Tina. Unfortunately, getting angry is a fact of life."

"I didn't flip out!"

Again Maxine didn't reply.

Tina gave a shuddering sob, seeming to collapse before Maxine's eyes. "I scared them. Oh, it was *me* who scared them!" She put her hand over her mouth to stifle her sobs.

Maxine put an arm around her. "They're fine. They're just worried about you. That's all."

"I won't see him again." Tina lifted her chin, finding strength from somewhere inside. "Then it won't happen."

Maxine didn't like the direction this was heading. "So you're going to avoid all men? All people? What if I get upset one day and make the mistake of getting angry around you? Please, Tina."

"I met a doctor the other day at the hospital. He was nice. Gave me his card. I bet he wouldn't get angry. He's used to dealing with stress."

"Yeah, right. He's a man, honey. He's human. Just because Scott got angry doesn't mean he's an abuser."

"Then why did his wife leave him?"

"I don't know. Why would she arrange for Callie to go see her without Scott's permission? Look, if you really believe Scott's abusive, we need to call the police—for Callie's sake if for no other reason."

Tina remained silent.

"You should have told him, Tina. Maybe then he would have understood how he should vent his anger when he's around you. He had no idea. You need to talk to him."

Tina was shaking her head. "I don't want to. I can't. You told him to leave, didn't you?"

"He's talking to the police right now about Callie, but he's really confused. Are you sure you won't see him?" Maxine was certain if she could get them into the same room, their love for each other would help them take the right course.

"No." Tina didn't meet her gaze but stared at her fingers.

"What about your relationship? You're not going to throw all that away, are you?"

Tina hesitated, and Maxine's hope grew, but then Tina shook her head. "I can't risk it, Maxine. You saw what happened. I can't do that again to the children."

"So that means you're going to see someone, right?" Maxine had to make her understand that Scott's going away wouldn't solve anything.

"Maybe." Tina shrugged, and her eyes met Maxine's. "Will you go out there and make sure he's gone? Please?"

Maxine noticed she didn't ask her to check on the children, which meant she believed they were okay, even alone with Scott. That was something, at least.

"Sure." Maxine rubbed Tina's hands. "I'll talk to him while you wash your face. The pizza will be here soon."

"Thanks, Maxine." Tina hugged her.

Maxine left the bedroom, wishing she had been more successful. Tina and Scott loved each other, but did they love enough to conquer Tina's past? Things weren't looking good. Unless . . . Maxine smiled grimly. She might not get through to Tina, but Scott was another story. Maybe she could work on him.

Scott and the children were talking in the kitchen, but everyone fell silent when Maxine entered the room. No doubt they'd been discussing Tina. "Have you finished calling?" she asked brightly.

"Only a few more," Ashley said.

"Good. Then why don't you wait out on the front porch for

the pizza man and make those few calls." Maxine met Ashley's eyes and the girl nodded, glancing once toward Scott.

"Can I give him the money?" Ronnie asked his sister.

"I want to carry the root beer," Dallin shouted. The little boys ran toward the door, with Skip and Ashley following behind.

"So," Maxine began when she was alone with Scott.

"I never had any idea," he said. "The kids, they told me everything—just now. I can't believe it."

"They've had a lot of counseling. They're used to talking about it."

"No, I mean, I can't believe they didn't say anything before."

"Unfortunately, they've also learned how to keep secrets. They kept their father's for a long, long time." *And now they'd kept Tina's,* but Maxine didn't say that aloud. Neither did Scott.

"I shouldn't have been so upset." Scott rubbed his temples as though he had a headache.

"Glen used to get upset a lot. More than upset."

Scott's face was bleak. "It makes me furious to think about it, but can't she give me the benefit of the doubt? I shouldn't have to pay for what he did."

"Oh, but you do. You made that choice when you started dating Tina."

"I didn't know."

Maxine looked hard at him. "Are you saying you would have made a different choice? Because you still can. She thinks it's over. You could walk right out that door and forget everything."

His eyes blinked rapidly, but the tears came anyway. "I love her."

"Then you're going to have to learn how to deal with it, and it won't be easy. Her problems aren't simply going to disappear. She has a lot to deal with still—memories, fears. Things people like us don't even understand." Maxine took a step closer to him, her voice lowering. "I'll never forget the time she told me about buying a new dress to attend one of Ashley's school concerts. Glen saw her all ready to go and became offended that she was going without him—but he never attended events like that, so she hadn't even thought to invite him. He ripped the dress right off her, buttons popping everywhere. The fabric cut into the back of her neck. She still has marks." She paused to let the words sink in.

"I want to kill him," Scott growled.

"Someone already did." Maxine allowed herself a small smile. "Not on purpose, of course, but he's dead all the same. However, I want you to know that she was leaving him, anyway. She had money saved, and she was going to take the children to a shelter. She'd realized by then that nothing she could do would change Glen and that the children had to come first. *She* had to come first."

Scott shook his head. "If I had known . . ."

"You'd never get angry?"

"Well, I'd try."

"She needs counseling. She needs to recognize the triggers and find ways to deal with it."

Scott looked hopeful. "Will she go?"

"She did for a while right at first, but apparently not for long enough, and I don't think she will now. That's why you'll have to go instead."

"Me?" His expression was one of disbelief.

"Either that or walk out that door right now and tell those kids good-bye."

Scott closed his eyes for a moment, his face seeming to age. When his eyes opened, Maxine knew she had won. "I love her, Maxine," he said. "I'll do anything. But do you think it will really help?"

"I can't promise anything except that it certainly can't hurt. It might just be the start she needs."

"Okay, I'll do it." He glanced at the kitchen doorway. They could hear by Ronnie's excitement that the pizza had arrived. "Can I talk to her?" he asked.

"No." Maxine couldn't let him. Despite her own wish, she had to abide by her friend's decision. "Not now. You go home, get things covered with Callie, and we'll be in touch."

"Can I call her, do you think?"

"You can try. But not until tomorrow."

His jaw clenched and unclenched. "At least I know why I've felt she was holding back all this time." He nodded once, sharply. "It's a good thing this happened because now I know. I'll be what she needs—somehow."

Scott left, looking small and forlorn despite his bulk. As he drove away, Maxine heard Tina in the hallway. She must have been looking out the window, waiting for him to leave.

"He's gone," Maxine told her. "I hope that's what you wanted." Would Tina miss Scott as much as she missed Harold?

Tina nodded, her face once again normal, her tone bright. "Well, where's that pizza?" she asked. "I'm so hungry I could eat a horse." But Tina ended up eating only half a piece, and the rest of the time she stared vaguely at something no one else could see.

CHAPTER

21

Evie

Time is rushing by. I still haven't asked Jack to go with me to the concert. Now I know exactly how men feel. I swear I will never turn down another date. I may drag a friend along with me, but I'll still go!

The worst thing is that this week I actually gained two pounds. It makes me feel sick, thinking of all the exercise I did and all the food I didn't eat—and I still gained. Rosalva said I should measure myself and that would make me feel better, seeing all the inches I've lost—and it did—but still I can't believe I've gained on the week I MUST ask Jack out. What if I'm too big for him to take seriously?

I've actually talked to him quite a bit in the past weeks, but he's never asked me out. It would make things so much easier if he had.

Is he so blind that he can't see I'm crazy for him? Maybe crazy is right.

Cecilia's divorce has just been made final. She says she's through with men, but I remember feeling the same way. It's hard to think of sharing your soul with someone when the man who promised to love you for eternity doesn't uphold his part of the bargain. Sometimes I wish instead my husband had died, like Maxine's or Bernice's. At least they know they were loved and have the hope of eternity.

I feel like such a slob! On days like this I get the feeling maybe Jason was right to leave me, even though I know he was wrong. After all, I'm the same person I was before I got on the scale this morning. Oh, why did I have to eat that cookie yesterday? I tried to stay off sugar, but it was too hard. Besides, it was only one cookie! I wish I could feel pretty, but I really don't today. There's no way Jack's going to say yes. I wish I'd never had this idea of asking him at all.

If today were Wednesday I could talk this out with the ladies, but I'll have to wait until tomorrow when we're all together. I'm so glad to have the ladies of the Independence Club—and Cecilia, too, of course. (She would have joined us by now if she didn't have to teach during the day.)

Maybe by tomorrow one of us will have figured out a way to help Tina. When I saw her Sunday on my walk with Maxine, she was horribly depressed, though she tried to hide it with all the cheeriness that I'm beginning to see is only a front. She and Scott broke up, apparently, but she won't say why. Maxine knows, so I'll follow her lead and just be there for Tina. My heart really goes out to her.

What's happening with all of us? Things seem to be going wrong right and left. Well, for all of us except Rosalva, who is happy at last. She's finally given up talking about letting Willard find another woman—thank heaven. We can all see she loves him too much to let him go. But speaking of Rosalva, she's still acting a little odd. She

*came to my house last week when I had my grandchildren over—
she rarely does that anymore. Little Andrea sat on her lap for an
hour. Cecilia was put out because usually Andrea sits on her lap.*

*Two entire pounds—yuck. I think I'm going to be miserable all
day. Only a miracle could make everything better.*

E vie walked on the treadmill, feeling heavy and sad. *Two
entire pounds,* she thought for the hundredth time that
day. That was a lot, and it set back her progress at least
three weeks, counting this one, because it would take another
week to lose the weight she'd gained and another week to lose
more to show progress. That would be after the Billy Joel concert. She wanted to cry.

Cecilia came in and waved. She stopped and talked a
minute to Christopher, who was already sweating away on his
treadmill. Did they like each other? The thought made Evie
uncomfortable, though she couldn't understand why. Why
wouldn't she be happy to see two of her good friends together?

I've had enough! Evie punched the off button on her treadmill. She'd already gone two miles more than her usual three,
and she was feeling sick to her stomach. Besides, the extra
miles couldn't take away those two pounds in a day.

"All done?" Cecilia was smiling—she'd been doing that a
lot since Jason had been forced to leave their house. She'd lost
a bit of weight herself, and she'd restyled her hair in a short
bob, something she'd always wanted to do. Evie felt proud of
her progress, as if it were her own. Strange how she owed Jason
this wonderful friendship with Cecilia.

"I came in early," Evie confessed. "I gained weight."

"Oh, no!" Cecilia squeezed her hand. "You wouldn't know
it, though. You look fabulous!"

"You think so?" Evie was hungry to hear the truth—as long as it was positive.

"Absolutely. And I love that outfit, especially the pink shirt. Is it new?"

Evie nodded. "I'm trying to get up enough courage to ask Jack to the concert. But the truth is, I'm thinking maybe I shouldn't ask him after all."

Cecilia squinted at her. "Huh? Did I hear you right?"

"Well, what if he says no? And two weeks isn't exactly a lot of notice."

"I said I'd ask him for you."

"I know, but I was hoping he would ask me first, and now . . ."

"You're having second thoughts."

"I think part of the problem is that I don't know him really well."

"You don't have to know him well," Cecilia said. "Put it this way. If you were going to recommend a guy to a friend, would you recommend Jack?"

"Well, yeah, I guess. Why not?"

Cecilia frowned. "Look, I wasn't going to say anything, but since you're having second thoughts, I think you ought to know that Christopher got those tickets because he really loves Billy Joel. He was planning on going to the concert, and it was my big mouth that made him sell the tickets to you."

Evie wanted to deny Cecilia's words, but she recalled all too clearly how excited Christopher had been about Billy Joel, and now that she thought about it, he had seemed to hesitate briefly when Cecilia proposed that he sell Evie the tickets. Of course, she'd been too wrapped up in her obsession with Jack to really notice. "Oh, no," she moaned. "I've become Jason, haven't I? Not caring about anyone but myself."

Cecilia laughed. "Hardly, but maybe you should ask Christopher to go with you. You can always ask Jack to something else later."

That was nice of Cecilia, seeing as she and Christopher had become so close. By rights Cecilia and Christopher should have the tickets. If he'd kept them, he would have asked Cecilia to go with him, anyway.

Christopher was coming their way, and Evie vacillated. What should she do? Too late she noticed Jack at his side, walking slightly behind as though Christopher was leading him somewhere.

To her.

Evie swallowed hard. This was the moment of truth. "Hi," she said, forcing a smile as they approached.

"Is it true?" Jack asked, his handsome face alive and friendly. "You have tickets to Billy Joel?"

"Well, yeah."

Jack waited a moment, but when she didn't speak he added, "So, Billy Joel, huh? That's cool. I'd love to see that concert!"

"Funny you'd say that," Christopher winked at Evie, "because I hear Evie is looking for someone to join her."

"Really?" Jack asked, his eagerness all too apparent, and in that moment Evie knew she had him. Whatever his feelings for her now, this concert would really put her up a notch in his estimation. He might even ask her out after they returned.

Yet what about Christopher and Cecilia? By rights, these tickets were theirs, and they had been good enough friends to sacrifice their pleasure for her.

Both Christopher and Jack were looking at her expectantly—Christopher with the excitement of someone who had done a good deed, and Jack with the expectation of a man who knew he stood in front of a woman who admired him and who would do almost anything to impress him.

But would she? Suddenly Cecilia's words returned to her. If she were to recommend one of these men to a friend, who would she choose? Jack was an enigma, a handsome, dashing, successful man who had no end of admirers. He expected to be chased, and he was confident of his place in the world. Christopher wasn't as sure of himself, but he was a strong, funny, kind, loyal man who'd sacrifice his own desires to make a friend happy. No contest. If any of her friends needed a date, she'd recommend Christopher in a heartbeat. He wouldn't break a woman's heart or take advantage of her. He was real.

"Uh, Evie?" Christopher prompted.

She met his gaze, surprised at the flood of emotions that waved through her. She recalled his laughing at the movies with her grandchildren, barbecuing steaks on her patio while she and Cecilia waded in the children's small pool. How he drove by her street on his way home from his beat in American Fork, flashing his headlights if he saw the light on in her room. How he sang Billy Joel with her and shared stories about his job.

What have I done? she thought with dismay. Her heart felt as heavy as the extra pounds she still carried. Christopher had been here all along, but she had overlooked him exactly as Jason had overlooked her. She only hoped that Cecilia had not been as blind—at least Christopher might find happiness with her.

"I do have the tickets," she said slowly, "but they're not

mine. I'm sorry, Jack. The tickets belong to a really good friend of mine, and I would feel horrible if he didn't get to see Billy Joel because of me." She stared at Christopher as she spoke, saw his eyes widen in understanding. He opened his mouth to protest, but she shook her head at him, already knowing that he would respect her wishes. He was that kind of man.

Disappointment registered on Jack's face but quickly smoothed into nonchalance. "Well, have fun." Without regret, Evie watched him walk away.

"Evie," Cecilia began.

Evie shook her head. "He could have still asked me out. No, I don't want to go with him." She smiled at Christopher. "The tickets are yours again. I'm sorry I was so selfish. I hope you two go and have a lot of fun."

"Us?" Cecilia began laughing. "Oh, I don't think so. That ticket was never meant for me, although I'm still planning on going along for some shopping in Las Vegas." She looked at Christopher. "I'm leaving this to you. Don't blow it." With that, she walked toward an open treadmill, still chuckling as she went.

Evie shifted her gaze between Cecilia's retreating back and Christopher's smiling face. "So," she said, hardly daring to hope.

"So, will you go to the concert with me?" he asked.

She smiled, the heaviness in her heart lifting. "Tell you what. I'll let you buy back one of the tickets, and then we'll go from there." That's better than she deserved, seeing how hideously she'd acted.

"Deal," he agreed. "But let's blow this place and go have a soda."

She wrinkled her nose. "I still have my weights to do."

"They'll wait for tomorrow." His grin wavered and his voice became serious. "Besides, you're already the most beautiful woman here."

Evie had the feeling he would think that regardless of what she weighed. She knew she felt that way about him.

"Okay," she said, hooking her arm though his. "Let's go."

Less than fifteen minutes later, freshly showered and dressed, she walked out of the gym feeling that she *was* the most beautiful woman in the world.

CHAPTER

22

Bernice

I will tell them today. Well, that is if someone asks. I mean, now with Tina being so sad about Scott, telling the ladies today could be like rubbing it in her face. Sheesh, first Maxine—who seems to be doing better these days, by the way—and now Tina. Am I just using them as an excuse? I know Clay would love to meet the ladies, and I would love to share that part of my life with him because those women mean more and more to me every day. Just like he does. This will teach me to be such a hypocrite. I know I've let it go way too long. We've set our wedding for the end of June, and I would like my friends to be there.

I think Maxine knows a lot more about Tina's breakup than she's letting on because she's been having all of us check up on Tina whenever we can. We've gone by her house the past two mornings on the pretense of a walk, and Tina seems okay but not all there. Almost like I remember feeling after David died. Numb. I've been so worried about her that I went to see her on my own last night, but she was with her children and acted a lot better than in the morning. I'm praying for her.

I'm also praying for Maxine. Like the others, I sent something to Harold. I won't say what because I'm feeling a little embarrassed about it. I think my engagement's going to my head.

So who's first?" Bernice asked. She was surprised when no one suggested that she go first because she knew how eager they all were to hear of the great insights she'd gained while studying the books of Samuel in the Bible. Well, that could wait.

Evie raised her hand near her face, bouncing like a little child. "I have news," she sang.

"You finally asked him?" Rosalva turned to her with wide eyes.

Evie giggled. "Well, I asked *a* him."

"What do you mean?" Tina came from the silent place in her mind where she had spent the first ten minutes of their brunch. Bernice suspected she wouldn't even have shown up if Maxine hadn't elicited a promise from her yesterday.

"I asked Christopher. Now don't say anything, because when it came right down to it, I decided that if it was one of you, I'd recommend Christopher over Jack. I thought he wanted to go with Cecilia, but it turns out it's me he's been wanting to date."

Bernice was confused, but Evie immediately launched into the rather convoluted story of how she and Christopher ended up as dates for the concert.

"And he said you were the most beautiful woman at the gym?" Tina was glowing almost like her old self. "Oh, that's so romantic!"

"Well, not if you take into account that they were all sweating," Bernice said, "but it's good to know that he likes you for who you are and not for what you weigh."

"I'm not going to quit working at it, though." Evie shook her head when Rosalva passed her the breadbasket. "I want to be healthy and follow my doctor's advice. After that, well, maybe I'm not going to be as focused on my weight."

"Amen to that!" That was exactly what Bernice had been trying to tell Evie for the past months. They were women, and they didn't have to be as thin as supermodels to be of value. Clay didn't mind at all that Bernice was a bit round in the middle. So was he, for that matter.

"What about you, Rosalva?" Evie asked. "Are you or are you not getting married?"

"I am!" Rosalva drew out a hand that she'd been hiding under the table. On her finger was a diamond that made Rosalva's slender hand look overloaded. "We've decided to take the plunge in July! I still worry, though, about what he'll say ten years down the road." She frowned but then waved it away. "Well, I'm not going to worry about it now. I did reach my goal, though. I found a good role model for my son—two, actually, since Lucas has been working with Spencer doing yards. I'm pretty content for now."

Maxine cleared her throat. "After looking at some of Tina's tour suggestions, I've decided that this fall I'm going to Paris after all. I'll be fresh from my French class, and why not?"

"Do you still want me to go with you?" Evie asked.

Maxine bit her lip. "I haven't gotten that far yet. But I don't really want to go alone."

Bernice wondered if Maxine was hoping Harold would come around, which would be a good thing, judging by the light in Evie's eyes. She might have other plans herself this fall.

All at once Bernice didn't feel like telling her friends about the books of Samuel. She wanted to tell them about Clay and show them her own ring. But Tina was sitting there staring vaguely again into the distance, and Bernice couldn't bring herself to do it.

"Tina?" Maxine said gently.

"Yes?" Tina blinked.

"What about your goals?"

Tina shook her head. "I haven't felt like doing many presentations, so I haven't signed up any new consultants."

Bernice felt a lump in her throat as she shared sympathetic gazes with the others. Tina's problems had nothing to do with consultants, nor, she was beginning to believe, with Scott. "I'll sign up," Bernice found herself saying. Tina might not have ended up with the husband she'd wanted, but she would at least get a new consultant.

Tina laughed. "You?" Though the reaction was only a shadow of Tina's former bright self, Bernice was glad to see her focus on something besides her problems.

"No offense, Bernice," Rosalva said, waving a fork in her direction, "but you would make the worst consultant ever." Bernice agreed, but she'd already spoken.

"No, I think she'd be great!" Tina said. "We'll sign you up right away, and I'll even send you a few customers to help you get started."

Bernice wondered what she'd gotten herself into. "Okay, but now let me tell you about my reading in Samuel."

By the end of brunch, Bernice had told them all about Eli, Samuel, Saul, and David, but nothing about Clay. *It's simple,* she told herself. *You just say, "Hey, I'm getting married next month."* But before she could gather her thoughts, the ladies had scattered. "Next week for sure," she muttered to herself. "Or maybe I should send them a letter. That way they could get their laughing over before our brunch."

In the parking lot Maxine and Tina were talking beside Tina's car. Tina's door was open, and she looked ready to get inside. Because Bernice had ridden with Maxine, she headed in their direction.

"No," Tina was saying, her voice agitated. "I'm not ready. I don't want to go."

"Please, Tina." Maxine put her hands together in front of her chest. "You know it's the only way."

"I'm doing fine—can't you see that?"

"That's not what I see at all."

Tina shook her head and looked away.

"I can't force you, Tina, but remember that admitting something is wrong is half the battle. You don't have to live like this. You'll have to face it eventually—if you want to be truly happy again."

What did Maxine mean? Bernice went a few steps closer, knowing she was intruding but unable to stop herself. "Is something wrong?"

Maxine drew away. "Call me if you need me, Tina." As she passed Bernice, she whispered, "Try to get her to go to her appointment. It's very important."

Tina watched Maxine go.

"Well, there went my ride," Bernice said. "I hope you don't mind taking me home."

Tina smiled without a trace of the vexation she had shown Maxine. "Of course not. Glad to have the company."

So that was how she was going to play it—as though nothing out of the ordinary had happened. As though Bernice hadn't overheard any argument. Well, Bernice had let Maxine down in the past, but she wasn't going to let either of her friends down now.

"What's going on, Tina?" she asked when they were seated in the car. "Please tell me. Maybe I can help."

"Nothing." Tina tried to smile, but Bernice could tell it took a lot of effort.

"Please."

"What about you?" Tina countered. "You're the one with the secret, aren't you? Tell you what—you tell me, and I'll tell you." When Bernice didn't reply, she nodded. "See? It's not so easy." She started the car, put it in gear, and waited for a car to pass by so she could back out of the parking space.

Moments ticked on, and any second Bernice knew she would lose the opportunity of the bargain. She took a deep breath. "Okay, I'm getting married—next month."

Tina's eyes left the rearview mirror. "Married? Oh, Bernice, how wonderful! I'm so happy for you! How long have you known? Why haven't you told us? Oh!" She let go of the wheel and hugged Bernice tightly, and Bernice could tell that her excitement was real. Of course, that was Tina—she was always ultrapositive in all her outward expressions. How might the others have reacted?

"Let me see your hand." Tina grabbed it and opened her

palm. "I knew it! It is a different ring. Look at those diamonds. Very nice."

Bernice basked in her friend's support.

"So why haven't you told us?" Tina repeated.

Bernice pursed her lips, looking out the window at a couple who were making their way into the restaurant. "Well, I did go rather hard on Maxine for dating. You and Rosalva and Evie had a reason to find new husbands, but I really believed if Maxine and I were to date, we would be betraying our husbands. Well, you know how I was."

"I know," Tina said with a laugh. "But you haven't talked like that for months. We saw how you tried to help Maxine and Harold—you've changed." Tina hugged her again. "I'm so happy for you, and the others will be too, you'll see."

"If I can tell them—I've been trying for a month now."

Tina laughed again. "Poor Bernice. You hate being wrong, don't you? Don't worry. I promise you, no one will say a word. We want you to be happy. This is so exciting!"

Bernice couldn't help the tears in her eyes. She had known all along that her friends would be happy for her, hadn't she? It was just so hard to admit that she was wrong—to eat crow, as Clay had called it.

"We should tell them next week." Tina glanced over her shoulder and started backing out. "Just announce it right out of the blue. I'll help you, if you can't do it."

"Thank you." Bernice meant it. Whatever happened, she knew Tina would be on her side, rooting for her and casting aside any stray comments that might embarrass her. "I want to help you, too," she said. "Your turn to spill the beans."

Tina's smile fled. She stopped the car, halfway out of the parking space. For a brief, horrible moment Bernice wished she hadn't brought it up at all. But no, this was what friends were for—the bad with the good.

"You promised," Bernice said in her most strident voice. That tone always seemed to work with Tina, and it didn't fail her now.

Tina swallowed with apparent difficulty. "I've had several incidents—like panic attacks or flashback sorts of things. From my time with Glen. Maxine thinks I should see a psychologist. She even made me an appointment with one."

Bernice's tears spilled over. How trite her own problem was compared with Tina's! She was utterly mortified that she could be so shallow. "You have to go," Bernice said. "Please."

Tina looked at her, saw her tears. "I'm okay, Bernice. Really."

"No. It's not okay. Please." Bernice wrapped her hands around the strap of her safety belt, searching for what to say. This confession went a great deal toward explaining Tina's odd behavior of late. How could she help her friend?

Tina sat without responding. Her hands still gripped the steering wheel, but she didn't try to move the car from its awkward position. A truck honked, and Bernice waved for them to go around. "Look, Tina, if you can't face your fears, then why should I face mine? If you don't go, I won't tell the ladies." It was a weak challenge, Bernice knew. The two could hardly compare, and she half-expected Tina to laugh at her. "And I guess that means no one will be at my wedding," Bernice added, the words sticking in her throat no matter how she swallowed. "Please, Tina. I'll go with you if you want."

Tina stared down at her hands for a long time. They were white from her death grip on the wheel. "Okay, then," she said finally. "I guess I'll give it a try. But I get to tell the ladies about you."

"Deal." Bernice would rather have her do it, anyway.

"And you have to drive." Tina let her hands drop from the wheel and took a card from her purse. "Here's the address. It's in Provo."

They exchanged places, and Bernice drove from the parking lot. She glanced over at Tina, who stared out the window, her face pale and drawn and her hands laced tightly in her lap. With each mile that passed, Bernice could feel the tension in Tina rise. Had she made a mistake? Maybe Maxine was wrong.

"So," she said, hoping conversation would help. "Anything new with the kids?" She didn't really expect an answer, except for maybe a shake of the head, but to her surprise, Tina opened her mouth and words rushed out, sounding abnormally high and breathy.

"Callie's with Ashley almost constantly since she came back from Idaho. They follow me around like shadows."

"That's not too bad, is it? That means Ashley likes you. You don't find many teens who like to hang out with their mothers."

Tina continued as though Bernice hadn't spoken. "Callie talks about Rainbow—that's her mother. She told me about the times she left." Tina glanced toward her, and Bernice gave her an encouraging smile.

"She left more than once?"

Tina nodded. "The first time was when Callie was eleven, the second when she was fourteen. Callie went to live with her for six months when she left the second time, but there was no food, and her mom was always off doing her own thing."

"Motherhood was too much of a burden, huh?" Bernice's chest felt tight, thinking of that little girl waiting for her mother to come home and make dinner.

"I guess. Rainbow took Callie back to Scott—she was barely fifteen then—and said she was through."

Bernice stopped at a light. "It's good to know it was Callie's mom who had the problem instead of Scott, isn't it?"

"It doesn't change what happened between us." Tina looked out the window again, her voice sounding far away.

Bernice didn't know the full story of what had happened between Tina and Scott—only Maxine did. She knew they'd stopped seeing each other and now suspected the breakup had something to do with Tina's past with Glen, but that was all. How could she help if she didn't know everything? Well, she had to try. "I'm sorry about you and Scott," she ventured. "Has he called at all?"

Tina gave a delicate snort. "He calls all the time. He's left a million messages."

"You don't pick up the phone?"

Shaking her head, Tina crossed her arms over her chest and rubbed her bare arms. "He begs me to talk about it, says he's sorry for scaring me and that he's sure we can work things out. To make it worse, the children are confused because he's suddenly no longer around."

"And how do you feel?"

Tina sighed. "I miss him. Maybe Maxine's right and I should give him another chance." She gave a sharp, bitter laugh. "Or maybe you were right all along and no widow should ever remarry."

"I was wrong."

"Maybe you're not. Maybe Glen will make a change in heaven and become the man I once thought he could be."

"Do you believe that?"

A tear slid down Tina's cheek. "I think he's exactly the same, and I don't want to be with him." She looked out the window again as though wanting to hide her face. She didn't speak the rest of the way to the clinic, no matter how many comments Bernice made.

They walked into the clinic together and sat in the waiting room where the receptionist had Tina fill out a paper. There were a few other patients waiting to see other doctors, but they were called in almost immediately.

Just our luck, Bernice thought sourly. *The doctor must be running late.* "I'll go see what the holdup is," she told Tina. "You can just wait right here, if you'd rather."

"Thanks." Tina smiled at her, but the smile looked fake. Had it always been fake? Had this horrible sadness always lurked behind the smile?

No, Bernice decided. *Sometimes the smile is real.* Still, she wanted to kick herself for not seeing the times when Tina was so obviously hurting, but she had been too wrapped up in her own life to notice.

She hurried to the receptionist and learned that they were actually fifteen minutes early for the appointment. Why had Maxine insisted they arrive at this time?

Bernice decided not to tell Tina they were early, for fear she'd change her mind and want to leave. Better for her to think the doctor would be out any second.

"I know," Bernice said as she settled beside Tina on a chair to wait. "We can write in our journals. You've been doing it, haven't you?" It was something to say, something to fill the space inside her friend where fear threatened to overcome courage.

Tina frowned. "Some. But I don't have it here."

"No problem." Bernice took her own journal from her bag where she always carried it with her scriptures. She never knew when she might need to jot something down. She clicked open the small three-ring binder and removed a piece of paper. "I hope you got one like this. It'll be easy to slip the page in. Here's a pen, too."

Tina took the page without comment but did not begin writing. Bernice found another pen and pretended to write as she kept an eye on her friend. The minutes ticked by, and every so often Tina glanced at the time on her cell phone. What if the doctor was so late that Tina decided to leave? *Hurry, doctor,* Bernice thought.

As though someone had heard her thoughts, the door opened, and a female psychologist emerged with her patient. Tina followed Bernice's gaze—and gasped.

Ah, so this is part of Maxine's plan, Bernice thought. *That's why getting here early was so important.* Silently, she applauded Maxine's bravery, but she wondered if it would work. She waited to see what would happen next.

CHAPTER

23

Tina

Maxine believes if I talk to somebody about it I'll feel better, but the idea of reliving my life with Glen terrifies me. It terrifies me more than living the rest of my life alone.

Oh, I feel like packing up my car and moving to another state!

Tina sucked in a ragged breath when she saw Scott standing next to the psychologist. Her pen fell from limp fingers and rolled down the incline of her leg to the carpet. She leapt to her feet, ready to flee, but felt Bernice's steadying hand on her shoulder.

Scott looked good—as handsome as usual, though there were telltale signs of stress in the half-circles under his eyes and the hungry way he drank in her presence. He crossed the room in three steps.

"What are you doing here?" The words spilled from her accusingly, without check. She knew already that Maxine must be involved somehow. Maybe Bernice, too. That's why they'd been so insistent on her coming today.

A shadow passed over Scott's face, but after a moment's hesitation, he forced a smile, though his brown eyes remained sober. "Why am I here? Well, let's see. I guess it's because the woman I love has blocked me out, and I want to understand why." He stood staring at her, both of them silent. The quiet grew between them, an impossible gulf that Tina doubted they could ever bridge, regardless of how much she wanted to be in his arms.

"Plus," he added with a touch of irony, "I seem to have what they call abandonment issues, what with my wife leaving me. Apparently, I'm afraid of being left behind, and that's why I hate the idea of letting Callie visit her mom."

That Tina had left him, as surely as Rainbow had, hung between them, and there was no changing that fact. She took a step back. Maybe she should run from the office to spare them both this pain. Bernice was no longer at her side, holding her back.

"Tina," he said softly, "why didn't you tell me?"

She looked around, searching for a way out. Bernice had retreated to the far end of the room where she was chatting with the receptionist and the psychologist. No one else was in sight.

"Please." The hurt in Scott's voice cut deeply.

That did it. She couldn't run away from this. She tore her gaze from his and stared at the carpet, a dull gray, her fingers twisting together in front of her. "It's not you. I know that now. I just . . ." She stopped, her breath coming faster despite her determination to remain calm. "I didn't want you to think I was the kind of woman who would be abused."

"It wasn't your fault." He spoke without hesitation or doubt.

She dared to look at him then. "I should have been stronger. I shouldn't have let—"

He placed a gentle hand on her arm, and the warmth made her want to weep. "You're talking to a man whose wife walked out on him not once but twice."

"That's different. She was the one with problems. Callie has told me all about her. You're a wonderful man."

"Glen was the one with problems," he countered. "And you're a wonderful woman."

Tina felt her lips curve in a smile. Could it be so simple?

His hand slid down her arm until it reached her hand, which he held in both of his. Not too tightly, not to force—she noted that—but strong enough to tell her she was loved. "I want to be there for you," he said. "Whatever it takes, however long you need. We can work through this together. Can we at least try? Are we both brave enough to face our demons?"

He had apparently faced his. He was seeing a psychologist so that he could understand her. There was no sign of giving up or walking away.

She lifted her other hand and put it in his, all the answer she could muster. He smiled and pulled her into a hug. "I love you, Tina. I know we're in for some rough times, but I swear I will do my best never to hurt you."

His promise wasn't enough, not yet, but she believed it would become enough as she learned to cope with the past—a past that had nothing to do with him but that he was willing to help her confront. Taking his hand, she moved slowly toward the waiting psychologist. There would be a lot of baggage she would have to deal with alone, but he would be with her through these first difficult moments.

"I can't promise I'll never leave," she whispered, not wanting to hurt him but knowing she had to be honest. She wished she could give him more, but it was too soon.

He smiled and squeezed her hand. "You can leave any time you want, Tina. Just so long as you always come back."

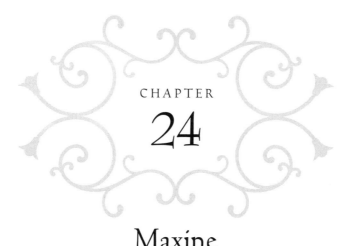

CHAPTER

24

Maxine

Today I'm remembering Harold and his kiss in the garage. This has gone on long enough. I'm driving down to see him today after our brunch at Mimi's. I didn't call ahead, but I think his daughter will let me in. Whatever happens, this will close an era for me. I'm moving on with my life.

Tina is doing well. She had three appointments with the psychologist last week and has the same for this week. Eventually, she'll be down to one per week. Scott went with her all last week, but this week she went to one alone. I think that's a good sign. Having Scott in her life doesn't change the past, but love gives her more courage to face it.

Even as she plans her wedding, Rosalva is still spouting dire predictions about Willard's future regrets. I don't like the direction that's heading. She needs to come to terms with things the way he has. Could it be that she has doubts about marrying him? Or maybe she has her own doubts about not having more children. Interesting to consider.

Evie's in love and she's glowing. Bernice . . . well, I'll get to the bottom of that today at Mimi's—I hope. I feel so lucky to have these friends in my life. I'm glad we decided to form the Independence Club.

I wonder if Harold ever thinks of me.

Maxine took her fork and banged it against her glass. "Attention, ladies. Tina just told me that she would like to make an announcement." Around the table everyone fell silent, eyes riveted on Tina. Maxine found herself leaning forward, as puzzled and eager as the rest. Surely Tina wasn't rushing into marriage yet. Scott knew better than that.

"This announcement isn't really for me," Tina began.

Maxine heaved a silent sigh of relief.

"Actually, it's for Bernice. She's getting married next month, and we need to help her with the wedding—she hasn't made a single plan!"

There was a swift united intake of breath, but in the next minute congratulations fell like rain over Bernice, who was crying and making apologies for not telling them sooner. Maxine laughed. One more problem to cease worrying about! "Oh, Bernice," she said, "this is absolutely the best news I've heard all week!"

Bernice beamed, not a trace of her usual sour expression in sight.

Seated next to Maxine, Rosalva opened her mouth, and Maxine knew that if anyone were to say something about

Bernice's past comments, even teasingly, it would be Rosalva. Maxine gave her a sharp kick under the table. "Ow!" Rosalva said.

"Oh, sorry." Maxine gave her an innocent stare.

"You're not fooling me," Rosalva whispered. "You did that on purpose."

"Well, you're not fooling me, either." Maxine countered, arching her brow enigmatically, and to her surprise it worked. Rosalva sat back in her chair, mouth shut. *What's that about?* Maxine wondered.

As the talk about the wedding progressed, Maxine kept an eye on Rosalva and was amazed to see her gaze wandering to the new baby with the couple sitting at the next table. She'd tear her eyes away, only to look again within a few seconds. The mother was holding the baby and eating at the same time, as though she couldn't bear to set the child down even for an instant. There was an undisguised longing on Rosalva's face.

So that's it, Maxine thought. *She's thinking about babies, and when I said she wasn't fooling me, she thought I could tell.* Well, Maxine *could* tell—now that she knew to look for something.

"Cute baby," she whispered.

Rosalva blinked. "Oh, I guess."

Smiling, Maxine refocused on the conversation.

"I'm sure we can pull it together if we all pitch in," Tina was saying.

Bernice looked pleased. "We don't want a big wedding or anything."

"Oh, show them the ring," Tina urged Bernice. "It's got three diamonds the same size. Absolutely beautiful."

"You only had a band before, didn't you?" Evie asked, admiring the ring.

The waitress came with their food, and Maxine had only taken one bite when Tina's voice rang out. "He's here! He came!"

Now what? Maxine thought. If any of these engaged ladies thought their men were going to crash this party, they had better think again. This club was for women only. She looked up to see the newcomer, and her jaw dropped.

Harold.

Now it was Rosalva's turn to kick her. "Close your mouth," she whispered.

Maxine obeyed, but her eyes didn't leave Harold. He'd changed a great deal in the many weeks since she'd last seen him. He was upright for one, moving slowly, supported by a handsome cane. His hair was whiter, and he'd gained a bit of weight with his forced inactivity, but he was still dressed smartly, and his eyes were exactly the same. Today they were as blue as his suit.

Willard Oakman walked a step behind him, looking ready to catch Harold should he stumble, but Harold's movements, though slow, were precise and sure. Willard waved to Rosalva, and she winked back.

"Hi, ladies." Harold sounded so much like the old Harold that Maxine wanted to weep. There followed a flurry of hellos. Only Maxine sat mutely.

Now what? She seemed to always ask that question where Harold was concerned.

Harold looked at Maxine. "Can I talk to you a moment?" His words came hesitantly but without any notable slurring.

"Sure," she agreed. If Harold's question had been a bid for privacy, it was in vain because no one moved. "You're looking well," she added.

"I won't be driving again soon, if ever, but walking is coming along."

He stepped around Rosalva's chair ever-so-slowly. "I know I've been a little bit of a fool."

"A little?" Rosalva said with a snort.

Harold smiled. The left side of his face drooped a little but was clearly working much better than it had in the hospital. Apparently his physical therapy was helping all his muscles regain their ability. "More than a little," he conceded. He looked again intently at Maxine. "Fortunately, we have good friends who've helped me realize it was more my pride getting in the way than my concern for you." He lifted his left hand with a bit of difficulty, as if to stave off her vocal agreement. "Although I was concerned about you, don't ever doubt that." His voice had grown gruff, but Maxine didn't respond. Why was he really here?

Harold changed his cane to his left hand and began unbuttoning his shirt with his right.

"Harold!" she exclaimed. She'd heard that right brain strokes often caused rash behavior, but surely he had more control than this—especially in a restaurant.

He only smiled and kept unbuttoning. Maxine stared, surprised to see that underneath he wore a T-shirt bearing her face. He smiled at her expression. "Thanks to Rosalva, I've had you with me every day."

Rosalva gave Maxine a smirk.

"But that's not all," Harold said. Willard proffered him a large brown paper bag with a handle, the kind used by upscale stores. Harold clumsily drew out a binder and placed it in front of Maxine. She opened it to reveal page after page of pictures of her—some with other people, but most of her alone or with Harold.

"Turned out quite nicely, didn't it?" Tina said with a satisfied smile. "If I do say so myself." No doubt who was responsible for that piece of work.

Next, Harold handed Maxine a letter containing a suggestion for a trip to France. Maxine recognized Evie's writing, though she didn't confess.

"Of course, this was the best," Harold said, removing something else from the bag. "The softest pillow I ever had—and the best company."

Maxine blinked in amazement to see a closeup of her own face staring from the pillow—an exceptionally good picture, yes, but embarrassing all the same.

The ladies looked back and forth at each other in confusion until Rosalva snapped her fingers. "Bernice, that was you, wasn't it?"

Bernice turned a bright, unbecoming red.

Harold laughed. "Yes. Thank you, Bernice. I loved it so much, I had Willard here help me make up another—Willard's my lawyer, by the way, but he's not above helping me out in other matters." This time the pillow he took from the bag had his own picture on it. And bold letters next to the photograph said, Will you marry me?

"I'd get down on my knees," Harold said, eyes holding Maxine's with a power she had quite forgotten, "but I don't think I'd be able to get up. Maybe in a few months, after more therapy."

Maxine's heart felt light. "Oh, sit already." She motioned for Rosalva to give him her chair. "You look like you're about ready to fall down."

"Not until I get an answer. I owe it to these ladies . . . and to you. But I warn you, you'll probably have to take care of me—just a little. I promise to make it worth your while." With that he bent down and kissed Maxine in front of the whole restaurant, one hand on his cane and the other on the back of her chair.

"Stop that!" Maxine pushed him away but gently so as not to put him off balance. "You'll get us kicked out of here."

"Well?" He started bending over again, and as much as Maxine enjoyed his kiss, she wasn't about to put on a show for everyone.

"Of course I'll marry you!" she said. "Now sit down."

He sat, reaching out to take her hand under the table, a triumphant smile on his face. "I'm not sure I'll make it to France this year," he leaned over to whisper in her ear, "but I'll work hard so we can go next year."

Maxine squeezed his hand so tightly her own ached. Tears threatened to spill over.

"I'm sorry," he added. "Call me a blind fool—which I guess I am in more ways than one since I still can't tell how close or far away things are—but I had to be sure there would be some of me left to take care of you."

"We'll take care of each other," she said. "And when we can't do that, they'll take care of us." This last she said loud enough for everyone to hear.

Tina laughed. "Oh, Maxine, you'll be taking care of all of us for years and years."

"I will need a baby-sitter after all." Rosalva was standing by Willard, her hand tucked in his arm.

Willard looked at her, unsure if he'd heard correctly. "What did you say?"

"I've decided I want us to have a baby."

"A . . . a . . . a . . ."

"A baby," Rosalva repeated, turning so that she stood in front of him. "Maybe two, even if I have to get fertility treatments. You never know."

"But I thought—"

Rosalva put a finger over Willard's lips. "You were willing to give up everything for me, so why shouldn't I give up something for you? Besides, it's not really giving up anything. Lately I've started thinking about what the most important thing is in the gospel—it's children, family. An eternal family. What's a few more years of diapers compared to another baby to love? I've never heard anyone wish they hadn't had as many children as they do, but I've heard way too many women wish they'd had more." She glanced at Evie, who nodded her agreement. "I love you too much to ever let you—or me—live with that regret."

Maxine could see Willard was too choked up to speak. He hugged Rosalva to him tightly, lifting her off the ground in spite of her high heels.

"Thank heaven that's settled," Maxine said tartly. "Now if you two will please get the waitress to pull over another table and a few chairs, we can finish our brunch without being any more of a spectacle. But you men had better not get used to being here, because the Independence Club is only for women."

"We'll start our own club," Harold assured her.

"Yeah, right," Rosalva said with a snort. "And what will you call it, the Dependence Club?"

Harold and Willard were unfazed. "Exactly," they said together.

"We know our limits," added Willard.

Underneath the table Harold still held Maxine's hand, and this time she knew neither of them would let go.

About the
Author

Rachel Ann Nunes (pronounced noon-esh) learned to read when she was four, beginning a lifetime fascination with the written word. She began writing in the seventh grade and is now the author of more than two dozen published books, including the popular *Ariana* series and the picture book *Daughter of a King,* voted best children's book of the year in 2003 by the Association of Independent LDS Booksellers. Her newest picture book, *The Secret of the King,* was chosen by the Governor's Commission on Literacy to be awarded to all Utah grade schools as part of the "Read with a Child for 20 Minutes per Day" program.

Rachel served a mission to Portugal for The Church of Jesus Christ of Latter-day Saints and teaches Sunday School in her Utah ward. She and her husband, TJ, have six children. She loves camping with her family, traveling, meeting new people, and, of course, writing. She writes Monday through Friday in her home office, often with a child on her lap, taking frequent breaks to build Lego towers, practice phonics, or jump on the trampoline with the kids.

Rachel welcomes invitations to speak to church groups and schools. Write to her at Rachel@RachelAnnNunes.com or P.O. Box 353, American Fork, UT 84003–0353. You can also visit her website, www.RachelAnnNunes.com, to enjoy her monthly newsletter or sign up to hear about new releases.